TIMBERWOLF ON THE MOUNTAIN

WATCHDOG MOUNTAIN DIVISION BOOK 2

OLIVIA MICHAELS

FALCON IN HAND PUBLISHING, LLC

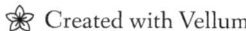 Created with Vellum

ONE

The little girl trembled in her seat as the six big men walked through the door. Their faces looked stern and unforgiving as they filed past her one by one, each making sure that she knew without a doubt they were there for her. The last man stopped and knelt in front of her, bringing his face to her level. He looked into her eyes as her bottom lip quivered. He took her hands in his—big and rough and warm.

"We're here, Laurie. When you go up to sit by the judge, you keep your eyes on us, on me," Gabe O'Neil said. "You don't need to look at *him*. What is he, Laurie? Do you remember?" His gaze moved to her lips as she spoke, watching every word.

The little girl's voice quavered as she said, "He's a worm."

"Yes he is, sweetheart. He's a worm. And worms are food. And you are a brave little bird who's going to feast on him today. You're going to sing out the truth, and you're going to help put him in a place where he can't hurt anyone else. This isn't all on you though, sweetheart, you remember that, too. A lot of people let you down, but we're not going to. No matter what happens today, we've got your back. He will never come near you again."

Laurie looked down. She murmured something that he couldn't hear or make out. But the tear slipping down her cheek told him volumes.

Gabe gently tilted her chin up until she was looking at him again. "You are so brave, Laurie. Someone like you should never have to be this brave, but here you are."

"I'm not brave. I'm scared, Uncle Gabe."

"You *are* brave, Laurie. Brave is being scared and doing the scary thing anyway. You are the bravest person in this room right now, do you know that?"

He couldn't hear her whisper but watching her lips Gabe thought she said, "As brave as you? As brave as Uncle Bear?"

"Braver than me and Bear put together on our scariest day."

Gabe felt his mouth go dry as a memory flashed through his mind, a brutal reminder of his and Bear's scariest day. He glanced up at his friend, Jon Behr, who'd filed in with the rest of them. Bear met his eyes and stood up.

And up, and up.

Bear was one of the biggest men Gabe had ever known. Underneath all that height and muscle beat a huge and gentle heart of gold—unless you were his enemy or threatening someone he cared about, then God help you. Bear sat beside the other contender for the biggest man Gabe knew, and the unofficial leader of their team, Benjamin "Moose" Massey. Ben looked almost comical trying to scoot back on the bench to let Bear get past him.

Bear lumbered over to Gabe and Laurie. The sound of people talking in the courtroom increased at the sight of the two big men with the star witness. Gabe frowned, wanting to adjust his hearing aids. They were new ones and he was still getting used to them and sometimes his brain couldn't block out all the ambient noise. But he didn't dare touch them in front of Bear, who still held on to the idea that he was responsible for Gabe's hearing loss.

Laurie watched Bear as he dropped to his knees in front of her.

"Everything all right, Piglet?" Bear asked. He pointed at the stuffed animals on Laurie's lap—a Pooh Bear and a Piglet. Gabe and Bear gave her the stuffies when they'd met a few weeks ago to try and gain her trust. The men knew they could be big and intimidating and Laurie was already afraid of most men, thanks to the walking scum who hurt her. They hoped Pooh and Piglet would help her feel safe when she cuddled them at night and remind her to be brave during the day. They'd told her that Piglet was small, but fierce and brave and loyal—just like her. The nickname Bear gave Laurie stuck, and the little girl smiled every time he called her that, including now. She had the sweetest smile, complete with a missing front tooth she'd traded for ten dollars to the Tooth Fairy a few days ago. The guys had wanted to give her more, but Laurie's mother refused, saying they'd already done so much to help.

Laurie nodded and clutched Piglet closer.

"You look at us, Piglet," Bear said, echoing Gabe's words. "And if that's too scary, you just look down at old Pooh Bear and Piglet when you talk."

"Judge'll let you bring them up with you, so you won't be up there alone," Gabe said. That at least was certain. The judge had let other kids bring their stuffed animals and security blankets up with them and they made doubly sure that was one of the conditions of her testimony.

Gabe just wished everything else was as certain. The scumbag's family had hired the best lawyer in the state of Colorado to defend Jesse Tobison. The lawyer had a reputation for finding loopholes and for intimidating young witnesses like

Laurie to make sure his clients never saw the inside of a prison. Sadly, he had a successful record. Even if the lawyer had never directly abused a child himself, Gabe thought taking on abusers like Tobison on the regular made him ten times worse than the criminals he represented. It killed Gabe to think that Tobison might go free after what he'd done to Laurie and to other children.

He needed more faith that it wouldn't happen today. For Laurie's sake.

The courtroom grew louder, taking away Gabe's chance to hear Laurie's response. He tried not to grimace and risk Laurie thinking he was upset at her. He smiled instead. Bear put his hand on Gabe's shoulder—a warning that Tobison had just walked in with his lawyer.

Gabe squeezed Laurie's hands one last time. "You aren't alone. And we won't let him near you."

"Look at us," Bear said, getting to his feet.

Gabe followed him back to the bench where the rest of his team sat. They weren't a formal team, but brothers in spirit, with a self-directed mission to protect people like Laurie from predators who slipped through the fingers of justice. They all hoped that today would be different, that Jesse Tobison would be put away so that he couldn't threaten Laurie. He'd already violated a restraining order which was what prompted Laurie's mother to get in touch with Mountain Division. Ben had received a call from one of their confidential contacts that a little girl needed protection from a monster. They answered right away, meeting Laurie and reassuring her that at least one of them would guard her around the clock until Tobison was back in jail.

It took three days before the bastard showed his face at her house. But they'd kept her safe, both physically and emotionally. She didn't even know he was outside, restrained by Gabe while Bear was inside reading her a bedtime story. Gabe had wanted to kill him outright, but that wasn't how it worked.

At least not yet.

Now it was time for her to testify and Tobison—and his bastard lawyer—would use every psychological trick in the book to keep her from talking, or to trick her into sounding unreliable.

Repulsive.

"All rise," the bailiff said, announcing the judge's arrival. Then he asked that all conversations cease. That was a relief to Gabe. Now he could make out individual voices.

Tobison's lawyer spoke first. "May it please the court, Your Honor, I'd like to ask for the witness to leave the stuffed animals behind when she testifies. They are a distraction."

Son of a bitch. He was already starting in, trying to make sure Laurie was as uncomfortable as possible. He'd already managed to prevent Laurie from testifying by closed-circuit television, causing her to appear in person in the same room as her abuser. And she wasn't allowed to have her wonderful mom, Diane Andrews, sitting next to her on the stand.

"Request denied," the judge said. Her expression looked neutral but even Gabe could pick up on the disgust in her voice. "Laurie, can you come up here now and testify, please?" Her voice had softened and Gabe felt some relief. He'd listened to other judges talk over the heads of their young witnesses and that only led to confusion. This judge seemed to know how to talk to kids. Things were looking up.

Laurie held her head high as she approached the witness stand accompanied by an adult attendant.

That's my brave girl.

God, she looked so small, so fragile as she climbed up into the chair and took her oath. She clung to her stuffed animals like a life raft. But she looked straight at Gabe and Bear who both gave her a thumbs up.

She smiled back and refused to look at either the lawyer or at Tobison the entire time. She kept her gaze on the team of men who she knew would take a bullet to defend her.

"My name is Laurie Andrews," she began, and kept going from there in a strong, sure voice.

"YOU DID SO GOOD, PIGLET," Bear told her on the sidewalk in front of the parking lot afterward. Bear, Gabe, and Waylon "Ram" Ramson waited with Laurie while Ben and Elias "Lion" Hunt escorted her mom to get her minivan and Shane went to get a surprise for the little girl. The three men stood blocking her from the door, forming a protective circle around her, even though Jesse was still in custody. The rest of his family was there, and they were...weird to say the least. Intimidating for sure. She didn't need them coming up to her. Gabe thought Laurie looked so much better now that the day was done. Not happy exactly, but more relaxed. He wanted it to stay that way.

Diane drove up with Ben, and Shane was right behind them in a Watchdog SUV. Watchdog was where Shane worked as a security expert. Watchdog also trained dogs for police officers and for the private sector to be service dogs and for personal protection. Shane got out of the truck and went around to the back. Gabe smiled in anticipation as he watched Laurie's face and he wasn't disappointed. The little girl lit up like the Fourth of July the second she saw the dog.

"His name is Pete but I call him Peetie," Shane said, giving the big dog a scratch behind the ears. "He's Peetie the Sweetie, right? Loves getting pets, loves treats, loves to be spoiled rotten by kiddos like you." He knelt down beside the dog. "Go ahead. Give him a scratch."

Laurie reached out and scratched Pete's ears. The dog groaned and leaned against her. The men laughed along with Laurie's mom. The girl was too enchanted with Peetie to notice.

What Shane didn't tell Laurie was that if anyone came near her, Peetie would not be so sweet. Peetie would turn into a barking, biting, attacking machine.

Much like the men.

Peetie licked Laurie's nose, making her laugh.

"You like him, huh?" Shane asked.

"I do. He's cute."

"Well, he belongs to my boss, a man named Kyle. And when Kyle heard that there was a little girl who needed a friend to protect her, he told me to bring Peetie to see you. And he also said that if you wanted, you could take Peetie home for the night. Like a sleepover. How does that sound?"

Laurie looked at Shane in awe. "Really? You mean it?"

"Absolutely. I'll come and get him in the morning. He's got some work to do tomorrow, but he's all yours for the rest of today and tonight."

Laurie beamed as she looked first at Pete, then back at Shane, then Gabe, Bear, and finally her mom.

"Is it okay, Mom?"

Diane nodded as she sneaked a finger behind her dark glasses—undoubtedly to wipe away a tear. "We already talked about it and it's fine with me." She smiled at Shane as he stood up and handed her a small duffel.

"Got all his food, treats, and a couple toys right in here."

Laurie flew at Shane and hugged him fiercely. Gabe watched Shane's eyes mist over—through the mist in his own eyes. Bear cleared his throat and looked away, the big softie, while all the other guys shuffled their feet.

Laurie gave Bear a hug, then it was Gabe's turn. He knelt down and squeezed her tightly.

"You did good today, sweetheart, We're all proud of you. Go on home and play with Pete. I'll see you in a couple of days when I stop over to keep an eye on you at the house, okay?"

"Okay." The little girl pulled away. "And Uncle Gabe?"

"Yeah, sweetheart?"

"I love you."

Gabe let out a surprised breath. His voice cracked just a little as he said, "I love you, too. We all do."

"Let's get you home," Diane said, her voice choked with emotion. "Could you—"

Before she could finish speaking, Ben had the minivan's door open and was helping Laurie and Pete get settled into it. She turned back to Shane.

"Thank you. Can I...?" She reached into her purse and pulled out her wallet.

"Nope, nope, nope." All the men backed away, palms up, as if she'd pulled out a live rattlesnake.

"We don't take money," Elias said. He pulled his coat back and plucked at the scrubs underneath. "We've all got jobs. We don't do this for a living."

"I know, but, for the dog at least? I know hiring a trained guard dog must be expensive."

"No way, Diane," Shane said. "Kyle specifically told me this is on the house."

Another thing Shane didn't tell Diane. The money for Pete's services came from something Kyle called The Widows and Orphans Fund. Kyle's old boss back in Los Angeles, a man by the name of Lachlan Campbell started it. It wasn't because Diane was a widow or Laurie was an orphan. It was because if someone qualified for it, Watchdog created widows and orphans on behalf of the beneficiaries. Jesse Tobison wasn't married or had kids—thank God—but everyone who knew about him would be happy to remove him from the face of the earth and that included Kyle.

Diane put her wallet away as she looked from one man to another. "We're just so grateful."

"This is...this is just what we do," Shane said.

"Because it's right to do it," Gabe added.

"Yeah," Bear said, nodding. "Let's get you home. I can stay as long as you and Laurie need me today."

Bear had a woman named Ellie who owned some land and a sweet cabin up in the mountains. He'd helped her fix it up when she had no other home but needed a place to hide from her terrible family. They'd all known her as kids, but she'd been gone from Colorado a long time. When she came back, Bear had fallen hard for sweet little Ellie and she adored him. Bear hated to be away from her, but he hadn't hesitated to take a shift to make sure that Laurie felt safe after such a hard day, and Ellie even encouraged him to help out. She understood better than any of them what it was like to be attacked by filth like Tobison.

Bear got in the car and they all waved goodbye to Laurie, who finally looked happy to Gabe. It was good to see. Now, all he wanted was to get out of Denver and back to his small town. The place made his skin crawl.

As a cop car sped by, siren wailing, Shane tapped him on the shoulder. From his expression, Gabe knew he hadn't heard the man say something to him and Shane was trying to get his attention. One more reason to head back home; things were much quieter there.

"Riversong?" Shane asked, a hopeful spark in his eye. They

often went to the coffee shop after carrying out their work, to relax and debrief.

But Gabe knew Shane had ulterior motives.

———

THERE WERE times when Gabe looked at his hearing loss as a blessing. Riding with Shane to Riversong Coffee after the courtroom was one of those times. Gabe had been glad to get out of Denver. The place was too loud and big and always made him feel like it was about to swallow him whole. He much preferred their little hometown of Lyons to the big city. Now Gabe just wanted to grab a coffee and maybe go for a brief walk along the St. Vrain river that skirted the town. It was quiet there. Peaceful. And Gabe wouldn't have to listen to Shane, who was riled up from their morning in court.

Then again, Shane always got this way when they went to Riversong.

It was bad enough when Shane was drumming along with Van Halen on the steering wheel and droning on about the merits of eighties hair bands. It got worse when he started talking about the woman in the window.

Gabe made a show of turning off his hearing aid.

"Dude! Come on, seriously?"

Gabe could still make out Shane's words over the loud music, so the man must have been shouting.

"You know I'm right," Shane went on. "You need to make your move." He stopped at the light right before the shop and glared at Gabe until he turned his hearing aid back on.

"Yeah, because all that non-stop flirting you're doing with April is getting you so far."

"Hey, at least I'm talking to April instead of just moon dogging at her."

"What the hell does moon dogging even mean?"

"Dude, go look in a mirror while you're thinking about Little Miss Window Seat and you'll know." Shane pulled an exaggerated face—he tilted his head, his mouth slowly dropped open, and his eyes grew wide.

Gabe resisted flipping Shane off and pointed out the windshield instead. "Green means go."

Shane went through the intersection and pulled into Riversong's parking lot. Gabe's chest tightened as he couldn't resist looking at the window on the far-right end of the coffee shop.

There she was, same as every day at this time, sitting in the window seat and reading, her back to one of the bookshelves bracketing the padded bench. He knew she'd have a laptop sitting on the table beside her, and the minute he got his coffee and headed for a nearby table, she'd quickly set her book down, open the laptop, and start typing away.

"Why don't you just go introduce yourself and ask her out?"

"Because she always looks busy, that's why," Gabe said.

Pointedly busy the second he got up his nerve to say hi.

They got out of the SUV and walked to the door. April was finishing up with a customer, giving him a smile and a cup of joe. Her smile disappeared when she saw Shane—turning into something a little snarkier—though her sweet smile reappeared for Gabe.

"Morning," she said, and without waiting, immediately dumped two spoonfuls of sugar into the bottom of a ceramic mug. Next she would pour in coffee and one shot of espresso—just the way Gabe liked his coffee.

"Good morning, beautiful," Shane said, leaning on the counter. "I'll have my usual."

"Oh, of course you will. What was that again? I don't keep track."

Gabe tuned out the rest of their banter and glanced over at *her*. The beautiful woman in the window. Brunette, not too thin, thick eyelashes, cozy cardigan in all kinds of weather. He didn't know what she was reading because her book was covered in brown paper. Was she embarrassed about what she read, or was there another reason? Gabe was dying to know.

He was dying to know *anything* about her.

She lifted her pointer finger to her lips and her tongue darted out, wetting it, then she turned the next page. The gesture was completely unselfconscious and at the same time, extremely sexy. Gabe had to turn away before he embarrassed himself.

April had finished making his coffee and was starting on Shane's drink. Gabe pulled out his wallet.

April grinned and put her hand up. "Your money's no good here today, my friend."

What? Did he misunderstand? *It must be all the ambient noise. I really need to acclimate to these new hearing aids.*

"Sorry, I don't think I heard you right. It's free?" he ventured. He watched her lips carefully.

She pointed at his coffee. "That one's already been paid for," April said a little louder.

"You don't need to buy me coffee, April," Gabe said as he continued to open his wallet, feeling like maybe he was somehow the butt of a joke Shane was playing.

April reached across the counter and put her hand on his. He looked up. "*I* didn't buy it for you. *She* did." Then April discreetly pointed over his shoulder. Shane's eyes widened as did his smile, but April's face was dead serious.

Gabe turned to find the woman in the window seat looking shyly up at him through her gorgeous black lashes. She set her book aside and this time, she didn't touch her laptop. The sweetest little smile graced her lips.

"I'll just get my coffee to go," Shane said, looking back and forth between April and Gabe.

"Oh, you don't have to do that," Gabe said, suddenly remembering that yeah, there were other people in the world and one of them was his buddy there for a debriefing.

"Are you kidding?" Shane grinned. "Unless I can hang around up here at the counter—"

"No chance, bucko," April said as she rolled her eyes. "You'll scare off the rest of my customers."

"What?" He grinned wickedly and placed his fingertips against his chest. "There is nothing at all scary about *any* of this."

April shook her head then pointed her chin at Gabe's coffee. "That's getting cold. Better go drink it now, know what I mean?" She glanced at Shane. "And you can vamoose." April turned away, done with both the conversation and Shane, but Gabe caught her fighting back a smile as she walked to the other end of the counter.

"See you, brother. I'm taking a walk by the St. Vrain." Shane toasted Gabe with his to-go cup and headed for the door.

"What about having my six?"

"Brother, me leaving right now *is* having your six." And with that, he was out the door.

Gabe grinned. It was true. He'd been wondering how he could approach the shy, gorgeous woman without scaring her off. If she wasn't interested or already seeing someone, he didn't want to chase her away from the coffee shop, which she obviously loved, to avoid any further awkwardness. *No way is she single*, he'd told himself. He also told himself no way would she be interested in him, especially early on while he suffered the growing pains of adjusting both to civilian life and his hearing loss. But that was months ago, and Gabe was becoming more comfortable with his new life every day. Sure, there were still challenges and frustrations, but yeah, things were getting better.

Especially right now.

Gabe picked up his coffee mug and walked toward the woman, who looked down at the table, now doubly shy. He hoped she wasn't regretting her decision.

She wasn't curled up on the window seat today but had her feet on the floor. The winter sunlight coming through the window directly behind her gave her a soft, glowing halo. This close, Gabe could also smell her perfume—something faintly vanilla, papery, but with a touch of polished wood.

She smells like books. Like a bookstore or a library. Only sweeter.

"Hi," he said when he got to her table. He hoped his voice wasn't too loud. He was still getting used to adjusting his own volume. "Thank you," he added, lifting his cup. "Mind if I sit down?"

Her eyes went round as he sat in the wooden chair. She opened her mouth and took a breath as if she were going to speak. Then she closed it again and blinked rapidly.

Oh no. What did I do? He wondered if it was his voice. Was he too loud?

She tried again. "This wha-was..." She shook her head as she stood up and practically threw her things into her tote bag. "A m-mistake."

"Wait!" Gabe jumped to his feet. "I'll leave you alone."

But she was already moving past him, her gaze fixed on the floorboards, and headed for the door. April watched her, looking distraught.

"Rochelle, wait," she called after the woman, but she was out the door. April looked at Gabe.

"I didn't mean to frighten her," he said. He walked back up to the counter.

April's expression turned apologetic. "It's my fault. I shouldn't have pushed her."

"Pushed her?"

"Yeah. I'm the one who encouraged her."

Gabe looked back at the door. "Her name is Rochelle?"

April nodded. "She's been coming in for a while now. I've been trying to coax her out of her shell." She looked at the front door. "I just hope I didn't break it."

So did Gabe.

TWO

Rochelle Carlson walked into Riversong that morning feeling more confident than she had in a long time. Work was going well, she'd just gotten an amazing compliment, and she was looking forward to seeing the extremely good-looking guy who made her knees go weak the second she'd made eye contact with him a couple months before. The one with the soft-looking brown hair and dark eyes, the kind smile, the solid physique under his winter coat. The same one who sent her running—if not literally then metaphorically—every time he looked at her. He was a living, breathing Book Boyfriend.

And she wasn't used to having a Book Boyfriend that gorgeous giving her a second glance.

Rochelle thought of herself as a mouse. Small, quiet, easily overlooked. And the minute she opened her mouth? Well, that often didn't improve the image.

"Hey, Rochelle." April greeted her in her usual cheerful way.

"Hi, April, how are you?" April on the other hand, made Rochelle feel just a little brighter, a little more seen. She'd started a bit of a friendship with the barista, even though they'd never met up outside of Riversong. April was always working in her family's coffee shop and she had a son to look after. That kid seemed like a handful. But Rochelle and April had started talking for longer than the customary, *What can I get you? I'll have the usual, thanks* banter. April knew everyone in town, or at least everyone who had the good taste to buy their coffee at Riversong. So, she was always full of gossip and good stories and there was nothing Rochelle loved more than to listen to a good story.

"Oh, I'm the usual," April said. She grabbed a mug and started on Rochelle's order without needing to ask what it was. Rochelle wondered if she was too boring, that maybe she should branch out and try something new. Then April added, "He's not here yet."

"Huh?"

April laughed. "Don't give me that. It was the first thing you did when you walked in. You looked around for him."

"Who?" Rochelle asked.

April snorted. "Gabe O'Neil."

Is that his name? Rochelle thought. *Gabe.* She rolled the name around in her brain before she said it. "Gabe."

"Thought you might like to know his name after these many months." April set the mug down on the counter as Rochelle paid with her credit card. "I can tell you all about him too, if you want." She raised her eyebrows mischievously. "Or, you could find out for yourself when he comes in later. They're probably on their way here."

Rochelle put her card back in her wallet. "Who's they? And how do you know?"

"Shane Foti told me yesterday. He's one of Gabe's friends. They all come in here to debrief after they...do things."

If April's goal was to get Rochelle's undivided attention,

then she'd succeeded. First, it was the way April said Shane's name—there was something there. And what did 'do things' mean?

"Okay, April, I'm intrigued. What do they do? Spill the tea."

"If I spill any tea I get fired," April joked. "So, it's a group of guys who..." she rolled her lower lip into her mouth and paused. She lowered her voice. "Actually, this really is kinda secret. They're great guys, don't get me wrong. They help out people in the community with their problems. You know, the kind that bang on your door at four AM demanding to see you." She wrapped her arms around her torso. "Or that won't leave your kid alone."

Rochelle's eyes widened. "Vigilantes?" she whispered.

"No. I mean, not really. They just help out, you know?" April shrugged. "I'm telling you because I think Gabe is a great guy and I think you're pretty terrific, and you two should, you know, do more than give each other googly eyes."

"I do not give anyone googly eyes." She tilted her head. "Wait. Does he give me googly eyes?"

April laughed and slapped the counter. "Yes, yes he does. You would know that if you'd just look up from your book or your computer at him for more than half a second."

The Book Boyfriend is named Gabe O'Neil and he gives me googly eyes.

"No. You're imagining things," Rochelle said.

Now her friend rolled her eyes. "Tell you what. Why don't you buy him a coffee and see what he does?"

Shocked, Rochelle actually took a step back. "That's so..."

"What? Forward?" She laughed again.

"Well. Kinda?"

"Rochelle. It's okay to be a little forward. It'll do you some good."

TIMBERWOLF ON THE MOUNTAIN   19

Rochelle looked into her steaming coffee cup. She'd spent her life being told not to stick her neck out and now April was telling her to buy a total stranger—a total, hot-as-heck stranger —a cup of coffee? Then again, in a world where people swiped right all the time, she probably looked totally old-fashioned.

It's just coffee.

"Come on," April coaxed. "He's a sweetheart, I promise."

"Okay. But, can I do a secret admirer thing? Like, I can buy it now, then not be here when he comes in and—"

"And that defeats the entire purpose, my friend."

And it keeps me safe from making a fool out of myself Rochelle thought.

April tried one more time. "Come on. He's really nice, I promise."

Really nice. And hot. And makes googly eyes at...me. Her pulse quickened and she felt her palms tingle just thinking about the what ifs.

What if he actually comes up to me? What if there's some-thing there?

She took a fortifying drink of her coffee. "Okay. Okay, yeah, I'll do it."

"Hee!" April did a mini victory-dance. "This is going to be great."

Now Rochelle felt light-headed. "Can I still do it as a secret admirer?"

April leveled her gaze at Rochelle. Then she smirked. "I could, but you know he'd figure it out immediately anyway."

"Why?"

"Googly eyes, girl. Googly eyes."

ROCHELLE PAID for Gabe's next coffee and took her seat in the window. At least the coffee shop was quiet at the moment so that when the whole thing backfired there wouldn't be many witnesses. She loved Riversong and hated the idea of finding another place to work. She loved the smell of the roasting coffee, the used books for sale along with cute mugs, the way the light slanted through the window, and of course talking to April. Rochelle was fairly new to the area and didn't have anyone else to talk to yet. That could change today. She pictured Gabe turning and looking right at her, then walking across the coffee shop and sitting down in the wooden chair across the table.

Today is the day I'm going to tell him hello.

She shivered and it felt delicious.

She also wanted to bolt, right now.

Rochelle reached into her tote bag and pulled out her current project, the best one she'd ever had. She smiled at the book covered in brown kraft paper that hid it from the world. She found her place and began reading the characters on the page, quickly becoming lost in the poetry. So lost, in fact, that she didn't even notice when two men walked in the door.

"That one's already been paid for," April said. Her voice snapped Rochelle out of her book and back into reality. She glanced up to see Gabe O'Neil and Shane Foti standing at the counter. Gabe's back was to her but he quickly turned his head, too fast for her to look away.

He kept looking. And then he smiled.

The Book Boyfriend was *smiling* at her. And oh my, was it a beautiful smile. Pure warmth, warmer than the sun shining on her back. Warmer than her coffee, warmer even than the feeling the book in her hands gave her—and that was saying a lot.

Rochelle set the book aside without thinking about it. She

watched Shane tease April, then watched Gabe suddenly look worried when Shane headed for the door.

Oh no. Did I misread his expression a second ago? It wouldn't be the first time.

And then he was walking toward her, coffee in hand, that same gorgeous smile firmly in place.

She'd never admit it to April, barely admitted it to herself, but Rochelle had rehearsed what she'd say if she ever got a chance to speak to the handsome coffee shop guy. All those words queued up now in her mind.

But, oh no, they'd forgotten what order they were supposed to be in, like a line of boxcars jumping the track and getting all jumbled up. She looked down at the table hoping to get the words straightened out before he got there.

"Hi," he said. Gabe stood right in front of her.

What was that funny thing I was going to say? Just invite him to sit down. No, just say hi. Stick with hi for now. No, wait—

She looked up and he added, "Thank you," as he lifted his cup. "Mind if I sit down?"

Then before she could say anything he pulled out the chair and sat. He was so close, his knee brushed against hers under the little table and she exhaled every last bit of air. Just the barest touch and he'd left her breathless.

She opened her mouth as all the words rearranged themselves—into a brick wall.

Oh no. No, no, no. Not now, please. She tried to push out even one word, one little hi. How hard was it?

Too hard. The muscles in her throat clenched. The words wouldn't come.

She closed her mouth and felt her heart race with anxiety and her face flush. He was going to think there was something wrong with her, that she was stupid.

She's always been shy. She's just so shy. Come on sweetie, say something, say hi, tell them hello, come on. Her mother's well-meaning but harmful words took over inside and she was right back to being a tongue-tied little girl.

God, now he was staring at her and she couldn't read his expression at all except that the warm smile she was already addicted to was gone. How much time had passed since he'd sat down? It felt like an hour. It felt like forever and he was wait-ing, waiting, waiting for her to say something.

Why did she let April talk her into this mistake?

"This wha..." *No.* Her stutter was out in full force. "...Was..." Rochelle grabbed her tote and threw everything willy-nilly into it. "A m-mistake."

"Wait!"

She hesitated only a fraction of a second before he added, "I'll leave you alone."

Right. I blew it.

She couldn't get to the door fast enough.

THREE

I blew it. Gabe beat himself up as he walked into the rec center. April had filled him in on how she'd encouraged Rochelle to make the first move, berating herself for pushing her.

"She's quiet. I knew she was quiet, and I just need to learn that not everyone is a bigmouth like me," April said.

Gabe reassured April it wasn't the case. "I shouldn't have just pulled out a chair and sat down before she invited me." He'd been so excited that Rochelle was interested. She was the first woman who'd caught his attention since he'd retired from the military, and she was so intriguing. "If she comes back in—and I hope she does—her next coffee is on me. And tell her that I'll leave her alone."

"No, don't say that. I know she's interested, obviously. Just, maybe, I don't know, pretend she's a skittish deer." April scoffed at herself. "I mean... Ugh, I don't know what I mean." The door opened just then and April quickly looked past Gabe to the next customer. "Hi, can I help you, or can I ruin your life?"

Gabe grinned and shook his head. "I'll see you later," he

told April, then went outside to find Shane. He texted that he was ready to go and Shane replied with a thumbs up. Shane had picked Gabe up that morning from the garage where he'd left his truck for a tune-up. Of all mornings, Gabe just wanted to be alone with his thoughts on the way to work.

"So. How'd it go?" Shane asked the minute he came up the steps leading from the river to the parking lot. "I expected things to go longer. I'm not even finished with my coffee."

Gabe caught about every third word until Shane got closer and he asked his friend to repeat what he'd said. Gabe hated the brief look on Shane's face—not impatience with Gabe, but with himself for forgetting about Gabe's hearing. Gabe waved him off when he apologized.

"It could have gone better," Gabe said. "I scared her off."

"What? You? That's more *my* speed."

Gabe snorted. "Not today I guess."

"Shit, man, I'm sorry. But hey, don't give up, huh?"

"We'll see if she comes back. I told April to buy her a coffee and tell her I'll leave her alone."

Shane tagged him on the upper arm. "Naw, she's into you, I can tell. Just give her time."

"That's almost word for word what April told me."

"Great minds, man." Shane chuckled and smiled wide. Yeah, he had it bad for April.

They got into Shane's SUV. "What time you need to be to work?" he asked as he started the engine.

"Another hour. But I don't mind going in early."

"You got it, brother."

When Shane dropped Gabe off at the rec center, he offered to pick Gabe up after work and take him back to the garage. Gabe thanked him and got out, then jogged ahead of an older couple so he could open the door for them. He was glad to see that Stephanie had salted the walk after the light snow they'd gotten the night before. Today was Senior Clinic Day and they would have plenty of people coming in using canes and walkers. The couple thanked him and headed for the meeting rooms at the back where two public health nurses and their volunteer were setting things up.

Stephanie looked up from her computer at the front desk and smiled at Gabe. "Hey, boss, you're here earlier than I expected."

It was hard to hear what she said over the pop song playing overhead, the clanking of weights in the exercise room, and one shrieking kid who wanted a snack from the vending machine. He really needed to go in and get his hearing aids adjusted. He didn't want to let on that he didn't hear Stephanie so much as lipread her last words.

"Got my errands done earlier than I thought," he told her, hoping that he'd understood her and what he said made sense. When she nodded, he breathed a sigh of relief. "Everything good?" He stood close to the desk. At least the shrieking kid and his mom were out the door. That helped.

"Yup. We've already got people waiting for the clinic."

Gabe nodded. "They like to get here early. I'm glad the VNA approached us about holding regular clinics here. We've had a bunch of new sign-ups for Silver Sneakers."

"Those old people are so cute," Stephanie said, which made Gabe laugh. She was looking at her seventy-third birthday in a month. She also ran in the Colfax Marathon in Denver every year and led a yoga class at the center.

"I want to be you when I grow up," Gabe teased.

She sat up straighter and shimmied her shoulders. "Of course you do."

He laughed again, waved, and headed for his office.

Gabe had first found the rec center when he was at his lowest point emotionally. Newly booted from the Rangers on a medical discharge for his hearing, Gabe felt like he had no purpose anymore. Worse, his best friend, Bear, blamed himself for Gabe's injuries, which was totally ridiculous. Gabe was only doing what Bear would have done if their positions had been reversed. But Bear's guilt had caused him to doubt himself and retire early. He roamed the country instead of coming home to Lyons. Gabe had tried reaching out to Bear to convince him there were no hard feelings. Bear had ignored him, which made Gabe feel even worse. He'd avoided Gabe and the rest of their friends for years, even as Shane, Elias, Ben, and Waylon had moved back to Colorado.

Gabe and Bear were the first to retire, Gabe the first to return home. Without his friends, he felt as adrift as Bear was out on the road. He wasn't sure if he wanted to see his other friends. What would they think of his hearing loss? Would they be uncomfortable around him? Avoid him? Gabe's parents had retired to Florida and he bought their house from them. He hardly left it at first, even as his friends started moving back. Ben called him, asking if he'd be interested in a little project he had going on. Gabe ignored the calls and sulked around the house.

But one day he'd gotten a flyer in the mail advertising the rec center. Something about it appealed to him. Stephanie was the first person to greet and welcome him. If it had been anyone else, he might have walked back out the door. He stayed though, and worked out, and felt better. He came back the next day, then the next.

When he saw the poster for a free American Sign Language class to be held once a week, he looked away at first, but finally decided that he was holding himself back for no reason except pride. He didn't want to admit to himself that his life had changed forever. Going to the class convinced him that while his life was different now, different didn't mean bad. He called Ben and reunited with his friends. And of course they never rejected him. That fear was all in his head, holding him back. When he discovered Ben's project was Mountain Division—helping people who fell through the cracks—he felt like his life had purpose again.

Gabe didn't have to think twice when a management position opened up at the center and they didn't have to think twice about hiring him. Gabe made new friends as life got better and better.

The only person left out was Bear. Gabe tried reaching out to him again, letting him know that another of their friends was KIA. That brought Bear home late last summer. He said he was only passing through but stayed on at Watchdog as a handyman. When he met Ellie, well, that was all she wrote. Bear settled down for good. He and Gabe weren't quite square— Bear was still quiet (even for Bear) around Gabe—but they'd been spending more time together since Mountain Division had stepped up to help Laurie. The little girl had bonded with the two of them especially, and it helped melt some of the frost between Gabe and Bear.

But not quite all.

Gabe was looking over the previous month's expense reports and trying to forget about what happened in the coffee shop when Stephanie buzzed him—something she never did unless there was a problem. He instinctively looked at the clock and noted that the clinic had started half an hour ago. He hit the intercom button on his desk phone.

"Steph?"

"I just called 911. One of the old folks is down."

"Fell outside?" Gabe was already up and out of his chair.

"No. Collapsed at the clinic."

"Roger that." Then he was out of his office and grabbing the defibrillator off the wall beside the door. One of the nurses was running down the hall toward him. He met her halfway and she grabbed the device from him with a thank you, then sprinted back to the clinic. Gabe followed on her heels past people waiting for their physicals. He didn't have to see their faces to know they were worried. The nurse dashed through the door and Gabe was about to follow her in when the volunteer sitting at her card table held up her hand to stop him.

"HIPAA," she said. "Sorry."

Gabe got a glimpse of the situation inside before the door closed. The other nurse working the clinic was on the floor with an elderly man, trying to resuscitate him. He turned and assessed the people waiting. Just like he thought, they were murmuring to each other and watching the door, nervous expressions on some of their faces, stoic resolve on others.

Gabe turned to the volunteer, Evelyn. "I'll help you get everyone out."

"Thanks. Do you have another room where I can reschedule patients?" Evelyn stood and grabbed her scheduler and a box of patient files. Then she lowered her voice and Gabe lost what she said.

Dammit. He leaned in closer, "Sorry, what?"

"I think we should clear out the hall before the paramedics get here. And it's never fun to, you know, watch what happens."

"Yeah, I'll get you set up." He turned and addressed the waiting crowd. "Folks, if you'll all follow me, we'll get you rescheduled for the next clinic. Just this way." He pointed to a branch in the hall that led to a smaller room they mostly used for storage.

To his surprise, a couple of the people actually complained about not being seen today as they moved to the other room.

Movement caught Gabe's eye and he looked back toward

the front of the rec center. The paramedics were here, Elias sprinting in the lead followed by Waylon.

"Hey, brother," he shouted as he dashed past. Waylon nodded his direction. He and Elias disappeared behind the door, followed by a third paramedic. Another glimpse told Gabe things were not going well in the room. The man was still on the floor hooked to the defibrillator and the look the nurses gave Elias told him they were relieved the cavalry had arrived.

Gabe helped the last of the crowd down the hall to the other room. Evelyn had things in hand, even with the ones she called the 'troublemakers' who still wanted to be seen today no matter what.

He headed back to the clinic, not sure what help he could give if any, but ready to do whatever they needed. Inside he could hear Elias' voice but he couldn't make out anything else. He felt a rhythmic thumping through the floor and knew they'd brought out the LUCAS, a heavy-duty chest compression device. Gabe sent up a silent prayer for everyone in the room.

Stephanie joined him. She laid her hand on his upper arm, her expression serene.

"It's in God's hands, friend," she said.

"It's in my rec center."

She smiled and nodded. "That's in His hands, too."

The door opened. Waylon and the other paramedic wheeled out a stretcher. The man was strapped to it, the LUCAS still doing its work. Elias stayed behind in the room talking to the nurses who, under their calm demeanors, still looked upset. Gabe imagined they were giving him a report on what happened. He rapped on the door before going in. He needed to know if the rec center was liable.

Elias was just finishing up. He smiled grimly at Gabe.

"What's his chances?" Gabe asked.

One of the nurses wiped her eyes. "Not good." She looked at Elias.

"You all did everything you could. Massive heart attack, he should have died instantly, but you kept him going until we got here. I gotta run. Thanks for the medical history." He tapped his tablet.

"Thanks, brother," Gabe said.

Elias nodded and sprinted down the hall to catch up with the others.

Gabe turned to Sue, the nurse in charge of the clinic. "What happened?"

She looked at the other nurse, Fran. "He's one of our regulars. Just a sweet guy."

"He brings us homemade fudge," Fran said. "A different flavor every time. He has a sweet tooth, but he can't eat sweets anymore."

"Anyway, he was...there was just something a little off about him today," Sue said.

"I was listening to you talking to him, and I could just tell," Fran told Sue. "Nurse's intuition. I got done taking a BP and came over."

"And that's when he clenched up, like this." Sue threw her head back and drew her arms up.

"We thought he was seizing at first." Fran sniffed and wiped her nose with a tissue. Gabe noticed her shaking hand. "But his heart had stopped. Massive cardiac event. I don't think he's going to make it."

Sue put her arm around Fran. "It's all right. We did everything we could."

"Thank God for the paramedics."

Gabe nodded. He was very thankful for all his brothers.

Gabe spent the rest of the day writing up an incident report. Stephanie brought him coffee. She meant well, but it only reminded him of Rochelle. He hoped she'd come back to Riversong.

I should call April, see if she knows Rochelle's phone number. Not that he would call Rochelle, but maybe he could ask April if she would let Rochelle know that he wouldn't show up while she was there if he made her uncomfortable. He finished his report, made a couple of other calls, then looked up the number for Riversong. Before he had a chance to punch the number in, the light lit up on his desk phone, letting him know Stephanie was forwarding a call.

"Gabe O'Neil, how can I help you?"

"Hi, Gabe, it's April."

"April?"

"Yeah, from Riversong. The obnoxious one."

Gabe laughed. "I know who you are, April."

"Hard not to. Anyway, I want to apologize again."

"No need. I was just going to call you and ask for Rochelle's phone number so I can tell her I'm not an ogre and I'll leave her in peace."

"Uh-uh, no. Let me handle her."

"That sounds ominous," Gabe joked.

"Not at all! I'm just going to tell her she has a free coffee waiting, that's all."

"I would love that," he told her.

"Perfect," April said. "I warn you though—she's going to want to pay."

"Don't you dare let her pay this time. This round is on me."

"I know, and that's why you're letting me handle it."

Gabe smiled wide. Some of the weight of the day evaporated right off his shoulders. "Thanks, April."

"No problem. See you soon."

FOUR

Rochelle felt her face burning all the way to her car. She'd parked at the very edge of the Riversong parking lot—any extra steps she could get in during her day helped. Her job left her sitting a lot and she needed the exercise to stay in shape.

If only embarrassment burned calories, I'd be in the best shape of my life.

She tossed her tote into the passenger side, went around, and got in.

I'll just work from home for the rest of today. Maybe for the rest of every day.

By the time Rochelle pulled into her apartment's parking garage, she felt a little calmer, if a little more embarrassed. She'd totally overreacted, behaving like a child and running away.

What you need to do is go right back to Riversong and apologize.

But apologize for what? She recognized her Maman's voice in her head telling her what to do. Her Maman had usually acted mortified at Rochelle's 'bad behavior' as a girl. Rochelle could never measure up to her parents' standards, especially after her sister was born. But, the goal posts moved constantly. Rochelle was either too quiet or too excitable. Too shy or too friendly. Too slow to learn or too smart for her own good. Too lazy or too focused on a task. And when she got nervous, sometimes she stuttered or her speech shut down entirely, like today.

Ironic, considering how much she loved words and languages. Her livelihood depended on them.

Rochelle unlocked her apartment door and went inside. Her cat, a huge Norwegian Forest Cat named Greg, sauntered up to her, surprised that she was home already. She scratched behind Greg's ears as he twined around her legs and purred loudly.

"You're just looking for an extra bowl of food, aren't you? Well, it's not time yet."

Rochelle sat down at her desk and plugged her laptop in to charge. She opened a writing program that helped with her job before she checked her email. Three small projects came in that would take her the rest of the day. Rochelle worked as a translator, mostly French to English for French companies breaking into the U.S. market or for French-Canadian brands. Translating websites, brochures, training and technical manuals, instructions booklets—they all paid the bills. She was beginning to translate novels from English to French too, and wanted to do that full-time eventually.

Then there was the special project, the one that made her heart flutter. She was hoping to receive an email today that would tell her she had the job for sure.

And there it was in her inbox—the official contract to translate one of her favorite authors. She quickly read over the terms, then forced herself to slow down so that she didn't miss anything. But the contract looked good, and it was what she'd agreed to in person when they'd met a couple months ago, so she signed it and sent it back.

Rochelle smiled at the memory of first meeting Huey, using it to distract herself from the coffee shop earlier. She had never dreamed that when she'd sent his agent what amounted to a fan letter that he would want to meet her. She'd had to go into Denver—which was not her favorite thing to do—but so worth it. The dim sum restaurant off Federal Boulevard had been packed even mid-afternoon—no surprise. They had the best Cantonese-style food in the area. Instead of taking a number to be seated, Rochelle looked inside to see if he was there already.

And yes, the man she'd only seen in photos was sitting at a table near the back—Chen Shu-Hui. He was sitting beside another man—tall, an American, or at least she assumed he was by his blond hair and fair skin.

Rochelle wove between tables, careful to dodge the servers and their rolling carts loaded with small plates and bamboo steamers full of dumplings and buns. The aroma was divine and made her stomach rumble. She was glad the restaurant was loud enough to cover it.

Shu-Hui spotted her and smiled. He and the other man stood up as she reached the table. Rochelle bowed her head slightly as she shook Shu-Hui's hand.

"*Hen gao xing ren shi ni, Chen Jiao Shou,*" she said, which meant, *Good to meet you, Professor Chen*. She spoke the words she'd practiced over and over without a single stutter.

"Good to meet you, too. Please, call me Huey," Shu-Hui said in English. "Like Huey Lewis and the News. "Power of Love." Good singer from the eighties." He nodded and gave her an infectious grin that made her laugh.

"You are my daughter's height," he added, beaming. "And a pretty smile like hers."

Aw! And *that* charmed her completely, as if she wasn't already won over.

The other man shook hands with her. "I'm Theo Firestone."

Okay, that makes sense now. "Oh, yes. Good to meet you." Theo was the literary agent that Rochelle had contacted months ago when she learned he was representing Shu-Hui in the U.S. He hadn't mentioned coming to the meeting but she respected him for watching out for the author.

As they took their seats, a server rolled a cart to their table. They picked out a selection of dim sum and spread the plates out across the table to share. Rochelle was sure she'd drop her chopsticks out of nervousness, but Huey turned out to be nothing but warm and charming—just like his writing. They spoke mostly in English for Theo's benefit. Huey's English was good, and he complimented Rochelle on her Mandarin as they switched between the two languages if Huey didn't understand an English word.

Theo finished a pork dumpling and set his chopsticks down on the edge of his plate. "How did you learn Mandarin, if I may ask, Rochelle?"

She dabbed at her mouth with her napkin. She had her answer prepared. "I spent a good part of my childhood in China," she said. "My Maman is French-Canadian and my dad American so I was already used to speaking more than one language. I was a sponge for languages and so I picked up Mandarin pretty quickly. I had to learn it for school and if I wanted any friends."

She turned to Huey. "And I always found the characters so beautiful. I discovered your poetry in China and I kept studying Mandarin even after we came back to the U.S. Like I said in my letter, I've always loved your poetry, Professor Chen."

"*Nali nal,*" he said, waving her off with a smile, telling her 'No, no' as if his poetry were no good and he couldn't understand how she might like it. "And please, it is Huey, I insist. I am honored that you enjoy my work. I appreciate the English translation you sent. It captures what I say in my poems."

"It was just to show my appreciation," Rochelle said. "Nothing more than a fan letter, really."

Instead of answering, Huey looked at Theo.

"It was lovely, Rochelle," Theo said. "Which is why we're here today. We've been shopping American publishers for Huey's poems ever since he gained his green card. We think an English translation would help."

Outside the restaurant, a police car flew by, sirens blaring. Huey jumped in his seat as his gaze darted around the room.

"Oh! Are you all right?" Rochelle asked in Mandarin.

Huey nodded. "Please, forgive," he said in English. "I am easily startled. And," he lowered his voice. "I am not fond of authority."

Rochelle nodded in sympathy. *So the rumors are true.* She'd heard through the grapevine that Huey had fallen out of favor with the Chinese government and been arrested and tortured in China. He'd escaped three years ago in order to seek asylum in the U.S. as a political refugee. That wasn't the *official* story of course, but seeing his reaction, she knew it to be the truth.

Rochelle brought the conversation back to Huey's work. "I thought you had a publisher already, one of the university presses?"

Theo answered, "For Huey's other literary and scholarly works, yes, and they've been translated. But not for the poetry."

"I see. Having the poems already translated to English might be an easier sell to a publisher."

Theo smiled and nodded. "Exactly."

"Would you be willing to let us use the one you sent?"

Huey asked. He looked so hopeful, and yet ready to hear her say no.

Before she could answer, Theo added, "You would be compensated, of course, but we can't promise that the publisher will use you for the rest."

"But, I would request it," Huey added. "I would insist." He smiled.

Theo grinned at the author as he shook his head slightly. "No promises, and I hope you aren't disappointed."

"No, I'm not disappointed at all," she said, clutching her napkin. "Like I said, I've always loved your poetry, Huey. I never even expected you to meet with me. I mean it, it was really just a fan letter."

Huey laughed. He looked at Theo. "You see? There *are* fans of poetry in the world."

Theo chuckled along. "I see that. Well, Ms. Carlson, I think we have a deal. If you'll email an invoice for your translation, we'll get you paid for that at least."

"Please, it's Rochelle." She couldn't stop herself from grabbing Huey's hand. "*Xie xie!*" *Thank you.* "It's an honor to have translated just one poem from a book rumored to have been on the short list for a Nobel Prize." There was so much secrecy around the selection process no one could confirm that he'd been in the running. "I hope it works and that you find the perfect publisher."

Huey looked at Theo. "I want to ask her now."

Theo's eyebrows rose. "All right then."

"Ask me what?" Rochelle looked back between forth at the men.

"There is another book." Huey smiled softly.

BACK IN THE PRESENT, Rochelle sighed happily as she looked at the confirmation that the signed contract was sent successfully. The publisher who had chosen to work with Huey had also agreed to take her on as his translator.

She'd loved Huey's poems all her life. Their beauty had made her feel less alone when she was a girl struggling to fit in. Reading one of Huey's poems was like stepping into a secret world where no one could tease or criticize her. Whenever she was feeling down, she would recite one of the poems in her head. She'd been translating them in her head, too, for many years, and now she had a chance to actually make them come to life in English and share them with other people who could use their gentle beauty to get through a rough day.

That was fantastic all on its own, but there was something even better. Rochelle lovingly ran her hand over a book wrapped in brown kraft paper sitting beside her computer.

Red Light on Barren Fields.

I can't believe I'm also translating brand-new Chen Shu-Hui poems into English!

"It is still a secret and must be kept that way. You'll be the first person who has read these poems besides me," Huey had told her at the restaurant when he gave her the book—a hand-written, hardbound journal, twin to the first one Huey used to compose them. "They are the poems I wrote here in America, waiting for my asylum to go through."

There was something in Huey's voice and it hadn't taken Rochelle more than a moment to figure it out. Unlike his other works, she'd never found Huey's poems to be political—at least not overtly—though they did praise a China that was long gone. Add that to his jumpiness, and Rochelle understood. She suspected the poems in the new book represented Huey's freedom—and if he'd been critical of China's government before, it was nothing compared to now. Her fingers tingled, wanting to open the book and read his new poetry.

The publisher wanted to feature both Huey's old poems and his new ones in one volume as a way of introducing his work to an American audience. Rochelle still couldn't believe that she'd been chosen to do the translations. All because she'd reached out as a fan of Huey's writing.

She'd spent the last month reading *Red Light on Barren Fields* in Mandarin and had translated the first three poems already in anticipation of getting the job. Now, she was free to translate the rest. And she couldn't wait—she'd been right— Huey's new poems sang of freedom and gratitude.

A call came in over her phone, breaking her out of her thoughts. The number had a local area code but was unfamiliar. She quickly hit accept, thinking that maybe someone from the publishing house was calling her to give her some more details.

"Hello?"

"Hi, Rochelle? It's April."

"April?"

"Yeah, from Riversong. Hey, I'm probably overstepping, but I got your number from your signup info for our loyalty program. You can hang up on me if you want."

Rochelle laughed. "That would be so rude." April's call took her by surprise, but she was in such a good mood, she wouldn't think of hanging up.

"Not as rude as what I did to you this morning. I apologize. I can be really bossy just like the rest of my family, and sometimes I forget that not everyone is as good at pushing back as they are, so I end up overstepping with my friends."

My friends? April thinks of me as a friend. Her chest warmed.

"You aren't bossy."

"You are a terrible liar." April laughed. "I'm calling because I was afraid that you might not come back into the shop and that would just kill me. So, this is me being all apologetic for being a pushy broad and hoping that you'll forgive me and come back."

"Of course! There's nothing to forgive, I promise."

"Good." Rochelle could hear the relief in April's voice. "Because you also have a free coffee coming to you and I'd hate if you missed out on it."

"I love Riversong, so you don't have to buy me a coffee to get me back in, I promise."

April laughed again, harder this time. "Why does everyone think I'm the one buying people coffee? I don't give them away, I sell 'em—I gotta feed Kevin, and he's a growing boy."

"Wait. Did...Gabe buy me a coffee?" She hated how her voice went up in pitch as she said his name.

"Sure did."

"No, I should buy him another—"

"I'm stopping you right there. He's buying it as a way of saying he's sorry, too. He thinks he scared you."

"What? Scared me? No, not at all." Rochelle sighed. "It's not him, it's me."

"Oh, shoot. *Are* you dating someone? Oh my God, I'm so, so, so sorry for putting you on the spot like that."

"No, April, no. I'm not seeing anyone. I just...choked... when he sat down. Not literally, but... I used to have a stutter. Well, I guess 'used to' isn't really accurate."

April's side of the conversation went dead. That was exactly what Rochelle *didn't* want. She didn't want to hear April stumble over some sort of apology, or get all weird about it. Rochelle didn't stutter as much as she used to as a kid. It had taken her completely by surprise when it happened. But Gabe was just so gorgeous. No guy in real life was that handsome *and* nice *and* paid her any attention. He was supposed to stay a fantasy—one she was embarrassed to admit she thought about before going to sleep every night. He wasn't supposed to ever actually notice her beyond a sweet smile she was sure he gave everybody. And he certainly wasn't supposed to come over, pull out a chair, and sit down to actually talk to her.

"I had no idea," April said, and for a moment Rochelle thought she'd read her mind and was commenting on her ridiculous crush on Gabe.

"When Gabe sat down, I couldn't speak."

April paused, then said, "Awwwww!"

"Stop, stop."

"That's so sweet!"

"It's not, it's embarrassing."

April must have heard something in Rochelle's voice. "Okay, okay, I'm sorry. Again."

"It's okay."

"It's just that I love putting customers together, and this was a grand slam, so I thought. And it's just so cute because he thought he'd scared you off with his voice."

"His voice?" Gabe had a fantastic voice, so why would that worry him?

"Yeah. He thought maybe he was talking too loud. He's hard of hearing and gets a little self-conscious about it."

"Really? I had no idea."

"Just like I didn't know about your stutter. You two are both way too self-conscious. It's adorable."

"It doesn't feel adorable."

"Well, it is. Truth is, Gabe's more than hard of hearing. He's got some sort of hearing aid or implant or something. He was injured on a mission. He's a former Ranger. Aaand here I go running my mouth again."

Rochelle wondered if Gabe had learned American Sign

Language yet. She knew only the bare minimum of ASL, just how to sign the alphabet and a few key words. Like any language, it intrigued her.

"No, that's okay. I won't tell anyone. Who would I even have to tell?"

"Oh, honey." Rochelle heard a trace of pity in April's voice. "Have I talked you into coming back or have I scared you away for good?"

Rochelle smiled. "I'll be in bright and early tomorrow. I love Riversong way too much to abandon it. And I'd miss my friend." *And my real-life book boyfriend* she added silently.

"Back atcha! So glad we cleared this up. *Kevin!*" Rochelle winced as April shouted her son's name. "Sorry, gotta go. Kevin just said something about a ball pit and we just got the new beans in. Kevin, get back here!" She hung up.

Rochelle shook her head, still grinning. She'd seen the whirlwind that was April's son Kevin. She pictured him tearing open a giant bag of coffee beans and jumping in like it was a pile of leaves—or a ball pit.

She turned her thoughts back to Gabe. She was shocked that he thought he'd scared her off with his voice. Then again, if his hearing loss was new, he must feel like he's in another country. Maybe he had trouble communicating sometimes, like anyone who didn't know the language. She remembered what that was like anytime her parents took her to a new country and she'd had to adapt.

Rochelle absently signed each letter in Gabe's name. It might be fun to learn more sign language. Another challenge to add to translating Huey's books.

And my hands don't stutter when I'm nervous.

FIVE

Gabe had just disconnected April's call when his phone rang again. This time, it was Elias.

"Hey, brother," Gabe answered. "How's the patient?" His stomach sank even as he asked. The man had been gray when they'd rolled him out.

"We didn't lose him on the way. They took him straight into surgery in Longmont. As far as I know, he's still alive."

Whew. Gabe needed to call Sue and tell her. The nurses had looked so devastated when they left earlier, Fran especially.

"That's good news. I'll pass it along to Fran and Sue. Thanks for letting me know."

"You're welcome. So, I figure after this morning at the courtroom followed by the excitement at the rec center, you and Waylon and I could use a drink."

Gabe smiled. He'd planned on going straight home and taking a walk on his property. His house sat on twelve acres, wooded with a beautiful view at the edge of a bluff overlooking a tiny stream. He was more comfortable there in the quiet with his thoughts than he was in town anymore. But, a drink with his brothers appealed to him as well.

"Come on, T-Wolf," Elias said, using Gabe's old nickname when he hesitated. "Promise it'll be fun."

"Yeah, okay, why not?" Gabe was about to suggest a quiet place in Lyons when Elias overrode him.

"Great! I talked to Shane and he said you still needed to pick up your truck. I'll swing by the rec center to get you, then we'll get your truck and head for Cocks and Strippers."

Gabe groaned.

"What? Why the groan?"

Two reasons, neither of which he wanted to share with Elias. First, it didn't take a genius to do the math. Shane talking to Elias, plus Cocktails and Chicken Strips—a total meat market better known as Cocks and Strippers—equaled all his friends knowing he'd struck out with Rochelle. Second, Cocks and Strippers was loud on a good night and deafening the rest of the time. On one hand, if a woman did approach him, he didn't stick out so much for not being able to hear her. On the other hand, he had exactly zero chance of holding a conversation with anyone, plus he'd be miserable the entire time. He'd learned pretty quickly that even though his hearing aids had different settings, loud bars wreaked havoc on his ears.

"Does it have to be there?" he asked.

"Come on. It's Friday. That's where all the gorgeous women are going to be."

Yup, Elias' answer confirmed that Shane had run his damn mouth.

"I don't think—"

"Stop right there. I'm already on my way down to pick you up." Gabe pictured Elias on the mountain road between Lyons and the small firehouse where he and Waylon were volunteer paramedics. "Unless you want to walk to the garage to get your truck."

"I could, actually. Lyons is small. I need the fresh air."

"Nope. You already said yes so it's settled. See you in ten." Elias disconnected before Gabe could keep fighting.

Bastards. And the best friends a guy could ever hope to have.

Cal, the evening manager, came in just as Gabe was putting on his coat. He walked Stephanie to her car as was his custom, especially with the shorter, dark days of winter, then waited for Elias outside, dreading the evening in front of him. There'd been a time when he wouldn't have hesitated to go out with his buddies and pick up a woman for some casual fun on a Friday night. Now, he was self-conscious.

It didn't help that the first woman he'd tried to pick up when his brothers returned to Lyons tried to stick her tongue in his ear without realizing he had hearing aids. At first she thought he was wearing earbuds or earplugs, but when he told her what they were, she looked at him funny and asked how old he actually was. Then she asked if he was on disability. Then, she was on to the next guy.

Humiliating.

The other, bigger reason why he didn't want to go was Rochelle. He was sure he'd blown it today, and that if she even wanted to talk to him, she'd probably only want to be friends. That was fine with him—for now. But if there was even the smallest chance of developing something more, he didn't want to ruin it. Besides, he already knew that any woman he saw tonight wouldn't be able to compare to her delicate beauty.

THE MUSIC POUNDED through Cocks and Strippers—and through Gabe's head. He'd given up trying to follow any conversation with his friends. He was doing his best trying to lip-read, but they often forgot to look directly at him. Even though movies often showed people reading lips with perfect accuracy, that was far from the truth. Gabe caught about every tenth word.

The chicken strips were fantastic though.

Gabe wondered how much longer he needed to stick around before he could leave without looking anti-social or else they'd give him shit and make him stay twice as long. His friends were blowing off steam from the stress of seeing Laurie in court today, even though everything went well and Bear had texted Ben saying that she was all right emotionally, though he was staying with her and Diane until she went to bed. No matter what, it sucked that Laurie had to see the son of a bitch at all.

Someone tapped Gabe on the shoulder, interrupting his thoughts. He turned and saw Waylon, who had wandered off fifteen minutes ago. He was back—with two women. Gabe had to give him credit—the man worked fast. And the women with him were both gorgeous. Waylon had his arm around one of them, and the other was sizing up Gabe.

Shit.

He lip-read the words *dance floor* and smiled and nodded at her. He slipped off the stool and felt Elias punch his upper arm, his way of saying *atta boy.*

No need to be rude to her. One dance and then I'm out.

Luckily, it was a line dance which meant he didn't have to try and make chitchat. Gabe actually liked line dances, always had. This wasn't so bad.

Until he realized that the DJ had strung a bunch of song clips—and their dances—together into a medley. Gabe did all right at first. The DJ's voice was low enough that when he shouted out the next song, Gabe could mostly make out the name, and he was good enough that he could watch everyone else's first move and catch on, but it took all his concentration.

The problem came when the DJ called up a woman halfway through to announce the next segment. Her voice was high-pitched enough that he couldn't understand her. Gabe ended up bumping into his partner and almost stepping on her toes. Shame flooded him, especially when she said something and he shouted, "I can't hear you." She gripped an invisible beer glass and tipped it to her mouth, then laughed.

Great. She thinks I'm so drunk that I can't dance.

The music mercifully ended. Gabe gave her a tight smile and beelined it back to the table and his jacket. He felt her hand brush against his arm as if to stop him, but he wasn't having it.

"Gabe?" Shane asked as he threw on his coat.

Gabe shook his head and raised a hand, warding him off. "See you later."

Then he was out the door and under the mercifully quiet stars.

GABE SPENT the rest of the weekend nursing his wounded ego at home in the mountains just west of Lyons. He was thankful Bear wasn't at Cocks and Strippers to see him, which probably would have kicked off yet another round of blaming himself for Gabe's injury. Bear was better now that he had Ellie, but Gabe knew things still weren't one hundred percent between them.

Gabe didn't need Bear's guilt or his pity.

He spent the weekend reading, an activity that had earned him a second nickname among the Rangers—The Professor. Gabe was a fiend for books—one more reason why Rochelle captivated him. *Nothing sexier than a woman who reads* he thought. When he wasn't reading, he walked the trails around his land like his namesake—a lone timber wolf patrolling his territory, enjoying the solitude and the quiet. Winter hushed the wildlife and froze the streams into silence.

By Sunday night, Gabe was calm again and ready to quit the self-inflicted pity party. His texts were full of wolf emojis sent by his friends. When they were kids growing up around Lyons, they'd imagined they were part of an elite squad of soldiers and sailors who all had animal code names. Gabe was T-Wolf—short for Timberwolf. Sending the wolf emoji was his brothers' way of checking on him, a reminder that they knew him better than anyone else in the world.

He texted each man back, reassuring them all that he was fine, just needed some space.

The only person who called was April and he let it go to voicemail. She left a message saying that he was missed at Riversong.

"But not by me, by someone else who's been here every day. Well, a little by me, but not like that. Eh, I'll let you figure it out."

The message left him smiling. Rochelle had not abandoned Riversong. Had not abandoned *him*.

GABE GOT to the rec center early Monday morning. Stephanie wasn't at the receptionist desk, which was unusual. She was obviously there because all the lights were on. She hadn't turned the music on yet, which was a blessing at least for Gabe. He went to his office, answered some emails, then checked up front even though he hadn't seen her walk past the big window looking out onto the center.

No Stephanie.

She wasn't in the weight room or the workout rooms, either. She wasn't playing racquetball or running laps up on the second-floor track. That left one place. Gabe walked through the building, past the offices, past the weight rooms, and into the pool area. And that's where he found Stephanie sitting on a folded towel at the edge of the pool. She had her swimsuit on and she lazily kicked her feet in the water.

As soon as Gabe saw what she was up to, he stopped in surprise and confusion.

And then he started laughing.

"Stephanie, what in the hell are you doing?"

"What does it look like I'm doing?" She held up a black box with a tiny steering wheel on it. She quickly returned her attention to the small remote-controlled boat skimming along back and forth in one of the lap lanes.

"It looks like you're enjoying your second childhood."

Stephanie snorted. She turned the little steering wheel on her remote control just as the boat reached the far end of the roped-off lane. It did a U-turn and started back toward Gabe. He studied it as it got closer.

"Stephanie? Why is your smartwatch attached to the top of the boat?"

"Doctor's orders."

Well, that's a new one. "Your doctor wanted you to attach your smartwatch to your boat and send it back and forth across the pool. Do I have that right or am I mishearing you?"

Stephanie didn't bother to look at him as she rolled her eyes. "No, my current beau, the semi-retired doctor, is just overreacting. He heard my knees go snap, crackle, and pop the other morning—don't ask where or how, a lady never tells—and he's worried about me running the Colfax Marathon this year because it might be too hard on my knees. Doctor Boyfriend suggested I swim for a week or two instead of run around on the track upstairs to strengthen my legs and give my knees a break."

"Okay...so what's up with the boat and the smartwatch?"

"Well, he's out of town right now but he's keeping an eye on my smartwatch to make sure I'm okay, and he figured out how to get it to measure swimming laps. I really don't feel like getting my hair wet today since I went to the beauty parlor yesterday, so here we are."

She turned the little steering wheel again, and the boat started its next lap.

Gabe fought back another laugh. "Is that actually working?" He pointed at the boat.

"You bet it is. He's very proud of me. I've already done fifteen laps, can you believe that?" Stephanie smiled sweetly at Gabe. "And since I have the best boss in the world, he'll never rat me out, will he?"

Gabe couldn't hold his laughter back any longer. "No way would I come between you and Doctor Boyfriend."

"That's a good boy." She turned the boat again. "Sixteen laps. That's a new record. He'll be so proud."

Gabe's lips twitched. "Anyone ever tell you you're shameless, Stephanie?"

Her grin made her look devilish. "Doctor Boyfriend has. But once again, a lady—"

"Never tells. I get it."

"One more lap, then I'll towel off and get back to work, right after I text him about how much fun it was getting my feet wet this morning." She kicked her leg and water droplets landed on her legs, which she quickly brushed off.

"I'll leave you to it," Gabe said and turned. Then with a devilish grin of his own, he spun, squatted, and splashed

Stephanie. She shouted and almost dropped her remote into the pool.

"Oh! You are terrible! If you messed up my hairdo, I'll never forgive you." She patted her perfectly dry silver hair.

"You're gorgeous, Stephanie," Gabe said as he walked back toward the men's locker room and showers.

"You know it," she shouted, making Gabe laugh again.

Instead of heading for his office, Gabe went back up front to unlock the doors and man the desk. The center opened in ten minutes and he didn't want to make Stephanie rush. She could have singlehandedly run the place and they both knew it. He was thankful to have her, thankful she'd smiled at him that first day, prompting him to come back the next instead of hiding from the world.

Speaking of beautiful smiles and another gorgeous woman who keeps me connected to civilization...

Gabe wondered if Rochelle was at Riversong yet. He hated that he'd wasted his weekend feeling sorry for himself when he could have been there instead. Just seeing her in the window always brought his spirits up. He thought of how she'd left Riversong on Friday, just like he'd raced out of the bar later that night. She had no reason to be embarrassed, not with him. Now, he just needed to make her understand that.

Gabe planned on taking an early lunch and heading for the coffee shop, hoping to catch Rochelle. He knew she often stayed for hours, reading a book or typing on her computer. He wondered if she was a writer or maybe a researcher tied to Colorado University. CU was in Boulder, not too far down the road.

I'll ask her today. His chest tightened at the thought. Or would that put her on the spot again? Maybe he'd just sit quietly while they both drank their coffee.

He caught himself chuckling. He felt like he was back in

seventh grade asking a girl out on what passed for a date when he was thirteen. He felt just about as nervous.

Damn, I should just write 'Do you like me, check yes or no' on a piece of paper, fold it up, and give it to April to pass on to Rochelle. Maybe after that I'll work my way up to asking her to the school dance.

Gabe signed members in until Stephanie took over the front desk and shooed him back to his office. After that, the morning dragged by as Gabe checked the clock repeatedly. He swore time not only stopped but was moving backwards. It took forever for eleven o'clock to roll around.

"Going to lunch," he told Stephanie without breaking his stride past her desk. She said something back but it was lost to the music overhead and the aerobics instructor shouting encouragement to her class. Gabe practically jumped into his truck and drove to Riversong. He didn't think about texting April to see if Rochelle was even at the coffee shop until he was almost there.

Maybe he felt out of practice because he hadn't dated since his medical discharge from the Rangers. Or maybe because he'd built up a little fantasy around Rochelle. He couldn't remember feeling this excited about meeting a woman for a date, and this didn't even resemble a date.

His excitement only grew when he saw her familiar silhouette in the window.

She's here. His heart thumped against his ribcage as if trying to escape and run in ahead of him.

She was engrossed in a book. Rochelle looked so soft through the window, like an old-time painting. He stopped just for a moment, long enough (but never long enough) to admire her before she could feel him looking. He didn't want to startle her. He remembered April's advice: *Treat her like she's a skittish deer.*

Today, he'd approach her carefully, which was what he should have done from the start. He chuckled as he caught himself closing his truck's door carefully, as if she were a flock of birds that would take flight at the sound. Sparks ran up and down his spine and he quickened his pace across the parking lot. The day was cold so he breathed into his hands to make sure they were warm enough in case she reached out a hand to his.

The first thing Gabe noticed in the coffee shop was the overhead music. It was usually tuned to one of two stations— classic rock or folk music, depending on who was on shift, with the occasional classical music thrown in. April usually had classic rock playing at a healthy volume, but today, the classical music channel was turned way down.

Bless you, April.

April smiled when she spotted him come through the front door. She grabbed two coffee mugs without a word. Gabe appreciated her discretion. He'd been ready for some sort of comment about how he hadn't been in all weekend, but she wasn't nearly as bracing when Gabe was there alone. She seemed to save up her snark for Shane.

Gabe braved a glance in Rochelle's direction while April made their drinks. She was already watching him, a look of anticipation on her face. And then she did something that took him completely by surprise. First she waved. Then she held her index finger and thumb a little apart, followed that with a loose fist, then raised her fingers with her thumb folded across the palm of her hand. She curled her fingers back down, and with that final gesture, she'd fingerspelled his name.

Hello, Gabe.

SIX

Rochelle watched Gabe's face as she finished signing his name. She hoped she'd gotten it right—she'd studied ASL and practiced all weekend, worried that he might come into the coffeeshop on Saturday or Sunday and she wouldn't be ready, would mess it up somehow and he'd decide that between her stutter and messing up ASL, she wasn't worth his time after all.

Two strikes she could hear her dad say in her head. There was no third strike in her childhood. Two strikes and she was out.

For a single moment Gabe stood perfectly still as if time had ground to a halt around him. Then his lips curved into a smile as his eyes sparkled. He held up his hand as if saluting then signed back her name.

Hello, Rochelle.

April watched behind him, looking amused. She caught Rochelle's eye and winked, then tapped Gabe on the shoulder. Their coffees were ready. Gabe grabbed the mugs and walked slowly across the coffee shop, noticeably cautious. Rochelle gestured to the chair across from her, then signed, "Sit, please."

Gabe set the mugs on the little table and sat down. "I didn't know you knew ASL," he said. He had such a marvelous voice. He could have been a radio announcer.

Rochelle didn't quite trust her voice yet, so she signed the words she'd looked up and practiced. "I'm still learning. I hope I've got it right."

Gabe nodded eagerly. "You do," he both said and signed back. His head tilted slightly and his gaze unfocused the tiniest bit as he looked at her. She felt her heart triple its beats.

"Thanks," she said, no trace of a stutter.

Gabe nodded his chin at her latte. "While it's still hot," he said and picked up his own cup. As they drank, he watched her over the rim. She'd never felt so seen. Instead of making her feel nervous, it energized her until her insides practically fizzed.

She opened her mouth to apologize for running away on Friday but what came out instead was, "April told me that you knew ASL, and I love languages, so I thought I'd give it a try. Would you mind giving me some pointers?"

"I'd love that," Gabe said. Then he signed the words. Rochelle copied his gestures.

"Good. Now try this." He signed again, and she caught *you*, *book*, and *reading*.

"Oh! What am I reading?" she said and signed. "Well, it's a bit of a..." She could almost remember the sign for *secret*, but not quite. Was it the index finger at the mouth, or was it the thumb? Afraid she'd be wrong and make a fool of herself, she fingerspelled the word instead.

Gabe tapped his thumb against his lips twice. "Secret," he said.

"Oh, right." She felt her cheeks heat up as she looked down at the table.

"Hey, it's okay. Do you know how long it took me to learn? And I'm still learning."

She tilted her chin up. "Like any language."

"Exactly. There's always something new to learn. Here." He took her hand in his, which was rough but warm, sending tingles up her arm. He folded her fingers in and raised her hand to her lips, tapping her thumb against them. "Secret."

"Got it," she said. His eyes went a little unfocused again as he studied her lips and then he blinked rapidly and let go of her hand. "Sorry," he said and signed. "That was really presumptuous of me."

"No," she shook her head quickly. "If I don't have it right, then I'll look like a fool. Thank you." She didn't dare add how good his hand felt holding hers, or the way her skin tingled when he brought his hand close to her face.

They went back to drinking their coffees, eyeing each other over the rims of their coffee mugs. Rochelle struggled to think of something to say before the silence stretched on too long, but Gabe saved her.

"Is your secret book for work?" he asked.

"It is. I'm a translator."

His eyebrows rose. "Cool. For the government?"

Rochelle grinned. "No. Mostly for businesses. I don't usually translate sensitive things. But this project is a secret for now, and very precious to me." Yet, she wanted to share it with Gabe. She had a feeling he might appreciate Huey's poetry.

"Do you interpret for people as well?"

"Oh, I'm not an interpreter at all. That's a totally different skill set. I translate mostly French and English. With some Chinese thrown in," she couldn't help but add.

Gabe's eyebrows rose. "So, you can read and write Chinese characters?"

"Yes. I learned them as a little girl. This project—" She stopped herself. She'd already said too much. Her contract specified that she wasn't to talk about the new book or about Huey.

"I won't push you," Gabe said. "Not on that. But...maybe while I teach you ASL, you could show me some cool characters?"

"I'd love to," Rochelle said. Gabe didn't know it, but he'd gotten right to the heart of what she loved—written words. Any language, any form. She grabbed a notebook out of her tote where she'd been translating the poems. She flipped it open to a blank page and took out a pen.

"Is it like memorizing a bunch of pictures?" Gabe asked.

"Sort of, but not really." Rochelle drew a figure on the page. "Chinese characters started out as pictures, but they've evolved into representing sounds. There are the basic forms—"

Gabe touched the edge of the page and she looked up at him. He looked pained.

"You were talking pretty fast and quietly, and the table next to us is being kind of loud." He tapped an ear. "And I need these adjusted."

"Oh." She realized she was looking down—he couldn't read her lips. "Sorry. I tend to talk quickly when I'm excited."

Gabe smiled. "It's okay. I like seeing you excited." A hint of color filled his cheeks that warmed her insides.

Rochelle spent the next forty-five minutes showing Gabe some basic characters and explaining their meanings before he glanced at his watch.

"Whoops. I need to get back to work. Stephanie will be drumming her nails on the desk."

Rochelle started. "I don't even know where you work." She scolded herself for not asking Gabe about his life. Instead, she just let her interests take over. What if he was humoring her and was actually bored to tears but too polite to mention it?

"I work over at the rec center part-time. I'm one of the managers."

"Really, a manager? I'm surprised you don't teach one of the workout or weightlifting classes." She glanced at his well-defined arms and her gaze lingered there. It wasn't the first time she wondered how they would feel wrapped around her.

Stop it. Just stop it.

Gabe graced her with a gorgeous smile. "Thanks." He stood and she followed. "Can I get you another coffee? I should have asked earlier."

"No, no, I'm fine. Thanks."

When Gabe furrowed his brow she realized her voice had gone high and a bit squeaky. She quickly signed, "No, thank you," and, pitching her voice lower added, "I've hit my caffeine limit for the day."

Gabe nodded, looking thoughtful. "So…" he started.

Here's where he says it's been nice and I'm nice, and that's it.

"…Will I see you here again tomorrow? Could I buy you another coffee then?"

Rochelle was so shocked that she just looked at Gabe. He wasn't bored with her? He wasn't brushing her off after she'd wasted his time? When she tried to tell him that she'd love that, the words piled up and formed a wall just like they had the first time. She watched helplessly as his face fell.

"Never mind then," he said, his rich, radio announcer voice full of deep disappointment. "I shouldn't have—"

"Please," she signed. "I would love that."

Now Gabe looked stunned before his face broke into a warm smile.

"Good," he signed back. "I would, too." Then he said, "I can't believe you studied ASL this weekend."

Still not trusting her voice, Rochelle just shrugged and

smiled. How could she tell him that she would have spent the entire week learning ASL if it meant she could communicate with him? Was that desperate of her? Would it scare him away?

He studied her face, his own expression going soft with the tiniest smile now. "Thank you," he signed.

Her words still wouldn't come, but her hands flew. "Tomorrow. Coffee. Good. Fun." She bit her lower lip, then let out a giggle. "A lot to learn," she signed.

Gabe glanced at the Chinese characters on the page. "Same here. So. Tomorrow."

Rochelle nodded. "Tomorrow," she said. Even though it came out as little more than a whisper, Gabe nodded, understanding perfectly.

SEVEN

Gabe was on cloud nine when he got back to the rec center. Rochelle was learning ASL just to speak to him. Even his buddies hadn't gone that far. It touched him deeply, only increasing his desire to get to know Rochelle better. And honestly, the signing seemed to help *her* communicate more than it helped him.

He'd drifted past the reception desk before hearing, "You look like you had a good lunch." Stephanie's eyebrows were halfway to her hairline.

Gabe stopped and turned. "You could say that."

"Atta boy, tiger," she said with a wink and went back to her book.

Gabe just shook his head and continued to his office. He wasn't sure how he was supposed to get any work done when all he could think about was spending more time with Rochelle tomorrow. As she'd shown him how Chinese characters worked, she'd relaxed and her voice had grown more confident. He liked seeing that in her and knowing that he was the one who brought it out. He'd watched the same thing happen in himself while learning to sign. Gabe had gone from thinking he was completely useless to feeling reconnected to the world, even if it was in a different way.

About an hour before the end of his workday, Gabe's cell-phone rang. It was Ben.

"What's up, brother?"

"Bad news. Jesse Tobison's family is at it again."

"What the fuck, Ben?" Gabe clenched the edge of the desk as pure rage shot through his veins.

"Diane spotted Jesse's uncles circling Laurie's school earlier in their car."

"Of course they did."

"And when they got home, there was a 'present' waiting for them on the front porch. A bag full of dog shit."

"Fuck." Gabe wondered if anyone would come running if he pummeled his desk. The whole family hated Laurie for testifying against Jesse. They blamed her for the fact that their whole chain of daycare centers was under investigation for abuse. She didn't just help put Jesse behind bars—she threat-ened the entire family business. Gabe wondered which family member would face charges next.

"Bear's already en route to Laurie's house," Ben said. "Kyle's offered Peetie again and Bear's swinging by Watchdog to pick him up. What's your schedule?"

"I can watch tomorrow, all day. I can even go over there after work today and take a night shift if Bear needs a break." He'd planned on checking on the little girl that evening anyway. He had no problem extending it to an all-nighter to make sure she was safe.

"Good. Bear says he's fine, so I think we'll keep him on, doubled up with you if he and Ellie don't object, at least through tomorrow. I'll let them know and tell Bear to expect you after work."

Gabe felt uneasy. Did Ben not trust Gabe to be able to protect Laurie and Diane by himself because of his hearing?

No, that's your old insecurity talking he told himself. *Think about Laurie, not yourself for a minute. She needs extra reassurance right now, that's all. Makes sense since she bonded with Bear and me the most.*

The uneasiness didn't go away. Pulling a night shift would force him and Bear into time alone while Laurie and Diane slept. They still hadn't talked—not really—about their last mission together for the Rangers. Bear had traveled the country for years to avoid it, and now here they were.

Suck it up. Again, think of Laurie.

"Thanks, Ben."

"Thank *you*, T-Wolf." The big man paused. "As always, I'm grateful to you and the rest for everything."

"My pleasure and my honor, Moose."

"One day, you know, I'll be able to pay—"

"Stop right there, Ben. You know that's not why any of us do this."

"I know. I also know it takes up your time."

"Time I would have spent sulking in my house." The words were out before Gabe could stop them. "When I came home from the Rangers, I was in bad shape, you know that. When you got to town and called—"

"You mean when you picked up the phone finally."

Gabe chuckled. "Yeah. When I finally answered, I'd been sitting there feeling sorry for myself. You gave me back my sense of purpose, Moose."

"You would have found it anyway, brother."

Gabe looked out the office window into the rec center. "Maybe. Anyway, yeah, tell Bear I'll see him tonight."

"Roger that."

After Gabe disconnected, he remembered he'd made plans

to see Rochelle at Riversong the next day. He'd have to let her know that he might have to change that. Then he realized that he never asked for her number. She didn't work for a company he could call, either.

He dialed Riversong's number and a gruff man's voice answered.

"Riversong, how do you like your coffee?"

It was April's father, Sonny Taylor. Sonny had started the coffee shop years ago instead of going into the Taylor family business with his parents, which had been growing and selling marijuana illegally back in the Sixties. Sonny's sister Luna and her husband did, and now they owned a legal grow house and dispensary, which kept them out of jail—sometimes. Despite Sonny going straight, his branch of the family was tainted with the sins of the parents down through Sonny and on to his and Luna's kids, who Sonny looked after whenever their parents flaked out or got arrested.

"Could I speak with April, please?" Gabe asked.

Sonny paused. "Anything I can help you with?"

"No, I just need to talk to April."

Sonny gave him a slightly menacing growl. "She's on break. Who can I tell her called and why?"

Most of the time, Sonny was like his name—an easygoing, sunny day if a little quiet, and good with the customers.

"This is Gabe O'Neil. I'm a friend of hers. I wanted to ask her if—"

"What kind of friend of April's, Gabe O'Neil?"

Before Gabe could respond, there was a muffled sound and a woman's voice. Then April came on the line.

"Gabe, sorry!" April said. "What do you need, hon?" She sounded exasperated.

"Hate to bother you, but any chance Rochelle's still there?"

"You missed her, Gabe, sorry. When she's working here, she usually heads for home around four."

"Dammit."

"What's wrong?"

"Oh, something came up for tomorrow and I might not be able to see her, and..." he trailed off, feeling like an idiot.

"And lemme guess. You still didn't ask her for her number or give her yours."

"...Yeah."

April laughed. "You guys! Honestly. What century is this?"

Gabe smiled ruefully. "So, I'm a gentleman. I guess you prefer aggressive guys like Shane," he pushed back.

"Pfft, don't even go there," she warned him. "Hang on."

While Gabe waited, he wondered if maybe that was why Sonny sounded so guarded. But Shane wouldn't be harassing April beyond flirting with her at the counter, would he? Not to a point where her father would be acting like any man calling and asking for April was automatically suspect. Before he could think on it further, April came back on the line.

"Got it. Ready?"

Am I being too forward?

"Maybe I should just have you call or send a text instead."

"Nope, I'm out on this one. Though, it's been fun watching you two dance around each other." Humor had crept back into her voice. "I suppose after this, you'll take her out to a restaurant where I can't eavesdrop."

Gabe laughed. "Maybe you want to be our chaperone?"

"God, no. I'd make the worst chaperone, trust me. Here's her number."

Gabe's phone buzzed with an incoming text.

"Got it," he said as he looked at the text from April. "Thank you."

"Welcome! Gotta go, customers piled up while I was sorting your love life." And she disconnected.

Love life?

No. Friends, maybe. Gabe honestly couldn't tell with Rochelle.

Other women he'd been with had always let him know right up front exactly what they wanted. How many times had he been at a bar and seen a woman look at him from across the room, her eyes letting him know immediately that if he approached, preferably with a drink for her in his hand, that she'd be down for a night in his bed? And maybe more than one night if things went well. Sometimes they did and Gabe would be in a relationship for months before the demands of being a Ranger led to The Talk, as he thought of it. Always initiated by her and always ending with some variation on what a great guy he was but she didn't want to wait at home bored or worrying that he wouldn't come back.

And even when he was home, there was always a part of him that was still out on a mission, never entirely there, never completely present.

We'll stay friends, right? Every woman always asked that question.

Spoiler alert: they never did.

With Rochelle, there wasn't that quick promise of a good time. Just a slow, simmering desire, at least on Gabe's part.

But they were only friends, Right?

At least for now.

Gabe added Rochelle's number to his contacts, opened a text, and spent the next five minutes trying to figure out what to say. He couldn't tell her exactly why he'd miss their not-a-date because he wanted to preserve Laurie's privacy. But he also didn't want Rochelle to think he was blowing her off for no good reason, or that he'd changed his mind.

Finally, he figured it out.

> Rochelle, hi, it's Gabe. I asked April for your
> number because you'd already left Riversong.
> I hope that's okay.

He hit send and set his phone down. He made a pathetic attempt to work while he waited to hear his phone buzz.

Fifteen minutes later, he got a response.

> That's okay. I should have thought of giving
> you my number.

The three dots kept bouncing while she typed more.

> I'm new at this.

She added a blushing face emoji that only made Gabe like her more. He typed back:

> And I'm out of practice. So out of practice
> that I hate to do this, but I might not be at
> Riversong tomorrow.

He paused, then added:

> I made a promise to someone who

Gabe deleted the line before even finishing it. *Makes me sound like I already have a girlfriend.* All he needed was for Rochelle to misunderstand *that.* He started to type that it was work-related, but that was a flat-out lie. He went back to the promise.

> I promised I'd spend the day with my niece.

True enough. Laurie did refer to all the guys as her uncles.

His knee bounced up and down like the three dots while he watched as she answered, hoping she'd understand.

> That's sweet! I hope you two have a wonderful day!

Gabe blew out a breath. Yeah, they were definitely just friends. In Gabe's previous experience, any woman he was dating would've acted passive-aggressively jealous or outright demanded that he cancel his plans. He didn't think Rochelle was pulling anything passive-aggressive in her text, but he'd been wrong about women before—God knew that was true. He and Bear were a lot alike in that regard. But Bear had found his sweet little Ellie. Maybe Rochelle was made of the same cloth. He should ask her out, take her to dinner, go on an actual date.

Don't push it. Stop assuming there's a chance here. Be casual. Friends.

The memory of the woman at Cocks and Strippers thinking he was drunk pushed into his mind and he gritted his teeth in shame.

Why get my hopes up with Rochelle?

Gabe's thumbs flew as he typed:

> Thanks for understanding. Maybe I'll see you at Riversong next week?

He waited. And waited. His desk phone rang and he picked it up, his eyes still on his cell phone, watching for the three bouncing dots to make another appearance. He answered some questions about the incident at the clinic on Friday for insurance. The conversation ended and he waited some more. Gabe opened a spreadsheet, typed in some numbers, then tapped his phone since the screen had gone dark.

No response.

Jesus, get a grip. She's got a job too, you know. She's not sitting around waiting every second for your ass to text her. Casual, remember?

He went back to staring at his screen.

Or, she really is pissed like every other woman you couldn't make time for. Can you blame her?

"I said, why the sourpuss, boss? It's almost quittin' time."

Gabe startled and looked up at Stephanie standing in the doorway. How long had she been there?

"Nothing," he lied. "Just...numbers."

Stephanie crossed her arms and leaned against the door-frame. She obviously wasn't buying it.

"Didn't think anything could bring you down from lunch. What's the matter, she don't wanna go out with you again?"

"Dammit, Steph."

She grinned. "I'm right, aren't I? Well, she's not worth it."

"She's just gone quiet, that's all."

"Okay. Sure."

"We're not even dating. She's just a friend."

"Yeah, and I swam actual laps this morning."

"Is Doctor Boyfriend still falling for that?"

"Don't change the subject, Sunny Jim. Nobody comes back from lunch with a *friend* floating past my desk like you did."

Gabe didn't answer. He just finished typing in a note summing up the day for Cal.

Stephanie rolled her eyes. "Just walk me out, big fella."

Gabe stood up and grabbed his coat. He waved to Cal coming in on the way out. The parking lot was pretty full for the time of day. The night manager would have his hands full.

"So what did you say to her?" Stephanie waited until they'd gotten to her car to say anything else.

"You're not going to let it go, are you?"

"Nope."

"Fine." Gabe pulled out his phone and opened it to his texts with Rochelle, noting that she still hadn't answered. He handed the phone to Stephanie. She held the phone out at arm's length to read it. Then she laughed.

"Dum-dum!"

"What?"

"You left her hanging."

"I did not."

"Yeah, you did." Stephanie studied the messages another second before handing the phone back to Gabe.

"Trust me, you left her hanging. If she was just a friend as you insist, she would have texted back with a thumbs up or something. Instead, you've got silence. You need to ask her out," Stephanie said. "And after friend-zoning her, don't be surprised if she just says she'd like to keep meeting at Riversong."

Ooof! And here I thought I was the one getting friend-zoned.

"All right. I'll text her again." Gabe typed while Stephanie stood on her tiptoes at his elbow and watched.

"No, don't type that," she said.

Gabe turned the screen away from her. "Do you mind?"

"Do you want to mess this up again?"

He blew out a breath. "Why does everyone think they know how to handle my lov...I mean, my *friendships* better than I do?"

"Honey. You just answered your own question."

Gabe growled as he erased the message and typed in:

Actually, I'd love to take you out somewhere.
Or if you'd like we can keep meeting up at
Riversong, your choice.

"Better?"

Stephanie pursed her lips and gave a curt nod. "It'll do."

His phone buzzed almost immediately.

"Must have been good enough," Gabe said as he read the text then showed it to Stephanie. "And it looks like you were right."

> Oh! Yes, we can keep meeting at Riversong.
> That would be great.

Stephanie just smiled as she clicked on her key fob and her car door unlocked. Gabe grabbed the door handle and opened it for her. He waited for her to get her car started—the battery could be fussy in the cold—and then she rolled down the window.

"Oh, and to answer the question you asked inside?" she said. "Of course Doctor Boyfriend's still buying that I'm swimming laps. I'm a very trustworthy person."

Gabe was sure Stephanie could hear his laugh all the way to the edge of the parking lot.

He turned and headed for his truck, his good mood dissipating when he remembered where he was going. Gabe hoped Laurie and Diane were all right.

I probably shouldn't worry too much. Bear has a way of putting people at ease. Despite the big man's size, he could be gentle and he was almost always quiet, a listener. *Maybe I should call and see if they want me to pick up something for dinner. Laurie loves chicken nuggets like every other kid—*

Gabe's thoughts were interrupted when a car door opened and a woman stepped out. She was bundled in a heavy puffer coat and a beanie with a ridiculous pompom on top, but he'd know her shape anywhere.

It was one he had come to loathe.

EIGHT

Rochelle watched Gabe walk through the parking lot on his way back to work.

I think that went well. She swallowed down her doubts as she mentally went back over every moment of their time together. She lingered on the memories of Gabe's smile and his laugh.

Then her stomach lurched when she remembered how she'd almost ruined everything at the end. She hated it when her words failed her.

But I didn't ruin it. I'll see Gabe tomorrow.

Rochelle looked down at the notebook she'd been using to teach Gabe Chinese characters. She smiled at his somewhat clumsy efforts to copy her and wondered if that's how her attempts at ASL looked to him.

Nope, don't let that throw you. Gabe O'Neil spent lunchtime with you. You're translating Huey's latest poetry because he liked what you'd done already. You've come a long way from being a shy little girl in the shadows.

Rochelle smiled to herself as she carried her empty mug to

the counter and ordered a sandwich for lunch from Sonny. After eating, she opened her laptop and the brown paper-covered book and got to work on translating. She was well into her work and completely focused when her phone buzzed—the notification that it was time to pack up and head home startling her out of her work trance. She looked up to see that it was already getting dark outside. She'd started setting a timer for herself because otherwise, she got so involved with her work that she'd forget where she was or that it was time to leave. She packed up her things, waved to April, and headed out into the cold air.

The first stars were just coming out overhead. Rochelle could hear the St. Vrain splashing over the rocks nearby. Lyons was so beautiful and peaceful and she was glad she'd chosen to settle there. It wasn't flashy and fast like New York or Los Angeles and it wasn't too remote like some of the places where she'd lived growing up. It wasn't on anyone's top ten bucket list to visit, which meant her family wouldn't be visiting anytime soon. She wondered where they were right now. It would have only taken her a minute to look at Instagram to find out, but why bother?

Rochelle started her car and noticed another vehicle leaving the parking lot just behind her. She thought back for a moment and didn't remember anyone walking out of the shop after her. Come to think of it, that was the second time it happened.

Head in the clouds will get you killed she could hear her father say. She shook off his voice and drove to the grocery store in nearby Longmont. But the feeling didn't leave her. She kept glancing back and watching the car behind her. When she pulled into the grocery store parking lot, the other car kept going.

See? It was nothing.

Rochelle parked under a light as close to the store as she could get, telling herself it was just because she didn't want to walk that far.

As she filled her shopping cart, she couldn't shake the feeling she was being watched.

Just old habits.

When she was a girl in China, her family was constantly watched. All visitors were, along with regular citizens. Whenever her parents held or attended religious ceremonies at someone's house, they had to stay low key and keep the gatherings small. Even then, they were sometimes infiltrated by someone from the government. When Rochelle's mother had gotten pregnant, they decided to leave China altogether for the safety of the baby on the way.

Back in the U.S., life changed completely after Rochelle's little sister was born.

Rochelle shook the past from her thoughts and focused on the store. There was absolutely no one watching her.

The car that followed me out of Riversong's parking lot kept going, just like the time before. It's just nerves. No one is spying on you.

She paid for her groceries and left. She had an uneventful walk to the car despite the hair on the back of her neck prickling, which she ignored. When Rochelle got in her car, her phone buzzed again. She was surprised to see a text pop up from an unknown caller, but her surprise turned to delight when she read Gabe's name. Until she realized he was canceling on her. Disappointment set her back on the roller coaster of emotions.

What if he had to cancel because he has an actual date with someone else?

Then he gave his reason. He was seeing his niece.

Relief flooded her. It was actually sweet that he was

spending time with his family like that. She texted him back, reassuring him that it was okay. He returned with:

> Thanks for understanding. Maybe I'll see you
> at Riversong next week?

Her heart fell again. He sounded like he wasn't that into her. That question mark told the story along with the maybe.

Book Boyfriends aren't real she reminded herself. *And if they were, they wouldn't be into a scared little mouse like you.* She thought about texting back, attempting to be casual, but she couldn't think of the right words.

Sighing, Rochelle started the car.

It wasn't until she'd put away most of her groceries that Gabe texted again.

> Actually, I'd love to take you out somewhere.
> Or if you'd like we can keep meeting up at
> Riversong, your choice.

Rochelle felt like the sun had just risen above a tall mountain, flooding the valley her heart was trapped in with light.

He does want to see me.

Maybe there are real Book Boyfriends after all.

Then she bit her lip. The idea of going out with Gabe both delighted her and scared her to death. But, he'd left her the option of Riversong. A safe choice.

Or, was it a just-friends choice?

God, I really am terrible at this. Why is it so much easier for other people to figure out?

Play it safe. This might just be a pity date.

She finally texted that Riversong would work, then put her phone away before she could second-guess and make things worse. She made herself dinner and turned on the TV for company. *Friends* reruns were on. At least their misunderstandings made her laugh, unlike hers, which only left her feeling anxious.

I really don't want to mess this up.

Watching TV relaxed her until it was time to go to bed. When she turned out the light beside her window, she glanced outside in time to see a vehicle pull away from across the street, its headlights off until it was halfway up the hill.

Is that the same car from earlier? It was too dark to see for certain.

No. Just teenagers sneaking out she told herself. *You're in America, not China.*

She shook her head at her paranoia and went to bed.

NINE

Gabe didn't recognize the car parked next to his truck so she'd gotten the jump on him. He braced himself, clenching his fists to keep from throttling her when she turned and stared him down.

Velna Tobison. Jesse Tobison's mother.

Gabe had seen how Velna could turn on the charm when she needed to, and it was very convincing. She could come across as caring and protective—gaining the trust of so many parents who left their children in the care of her family's daycare centers. Parents like Diane, who Velna tricked into trusting her, into trusting her daughter would be safe with Jesse.

Standing there in the parking lot, Velna didn't bother trying to trick Gabe with her false charm.

Evil had a look that Gabe knew well. He could see it now in her eyes—a high, white glimmer of light that had nothing to do with sunlight or stars or anything good. It was a light straight out of hell—cold and piercing, like a poisoned needle. Maybe Velna had a soul once, but it had burned away in the glow of that malevolent light. And worse, Gabe figured she'd burned away her son's soul too when he was a child. Jesse had not been born evil—no baby was—but Gabe had a feeling that he'd been made that way by the woman standing in front of Gabe. Staring into the cold light of her eyes, he felt that evil down to his toes.

The one good thing was that if Velna was here it meant she wasn't off harassing Laurie. Gabe quickly looked into her car. She was alone, no brothers or cousins. Was Velna here to distract Gabe while they pulled some sort of shit at Laurie's house?

Dammit.

Gabe pulled his phone out of his pocket as he calmly walked toward Velna. He texted Bear one number—six. That was Mountain Division's signal to watch your six. It also represented the six of them, and that they had each other's backs. He put his phone away and stopped in front of Velna.

"What the hell do you want?" he asked her.

She smiled sadly. On any other face, her expression would have invoked pity but somehow, she made it look like a mask hiding diabolical laughter.

"Are you a father?"

"What? No."

"Then you can't possibly understand what I'm going through."

Gabe's jaw clenched before he said, "Yeah, you're right, I can't understand what you're going through. I can't understand how someone could abuse a child the way Jesse abused Laurie. Which means I can't understand what's going on in that sick, squirming mind of yours. I know he's your son, but how can you harass an innocent little girl?"

The high, white light in her eyes flared and her mask cracked the tiniest bit, showing him the rage lurking beneath it.

"We're still fighting to set Jesse free. I'm here hoping you can see your way to softening your heart toward my son."

Gabe almost staggered backward.

"Softening my heart?"

"Yes. He didn't do anything. She's not an innocent little girl. She's a liar. That horrible little girl is lying. Tell her and her mother that I want a public apology to both my son and me, and I want them to say he's innocent so he can go free." She ticked off on her fingers. First, I want my son back. Second, I want my business free from false allegations."

Yeah, supposedly false allegations that just keep coming— from other kids now that Laurie was brave enough to testify.

"You really are batshit crazy, you know that?" Gabe said. "Why the hell would I ever do that?"

"I'm asking *you* as a mother, since Diane can't seem to understand what I'm going through. The lawyer bills, people talking behind my back, parents pulling their kids out of our daycares—"

"Well, I'm here to say to your face, stay the hell away from Laurie and Diane. And tell your piece-of-shit son that I'm glad he's behind bars because he's guilty as sin."

Velna kept talking over him as if he didn't exist. "—and Jesse's just so sad. Everyone's judging him in prison."

"Oh, poor fucking baby. He deserves to be locked in a cell alone where he can rot to death. And so do you."

Velna pressed her fingers against her puffer coat, covering her heart. "How dare you? I'm his mother, and I love him, and I won't stand here listening to him get slandered."

"Then don't stand here. Get in your car and go drive it off a cliff. If I see you in this parking lot again, I'll tow your fucking car." He took a step forward until he loomed over her. "And if he, or you, or any other member of your fucked-up family comes anywhere near that little girl, there will be hell to pay, understand?"

"Is that a threat?"

Gabe almost told her it was a promise, but he stopped. For all he knew, her lawyer had made sure she had a wire under that coat.

"Not from me. There's still a restraining order against all of you. You would be breaking the law if you came anywhere near her—*that's* the hell you'll pay."

Velna's face squinched up into a wrinkled scowl. She looked for all the world like a baby about to throw a tantrum. She pointed at him.

"You'll see. One day, you'll have a son and someone will hurt him, and then you'll see. God will punish your hard heart, and you'll remember this night."

"I doubt it. God sounds ugly coming out of your filthy mouth. Now get the hell out of here." He took his phone out again. "I'm calling a tow truck."

"I warned you." She smirked and got into her car. Whatever Velna wanted to accomplish, she seemed satisfied.

Gabe watched her car until it disappeared from view. He studied his truck. The tires looked okay. Nothing was keyed. The windows were all intact. He even went so far as to turn his phone camera and flashlight on to examine the undercarriage for explosives.

Old habits were hard to break. But in Velna's case, he thought he was justified.

The last thing Gabe did was call Cal, giving him a description and the plate number of Velna's car, and asking him to make a copy of the video from the parking lot's camera. Gabe wanted to know when Velna got there and if she'd gotten out of the car at all. When Cal asked why, Gabe told him he'd explain later, but that the woman in the video was a known problem.

Then Gabe got in his truck and calmly texted Bear, telling him he was picking up nuggets and burgers for dinner.

BEAR OF COURSE was having none of Gabe's calm when he walked through the door with a couple of big fast-food bags and a smile on his face for Laurie.

"Uncle Gabe!"

"How's my girl?" Gabe said as he dropped to his knees when Laurie ran up to him. He set the bags aside and gave her a big hug. Bear swiped the bags off the floor before Peetie could get his paws on the food. Gabe knew the glare Bear gave him wasn't just for Gabe's carelessness with the food. He hadn't answered Bear's texts concerning the six until he'd pulled into the driveway.

> We'll talk later.

Was all he'd texted.

"Uncle Bear said you got nuggets."

"Just for you, princess."

"Sweet and sour sauce?"

"Sweet and sour sauce." Gabe swept the little girl up with one arm and followed Bear into the kitchen, Peetie trotting at his heels. Diane sat at the counter. The smile she gave Gabe was offset by the look of worry in her eyes.

"Thanks for dinner, Gabe," she said as she stood. She started to head for the cabinet where she kept her dishes but Bear was already there. Gabe set Laurie down on one of the stools lining the long counter dividing the kitchen from the TV room. *Friends* was on the screen but muted. He knew from previous stays that it was Diane's 'comfort show.'

Laurie seemed upbeat, making Gabe wonder if she didn't know that Jesse's family wasn't letting up. But, she had to know something, since both Gabe and Bear were there for the night. That had only happened during a court date or when there was a higher chance of Jesse or Velna or someone else from the family showing up and bothering them.

They ate while Laurie talked about her day at school. Gabe watched her for any signs of stress, but she chatted happily between bites of chicken nuggets. She didn't argue when it was time to do her homework or go to bed.

She must not know.

Gabe wasn't sure he was good with that. They'd always told her in the past—not to scare her, but to stay honest and keep her trust. Without honesty, a kid could stop trusting their gut when danger was near.

Laurie got into bed with her favorite stuffies—Pooh and Piglet—and Pete curled up at the foot of the bed. Laurie asked Gabe and Bear to each tell her a bedtime story. When they finished, Bear kissed her goodnight first, then Gabe knelt beside the bed and kissed her forehead.

"Everything okay?" he asked her, unable to help himself.

Laurie nodded. "Can you make sure Mommy's okay?"

"Of course." Gabe glanced at Bear, standing in the doorway and frowning, then back at Laurie. "Do you know why we're here, Piglet?"

She nodded again. "To make sure *they* don't come here. Jesse—I mean, *the worm*—is in jail and they're mad at me."

Gabe put his arm around Laurie and squeezed. "I'm sorry about that, sweetheart." He studied her face. "We're going to make sure you and your mom are safe."

"I know. You always have. That's why I'm not scared. But I don't want Mommy to be scared, either. And she looks scared."

Gabe's chest tightened, both from the trust Laurie placed in him and from anger that she and Diane needed their help at all.

"Uncle Bear and me, we'll talk to her. But I want you to know, we're not going to let anything happen to you."

Laurie nodded and cozied down into her pillows. She closed her eyes as Gabe tucked her covers in along her side, then turned out the light on her nightstand.

Diane was sitting on the couch with a glass of wine in her hand, blankly staring at another *Friends* episode. She looked over when Gabe and Bear came into the room.

"Can I get you guys anything?" she asked as she started to stand. Gabe waved her back down.

"What can *we* do for *you*?" he asked as he sat in one of the recliners to the side while Bear took the other.

"You're already doing so much." She wiped her eyes.

"Not as much as we'd like to do," Bear growled as he clenched his fists. "Sorry this is happening."

Diane nodded. "He's in prison. It was supposed to be over when that happened, and we could get on with our lives. I don't want to move. It would feel like we were on the run, like we were the ones who did something wrong. She has her friends and family here. She loves her school. I have a really good job and just the thought of trying to find another?" She shook her head.

"You shouldn't be forced to leave," Gabe said.

"I'm just hoping the rest of Jesse's family ends up in prison, too. There's so much evidence that they knew, and they didn't stop him. He wasn't the only one. And he didn't just hurt *my* little girl, but she's the first one who stood up against them. She wanted to help, to protect the other kids..." she trailed off, sniffling. Bear was already handing her a box of tissues, one of many scattered around the house. She took one and covered her face.

Gabe and Bear shared a look, murder in both their eyes. This is what Mountain Division did, this was their purpose, to protect the innocent. But right now, it didn't feel like enough.

They'd gone further than just protection before. But that was often done in the dark, and when they had no public ties to the victims. This case was different. If anything happened to Jesse's family members, the police would go straight to the six men who protected Laurie.

Diane uncovered her face and looked toward Laurie's bedroom. "She's so strong."

"So's her mother," Bear said.

"Laurie's more worried about you than about herself," Gabe said.

Diane flinched. "I hate that for her. No little kid should have to take care of and worry about their parents. But I just..."

She pressed the balled-up tissue to her nose again and sniffed. "I thought this was over and it feels like it's *starting* over instead. I can't hide it this time. I *am* scared."

"Then don't try to hide it," Gabe said. "We all went into this promising to keep everything transparent for Laurie. Jesse's lies, getting her to trust him, are what hurt her in the first place. She's *strong*, Diane. And smart, and observant. Let her know you're scared when you're scared, but that you're still fighting, that you haven't given up. I think that's what worries her the most."

Diane nodded. "You're right. I shouldn't hide what I'm feeling. I can't anyway; she knows."

"You still trust us, right?" Bear asked.

"Of course. You and Gabe and Shane. Elias, Waylon, and Ben. You all are the only reason I can sleep at night."

"Then trust us tonight, too. Go on to bed. Things'll look better in the morning."

She gave him a grateful smile. "Thank you." She finished

her wine just as the credits rolled. Bear and Gabe stood when she did, Gabe taking the empty glass from her hand.

"We'll take care of any dishes. You go on to bed."

Another grateful smile. "Thank you so much." She headed for the hallway but then stopped and turned. "When my husband passed away four years ago, I thought the last good man had died. I felt that even stronger when I discovered what Jesse had done to my baby. But, you all give me back my faith that there are still good men in the world."

Gabe and Bear said nothing, just nodded their thanks. Diane went on to bed and they went to the kitchen where Gabe washed her glass.

Bear didn't waste a second.

"So, what in the hell was the six for?"

"Velna. She came to the rec center. Bitch was lying in wait in the parking lot. Jesse wasn't with her so I texted in case he was slinking around here and she was just a distraction."

"I checked the cameras soon as you texted. No sign of him or anyone else." He opened the dishwasher and filled the cup with detergent.

"Then what do you think she was doing?" Gabe told Bear what Velna had said. "What's this softening your heart bullshit?"

"Like you said, bullshit." Bear closed the dishwasher door and hit the power button. "Tryin' to get in your head."

"Well, she did."

Bear grunted. "Kick her out." He opened the laptop sitting on the kitchen counter and studied the screen divided into four camera angles—views around Diane's yard and the street in front of the house. He scrolled back to the time Gabe came in the front door and sped through the video, looking for any sign of Jesse, Velna, or anyone else.

No movement in the yard, and no suspicious cars slowing

down or stopping along the street. They'd been known to park at just the right angle down the road so that their headlights blasted into the front windows in the middle of the night. They'd flash the brights on and off, then blast some godawful song, waking the entire street, before speeding off ahead of the cops. Sometimes, they'd throw cow patties at the house for good measure.

That was considered a mild attack. Another time, someone sneaked into the back yard and left a dead raccoon clutching a Pooh bear on the back porch. They'd caught footage of that one, and it was definitely a man dressed in dark clothes and a balaclava. Jesse was in custody at that point, so it wasn't him. They thought maybe it was another family member.

The family was sick, every last one of them. The only one who didn't seem to bother Laurie was Jesse's father, who had divorced Velna years before and moved away. Gabe didn't think he was much of a man, leaving his son with a monster, but maybe by then it was already too late. Like Velna had said, Gabe wasn't a father, so how could he know? He'd left that little jab out of his debriefing with Bear.

"Looks like they've left us alone so far," Bear said, setting the videos back to the live feed. He looked at Gabe. "Now what's eating you?"

"Nothing."

"Thought the Tobisons were the only ones who left bullshit around here." Bear sat down on one of the stools and it sighed under the weight of his frame. "What else did that bitch tell you?" He squinted, studying Gabe's face. "What poison did she pour into your brain, T-Wolf?"

"Telling you, it's nothing."

Bear looked away, saying something quietly that Gabe didn't catch.

"What was that?"

He looked at Gabe again, shame on his face. "Dammit, yeah, you didn't hear me. I said you're still uncomfortable around me."

Shit. Here we go.

"It's not me, brother, it's you. You're the one who waited so long to come back home after retiring, and then you weren't even gonna stay. You'd be down in Texas right now if it weren't for Ellie. When are you gonna stop blaming yourself for this?" He pointed to his ear. "I'd be dead if you weren't there."

"No, you'd still be a Ranger, and you'd have your hearing. I was the dumbass who triggered the explosion. Shoulda seen the trap. And then you took the brunt of it, saving my ass. You saved *my* sorry life, brother."

"Bear, that thing was so well-hidden, I would have triggered it if you hadn't done it first. Any one of us would have. Luck of the draw you were in the lead. If it had been me setting it off, you would have done what I did. And you were the one who carried me outta there."

"Yeah, which you woulda done for me."

Gabe grinned. "Are you kidding? You outweigh me. I would've left you right there, man."

Bear's eyes widened as he studied Gabe, who fought to keep from laughing. Then the skin at the corners of Bear's eyes crinkled, his mouth opened until his teeth shone white against his dark beard as he laughed. It was a rich, deep sound—rare, but less so now that he had Ellie.

"So," Gabe said. "Can we put this behind us finally?"

Bear continued to study him for a moment before asking, "Are you happy, T-Wolf?"

Gabe started to answer Bear's odd question but stopped. Was he happy? Sure, his life was looking up from when he was discharged. He wasn't moping around the house all the time, ignoring his friends anymore—last weekend being an exception. He had a job. He had a purpose, which he was fulfilling right now.

But am I happy?

Bear shook his head. "That's a no. Figured, from what I heard."

Gabe blew out a breath. "What? What'd they say?" Because of course his brothers had been talking about him to Bear.

"Told me about Cocks and Strippers."

Gabe looked away, practically growling. "I wasn't looking to hook up that night."

"Elias and Waylon, they didn't know."

"Know what?"

"How sweet you really are on Rochelle."

That took Gabe by surprise. "How do you know how I feel about Rochelle?"

"Shane. Told me you two have been circling each other. So, I'm wondering why you didn't make a move before now."

"I was going to, but she beat me to it. We had coffee together today. And I was supposed to see her at Riversong tomorrow," Gabe said, feeling defensive.

"She made the first move? The Gabe I know wouldn't have hesitated the second he saw a woman he wanted. But now?" Bear tapped his ear.

"It's not that." *Is it?* "She's very shy. Quiet."

"Different from your usual."

Gabe grinned. "Maybe."

"Sounds like my Ellie." Bear tapped his lips. "Maybe we could have 'em meet."

Gabe chuckled. "You mean like a double date?"

"Yeah. Ellie'd like that. She's been wanting to get out more, now that she's feeling better."

"Is she up at the cabin alone tonight?"

Bear shook his head. "She's down staying with Arden and Kyle at their ranch while I'm here. Arden's got other company staying there, too."

Gabe nodded. "I'd heard." Kyle's former bosses, Lachlan and Gina, were in town visiting.

"Arden and them are hoping they'll settle here. Ellie hopes so, too, now that she's met 'em. She says Gina reminds her of herself, just a little bit. A woman looking for a home." Bear looked surprisingly wistful. "Just like Ellie when she came here."

"Ellie's got a home now though, doesn't she?"

Bear just smiled. "Sure does." He shifted his weight. "So we're having that party for them all up at the cabin. Be good to see you there with a woman on your arm."

Gabe grinned.

"Especially a lady who makes you smile like that."

Gabe looked away. "We'll see, Bear. We'll see."

But he was already thinking about how he'd ask Rochelle if she wanted to meet his friends.

No. His brothers. His chosen family.

TEN

Gabe took first watch at Laurie's while Bear got some shuteye in one of the guest bedrooms. While he kept one eye on the split screen showing the camera feeds around the house, he looked up more information on Chinese characters. He wanted to impress Rochelle the next time they got together. The characters he'd attempted to draw had been awful, honestly. She was much better at ASL than he was at Mandarin.

He went back to thinking about how she'd taken the time to learn, just for him.

That's someone special.

After years of women who demanded things from Gabe, he wasn't sure what to do with someone who was the opposite.

Gabe and Bear switched places at three in the morning. Years of military training kicked in and Gabe fell asleep almost immediately. He woke to his phone alarm vibrating on his pillow and the smell of breakfast. He got up and ran a hand through his messy hair. He'd slept in his clothes so all he had to do was put his shoes on and join the others in the kitchen.

Bear had started breakfast at the end of his shift. Diane was already up—she'd had trouble sleeping for months—and Elias and Shane were seated at the island talking to her. Gabe figured Laurie was either sleeping in or getting ready for school. Seeing Shane and Elias there surprised him. He thought he'd be watching over Laurie all day with Bear.

"Wondered when you were gonna join us, Sleeping Beauty," Shane teased. Diane laughed, which was a wonderful sound.

"And good morning to you, Sunshine," Gabe answered Shane as he pulled out a stool and sat down. He grabbed a clean plate and piled it with bacon and toast. Diane started to get up to pour him coffee but Shane placed a hand on her shoulder.

"I've got it. My waiter skills are rusty," Shane said. Diane beamed at him.

"Thanks," Gabe said, taking the mug. "Surprised to see you here. Game change, or you just here to pick up Pete?"

Laurie ran into the kitchen as Gabe asked his question and hopped up onto a stool beside Elias. Pete curled up at her feet, hoping for stray crumbs.

"Both," Shane answered. "Peetie and me'll be accompanying Miss Laurie to school today. Special guests."

"It's career day at school," Diane said. "I'd totally forgotten about it, and forgot to ask for the time off. Shane offered to go."

"And I thought I'd tag along too, just for funsies," Elias added. He handed Laurie a plate with toast and scrambled eggs.

"Yay!" Laurie said. She picked up a triangle of toast.

Gabe nodded. He knew Elias wasn't going just for funsies, but to act as backup for Shane. They'd probably take turns in the parking lot and inside the school. The Tobisons were famous for showing up outside at recess, standing on a rocky hill in full view of the playground, just outside of the thousand-foot range of the school, but making sure Laurie knew they were there all the same. He looked out the window at the falling snow, knowing that wouldn't stop them from harassing Laurie.

"If you're sure, Elias," Gabe said. "Or I could—"

"It's cool, brother. This'll be fun." He exchanged a look with Bear. "You get on with your day."

When Bear avoided Gabe's eyes, he was pretty sure the big guy had called in a favor with Elias to make sure Gabe had a chance to see Rochelle. When he saw the look Shane gave him, he knew it for sure.

They finished breakfast, with Laurie chatting happily about how excited she was for her day. Gabe put himself on dish duty, and then it was time to go. He hugged Laurie goodbye and told her how proud he was of her.

"I'll see you guys later," he told his brothers.

"Hot date?" Shane joked.

Gabe just smiled back.

INSTEAD OF TEXTING HER, Gabe decided to surprise Rochelle at Riversong. The snow had turned to rain and the windows were cloudy with moisture and warmth inside the coffee shop. Gabe looked for her familiar silhouette. As always, he walked faster when he saw her shape in the window seat.

He ordered two coffees from Sonny and quickly made his way to Rochelle's seat. She was staring at her computer screen —no, make that staring *through* her screen. Her eyes looked glassy and she didn't notice him until he set the mugs down.

When she looked up at him, he noticed smeared mascara under her eyes and realized she'd been crying.

"What's wrong?" Gabe signed.

"It's n-nuth..." Rochelle pressed her lips together, shook her head, and slammed her laptop shut. She looked down into her lap.

Gabe didn't bother sitting across from her but scooted into the window seat beside her instead. As soon as he sat down he realized he might have made a mistake, but she didn't move away from him.

"It's not nothing," he said quietly. "You want to talk about it?" he signed.

She wiped her eyes but another tear fell immediately. She looked into his eyes, breaking his heart.

"Do you like me?" she signed shyly.

Oh my God. "I like you a lot," he signed back.

She smiled and her tears stopped. "Thank you. I needed that today," she signed. As she continued to look into his eyes, her gaze turned to wonder. A stray tear slipped down her cheek and he brushed it away without thinking. Her cheek was baby-soft. It had been a long time since he'd touched a woman's face. He dropped his hand.

She picked it up in hers and squeezed, then let go.

"I like you enough that I want to take you to a party to meet my friends," he signed before he lost his nerve.

She looked confused and he realized he'd signed too quickly. He smiled and asked again, this time slower while speaking the words.

Her mouth opened into a soft O. Then she closed it.

She's going to say no.

"What?" he quickly asked as he tilted his head. "I like you a lot," he reiterated. Then he grinned. "Do you eat with your hands? Is that why I can't take you?" he asked, then mimed picking up a glob of food in his fist and shoving it into his mouth.

She laughed. "No," she said.

He tilted his head again, trying to prompt her into telling him what was wrong. She only studied him, a wondering look in her eye.

Please, tell me what's wrong Gabe thought.

Finally, she signed back, "You like me," no question in her hands but in her eyes.

He nodded. "Yes." Then he clasped her hands. "Very much, Rochelle."

Her gaze went soft again as she studied his face.

I want to kiss you. Right now. Softly so I don't hurt you, because you're extra fragile today.

Gabe leaned forward, tilting his head slightly, eyes half-closed. And she closed the gap.

Rochelle's lips were softer than her cheek, and warm. He resisted deepening the kiss—he didn't want to startle her—or get kicked out of a public place.

She finished the kiss and pulled back. He opened his eyes before she did. Her eyelids fluttered. At last, she grinned.

He went in for a second kiss and she gladly let him. When they pulled back, he was happy to study her face, the blush that had crept into her cheeks.

Then Rochelle got up and he watched her, concerned that he'd done something wrong. But she smiled and signed 'walking to the bathroom' then frowned and made up a sign for washing her mascara-smudged eyes. He grinned and shook his head.

"You look fine. No, you look incredible."

She laughed and shook her head.

"One second," she signed, then walked away.

When she came back, she signed, "I looked like a raccoon."

Gabe thought there was no way she knew the sign for raccoon off the top of her head, so she must have looked it up on her phone while she was in the bathroom, and that touched him deeply.

He shook his head, laughing. He stretched his arm out. She grabbed a paperback off the bookshelf beside the window seat, sat back down, and immediately snuggled into him. Gabe wrapped his arm around her shoulder while his heart softly pounded and the rain fell outside. She opened her book with a grin as if they did this all the time and started to read.

Gabe never wanted to move again. He wanted to catch this moment up and keep it forever.

Is it possible I'm in love with you? he wondered. His heart and his gut told him unequivocally yes. But his head wasn't on board and started making its opinion known. He barely knew her, for one thing. And she barely knew him.

I don't care he realized. He knew everything he needed to know about her. She was kind and sweet and shy. She didn't judge or pity him. She trusted him as she sat there curled up next to him reading her book, and that brought out the protector in him.

And he knew that she made him feel good. So good, better than he had in a long, long time. And for that alone, he'd risk not knowing another thing about her.

Though he still wondered what had upset her so much today that she'd been prompted to ask if he liked her. He didn't think she'd been fishing for a compliment. No—she wanted to know, baseline, if he liked her. Almost as if she doubted anyone did. Had someone insulted her? Did she get some sort of rejection, maybe from a potential translation job? It seemed to go deeper than that, a fundamental wound. Something he was missing, something that he couldn't see.

Because to him, she was absolute perfection.

He nuzzled the top of her head and she wiggled, squirming closer. He noticed that she'd grabbed a romance to read. When he brought her to his house, she'd have plenty of romances to read since his mom had left so many behind.

I want to show her my home. The idea, the rightness and ease of it, made his heart pound.

Gabe reached across the table and pulled Rochelle's latte closer so she could reach it. She smiled up at him, then took the mug and sipped.

They sat there quietly for a while, finishing their coffees. Gabe felt her body relax more and more. She finally closed the book and set it back on the shelf.

"Better?" he asked.

"Better," she said.

"Good." He brushed his lips against her forehead. "So. Like I said earlier, I'd like to take you to a party a couple of my friends are hosting. Would you like to go?"

Rochelle sat up and grew thoughtful. Then she huffed and went for her purse. She pulled out the little notebook and a pen and started writing. When she finished, she stared frowning at the words. Then she reluctantly turned the notebook around.

Do you know that I'm different? Is it possible that you don't?

"Different?" he signed. He started to sign some more but grabbed the notebook instead. He didn't want to risk being misunderstood for a second and he was sure both his hands and his spoken words would betray him.

I don't know what you mean by different. Do you mean that you're kinder and sweeter and so much better than anyone I've ever known? Do you mean you're someone who doesn't treat me like I'm stupid or like maybe the deaf is catching? If that's what you mean, then yes, you're different—and I don't want you to be the same as everyone else.

He paused and studied her face before turning the notebook around for her to read. As she read his words, her eyes widened and then turned shiny. She bit her lower lip. She looked back and forth between his face and the words on the page.

Then she flipped to the next page and started writing. Gabe wouldn't have been surprised if her pen tore through the page. She handed the notebook back to him.

What if I freeze up or stutter when I'm trying to talk to your friends? What if I totally embarrass you and they think I'm stupid. That YOU'RE stupid for bringing me? What if this is just how it is now?

He felt his eyebrows rise as he read her words. He didn't care if she didn't speak a single word the entire time she was at the party. It didn't matter one bit.

But she must have taken his surprise the wrong way, because the next thing she wrote was:

I understand. You don't have to take me if you've changed your mind.

"No!" he both signed and said. He took the notebook out of her hands and set it aside. Then, he took her hands in his and brought them to his lips. He kissed the backs of her fingers.

"I care about you," he said. "So much. But if it makes you uncomfortable, we can start slower. Do you just want to go somewhere for lunch today?" Gabe asked. "What do you like to eat?"

He watched her lips move. "I care about you too," she said. She took her hands out of his and picked up the notebook. She wrote something then showed it to him with a smile.

How about Italian?

ELEVEN

If there was one thing that was sure to ruin Rochelle's day, it was a message from her parents.

The latest messages had come in during the middle of the night. Her family was eight hours behind her—no, make that one day ahead but seemed eight hours behind, since apparently they were in Japan—and didn't account for, or care about, the time zone difference. The second message was simply berating her for not answering the first one right away.

The first message read:

> Konnichiwa! We're in Kyoto! If you haven't already, go look on our page at your sister dressed up as a geisha! Isn't she adorable? We've gotten SO many likes!! This new tour is going great and we have new signups for the next one!

Then the next:

> Rochelle! Haven't you looked yet? I expected you to leave a nice comment on the page by now! Your sister is very upset that you haven't said anything! You need to be more social!!!

And the last one:

> Why do you always have to be so difficult? If you were more likable, you could come with us sometime.

They are who they are she thought. *They love you, they just...don't always show it very well.*

Rochelle wasn't hungry so she skipped breakfast, showered, and got ready for a day at Riversong. She wished that she could see Gabe today. His sweet smile could always bring her right back up.

As much as Rochelle tried not to, she let the messages get to her, until she found herself looking at her family's social media account between translating assignments. And there she was, Rochelle's younger, prettier, more socially acceptable sister showing off a kimono, Japanese-style rice powder makeup, and pretending to be a geisha. A short video clip showed her walking down the streets of Kyoto while her mother followed behind from a distance and narrated. When a couple of tourists stopped her sister to take her picture, her mother bragged about how they'd been fooled, and how perfect Sandra looked.

The tears welled up in spite of how hard Rochelle tried to hold them back. She loved her sister, she really did. And, she loved her parents. They just had different priorities from Rochelle. But dammit, sometimes it just hurt.

It was then Gabe surprised her at Riversong, as if she'd conjured a book boyfriend out of her desires alone. And yet, her feelings of being less than, of not measuring up, clouded her heart, choked her words before she could speak them. And her damned stutter came back, of course. The thing her parents most criticized her for when she was young.

She slammed her laptop closed out of a sudden fear that he would catch a glimpse of Sandra and fall in love with her—as totally irrational as that was. No, he wouldn't fall in love with a screenshot. But if he ever met her in person, Rochelle thought she wouldn't stand a chance against Sandra.

Her vocal cords might have been blocked but every last insecurity Rochelle felt rushed out of her through her hands when Gabe asked her what was wrong. Instead of rejecting her, he did the opposite. He touched her—softly, gently. He looked at her as if she were the most beautiful woman on earth. And when he kissed her, his lips were soft yet strong, reassuring, even a little teasing. And when he put his arm around her, she couldn't help but melt into him.

But at the same time, Rochelle felt like she was deceiving him. Didn't he realize how weird she was? How she never quite fit in wherever she went? How the only place where she felt safe was inside the pages of a book, dreaming about imaginary book boyfriends?

Was that normal?

What if she embarrassed him at this party he wanted to take her to? She could hardly believe she was trusting him enough to commit her fears to paper—asking him if he truly understood that she was different—and admitting what she thought was so obvious. But the more vulnerability she showed him, the brighter his smile, the kinder his eyes, the softer his touch. Yes, he wanted her there. Wanted her in his life.

There were many things she wanted to ask him, but the question she wanted him to answer the most was also the most ridiculous one.

Are you real?

BY THE TIME they got to the restaurant for lunch, Rochelle's difficult morning felt unreal, that her real life, her *true* life, was this: walking beside Gabe into the restaurant, her hand resting gently in the crook of his arm.

"Two, please," Gabe told the hostess behind the podium and she showed them to a table and gave them each a menu. Rochelle scanned the entrees, trying to narrow down all the delicious choices and realized she was starving from skipping breakfast.

Gabe asked her what she was going to order and without hesitating, she answered, "Everything looks so good, but I think I'll have the lasagna with the minestrone to start."

"That's what I was thinking of getting, too."

"And dessert. We have to get the cannoli. Have you tried it? Even if you're full, you'll have to get one to go."

She looked up to see Gabe smiling at her, his eyes sparkling.

That's when she realized her words were coming easy, flowing out without so much as a pause. Their waiter approached the table just then, and she ordered without a hitch. All the cloudiness in her heart was gone. The tightness in her chest had dissolved, leaving her words free to flow.

"Is everything all right with your niece?" she asked quickly, just to prove to herself that she could speak.

Gabe's eyes widened momentarily. "Oh. Yes. The plans just changed again, that's all." He looked at the table and frowned, making Rochelle wonder if Gabe had a difficult relationship with his family, too. He looked at her again and what he said next surprised her.

"I feel like I'm lying to you when I talk about her and I don't want to do that. She's...not my niece by blood. She calls me uncle—calls several of my friends uncle—because we're watching over her right now."

"Watching over her? What does that mean?"

Gabe sucked in his cheeks, then said, "It's not something I'm at full liberty to discuss. There are some legal issues. But, she needs protecting right now."

"A divorce case?" Then Rochelle waved her hand. "Sorry, no, it's none of my business like I said."

Gabe gave her an apologetic smile. "I'm sorry. I didn't want to mislead you, and I also don't want you to feel like I'm shutting you out."

Rochelle smiled. "Neither one is the case. I understand, I promise."

The waiter brought a basket of cheese bread and a small bowl of marinara. Rochelle thanked him and Gabe served her a plate with a thick slice of bread. She noticed him watching her and grinning to himself.

"What is it?" She both said and signed the words, as everyone at a nearby table started singing "Happy Birthday" to a woman with a candle-studded tiramisu in front of her. Rochelle was finding ASL to be incredibly handy.

"I liked today at the coffee shop," he said and signed back. "You, sitting against me."

Rochelle's cheeks warmed. "I liked it, too." She sucked in her lower lip. "I liked the kissing," she signed without saying it aloud.

Gabe's eyebrows rose and she realized that she'd just given away more than she'd wanted to. She knew the sign for kissing because she'd looked it up—along with a few other ones she'd like to try out with Gabe.

Rochelle swore she could feel her face catch fire, especially when Gabe signed, "Kissing?" back to her.

"Caught," she said and signed. The woman at the other table was blowing out her candles while everyone clapped.

In for a penny...

"I know a few others," she said when the clapping died down. Then she signed, "Hugging. Caressing." She looked around as if everyone in the restaurant knew ASL. She hunched over and made her gestures small. "Some...naughty ones."

Gabe started shaking and she realized that he was laughing silently. But the best thing was, he wasn't laughing at her, not exactly. Not in a way that hurt, but in a way that made her laugh, too.

Then his dark eyes smoldered as he signed, "Why did you want to learn those words, Rochelle?"

Heart jackhammering, she summoned up every ounce of courage she possessed. She smiled back and signed, "Just in case I need them." Then she asked, "Will I?"

The world shrank down to only her and Gabe as he studied her, his eyes growing even darker. His nod told her everything she needed to know.

The waiter brought their food, breaking the spell. Rochelle remembered where she was—not alone on Gabe Island but in a crowded restaurant. It had been a long time since anyone had so deeply captured her attention. She hoped it was the same for him.

"How is your project going?" Gabe asked.

"Good," Rochelle said. "Better than good. I sent some of my translations to the client a couple days ago and he's really happy with them. We're getting together at Riversong to go over some finer points next week. I'm hoping to have more poems done—"

Rochelle stopped and she clapped her mouth shut. Her

eyes widened and her eyelids fluttered as if she could blink away what she'd just said.

"Hey." Gabe reached across the table and grabbed her hand. "I won't say a word about your project to anyone."

Rochelle relaxed. "I know you wouldn't. I just..." She looked around the restaurant, suddenly feeling watched again.

Ridiculous. I'm fine. Just like the other night.

So why am I so jumpy?

"Rochelle?" Gabe squeezed her hand. "Are you all right?" His head was on a swivel as he reconned the restaurant.

She smiled self-consciously. "Yeah. You would think I'm guarding state secrets. It's just poetry. I'm translating poetry written by one of my favorite authors, but he wants to keep it on the downlow."

Gabe's expression went from high alert to soft and contemplative as he nodded. "You told me. Sounds like a dream job."

"It is. I've been working on it for a month now."

"A month?"

"I know it sounds crazy that it would take that long just to translate a handful of poems. But I have to capture his voice. The things he's trying to say, not just the words themselves. It takes thought and effort and understanding. Otherwise, we might just as well have straight AI translating poems and books."

"His soul. You're translating his soul."

Rochelle placed her hand over her heart as heat spread there. "You understand. You really get it."

Color tinged Gabe's cheeks. "It's important to be understood. A lot of people take that for granted. I certainly did before my accident. And it takes a lot of skill for someone to listen—really listen—to someone else's message. To hear what they're really saying and not what you want or expect to hear."

He smiled gently. "Your poet is lucky to have you as his translator."

Rochelle's chest bloomed with warmth. "Thank you."

The waiter approached with a dessert menu and Rochelle realized Gabe was still holding her hand. She jerked it out of his, startled at the interruption. She registered disappointment on his face a moment before he covered it up.

"Dessert?" Gabe asked almost absently.

Rochelle grabbed his hand again. "Speaking of messages getting misread. The waiter just startled me, that's all."

Gabe set the menu down deliberately, studying Rochelle's face again.

He leaned forward. "Just so we're clear, can I confess something?"

Rochelle tensed up at his seriousness. "Sure."

"I was never a regular at Riversong, not until the morning I saw you there in the window. When I walked into the shop and got a closer look at you, you intrigued me. I wondered what you were reading, what had you so captivated that the world seemed to disappear for you. I went back to work and couldn't get you out of my mind. So I came back the next morning. And the next. Does that make you uncomfortable?"

She relaxed and grinned, relieved. "No, not at all. While we're confessing things, I used to wait for you to come in. It made my day." Rochelle couldn't believe she was admitting to that. "I...used to imagine what it might be like to know you." She wasn't quite ready to say the words *book boyfriend* yet—or maybe ever. "So, does that make *you* uncomfortable?"

Gabe chuckled. "Not at all." His eyes flashed, causing heat to creep up Rochelle's chest. "As a matter of fact, right now, I'd like to—"

The alert from Gabe's phone vibrated the whole table. He picked it up, looking annoyed. As Rochelle watched Gabe read the message across the top of the screen, the annoyance shifted to rage like nothing she'd ever seen. She sat up straighter, her spine pressed against her chairback. She remembered what April told her about Gabe and his friends.

They're great guys, don't get me wrong. They help out people in the community with their problems. You know, the kind that bang on your door at four AM demanding to see you. Or that won't leave your kid alone.

Gabe glanced up and his ferocity quickly changed to alarm.

"Shit, I'm sorry. I'm scaring you."

"N-no, it's oh-okay," she said as she tried to relax her body. But she wasn't fooling Gabe. He'd startled her and she could tell he knew it.

Gabe's eyes filled with regret.

"I don't want things to end like this, but I have to go."

"What's happening? Is it the little girl? Is she all right?"

Gabe nodded as he took cash from his wallet and laid it on the table. "Yeah. It's her, and no, she's not okay. But she will be." He stood up and Rochelle followed. "Again, I'm sorry."

"It's okay, I understand."

But from the way that Gabe turned his face away, she knew he didn't believe her.

They reached the front door and Gabe held it open for her. He walked her to her car as the afternoon sun peeked out from behind a cloud. The silence grew between them with every step. Rochelle fumbled with her key fob but finally got the door unlocked. Gabe stayed silent as her own word-bricks piled up. At this rate, she wouldn't even be able to tell him goodbye.

Gabe reached for the door handle faster than she did and opened the door. He wouldn't meet her eyes and his jaw was clenched. The hand holding the door was white-knuckled and the other was balled into a fist. She moved around him to get in the driver's seat.

Am I really just going to get in my car and drive away like this?

Rochelle stopped and turned. Gabe's chin came up and he looked deeply into her eyes. She saw anger there, and frustration, and the beginnings of doubt.

So she stood on her toes and kissed him.

She wasn't settling for a light peck on the lips, either. This was a real kiss. She poured every ounce of her warmth—and yes, passion—into it. If she couldn't say the words out loud and she couldn't sign them, she would let him know exactly how she felt with her kiss.

Gabe's arms encircled her and pulled her close. His hand ran up her back and tangled in her hair. He deepened the kiss and she tasted his desire as his tongue pushed past her lips and he claimed her mouth. By the time he pulled back, she was breathless and her legs felt boneless. She opened her eyes and found him staring at her. The fury was still there—not aimed at her, never at her, she thought—but there was also passion and an intensity that made her skin bloom with heat.

"Please, just...be careful while you're taking out the garbage," she whispered. Gabe studied her lips as she spoke and his gaze softened.

So," he asked with a devilish grin, "Will you come to the party with me?"

"Party?" *Oh, right. A party.* "I would love to," Rochelle said without hesitating. "Just tell me when and where."

"When is this weekend. Where is in the mountains. Text me your address and I'll come by and pick you up."

And then he was gone, off to protect a little girl from whatever threatened her. But not before she watched the rage return to his eyes as he turned away.

Whoever's threatening the girl doesn't stand a chance.

TWELVE

Fury so strong it turned his vision red coursed through Gabe's veins as his truck tore through the streets on its way to Laurie's school. He forced himself to slow down when he saw the school zone signs up ahead. He turned off to the right as Shane had instructed in his text. He pulled up behind his brother's vehicle, out of sight of the hill and playground, got out, and got into the passenger side of the SUV.

"Fuckers," Gabe said immediately. "How long?"

"Twenty minutes now," Shane answered Gabe's question, telling him how long Jesse's family members had been spying on the school from the hill. "Three of them, including Velna."

"Do we know who the other two are?"

"Negative. Two men, balaclavas. Velna doesn't bother hiding her face."

"Probably her brother and a cousin," Gabe said, looking toward the school as if he could see through it to the hill on the other side. Then he glanced at the clock on the dash. "Recess in ten. Where's Elias?"

"Inside. He's been alerted, but he's also doing his presentation. I discovered the problem when I came outside with Peetie after mine. They got into place right after Elias and I changed guard."

Two dogs in the back whined from their kennels, Pete and a Malinois Gabe didn't recognize.

"So Elias has got eyes on her in there. Good." Gabe met Shane's glare and saw his own rage mirrored there. "Let's go."

Shane started the SUV and turned down a street away from the school. He took streets out of sight of the hill until he pulled up on the other side of it. Gabe noted they had eight minutes to make the Tobisons disappear. Shane parked and they scanned the street. Nothing but a couple of empty parked cars. Gabe assumed one or both belonged to the Tobisons.

They got out of the SUV and Shane went around the back to let the Malinois out—a female who looked at Shane for her next instructions.

"Heel," Shane said. She walked beside him as they headed toward the open space and started up the hill. "Good girl, good Valkyrie." They picked their way up one of several gravel trails between the snowy rocks.

Three figures appeared at the top of the hill. When they spotted Gabe, Shane, and the dog, they tore down the side, aimed toward a car parked across the street.

Well, shit.

"Halt, or I will release my dog!" Shane shouted.

They kept running.

"You warned 'em," Gabe said.

"Block," Shane commanded. Valkyrie flew across the hill and was on them in a flash, growling and snarling and blocking their way to the car as Shane and Gabe ran to catch up with her.

The three stopped in their tracks. "We're under attack," one of the men shouted.

Gabe laughed. "Not yet you aren't," he said, clenching his fists as the old battle rage made time slow down as he focused on his enemies.

Shane turned his head suddenly and looked behind them. Gabe glance back to see a man get out of the driver's side of one of the cars and run toward them.

Ambushed.

He smiled. This would be fun.

"Hello, Velna," he said to the woman who ignored Valkyrie, instead choosing to shoot hate-filled daggers from her eyes at Gabe. "I don't think you all belong here."

"Free country," one of the men spat. He was holding a sheet of cardboard nailed to a stake. A homemade sign.

"You're not free to harass a little girl," Shane said.

"We're not the harassers here," Velna said.

"Really?" Gabe ripped the sign out of the man's hand and turned it around. The words *Little Liar Laurie* were scrawled across it in red paint. "Then what the fuck is this?"

The man from the car reached them. Velna's brother, Michael. That's when Gabe saw the cell phone in his hand. He was recording the entire exchange.

Definitely ambushed.

"I've got it all," Michael said. He held up the phone, its camera pointed at Gabe holding the sign.

"No, you don't." Shane reached out, grabbed the phone, and slammed it against a rock, shattering the screen.

"I'm gonna sue you," Michael shouted.

Gabe tore the sign in half and dropped the pieces. "Velna, I'm gonna warn you once because I don't want to hit a woman. Get yourself and your fucked-up family off this hill and away from here and stay away."

"Soften your heart, Gabe," she said.

Freak. "Leave."

She put her hands up dismissively and took a step back. "All right, all right. Come on, cousins."

Then she swung.

Gabe easily caught her fist in his hand. It took everything he had not to crush her fingers. He turned her instead and wrenched her arm behind her back, just enough to cause some serious pain but no damage. Then he pushed her into one of the men who decided now would be a great time to attack him head-on. They went stumbling backward and fell into a snow-drift. A sound like a couple of coconuts knocking together told him the man's head had found one of the rocks under the snow.

Velna scrambled back up and started sprinting for the car. Gabe fought the voice inside his head telling him to let her go as the other cousin in a balaclava took a swing and hit Gabe squarely on the jaw. His head snapped back and the world went red. He was vaguely aware of Valkyrie's snarls as she defended Shane against Michael.

The man came in closer and Gabe kicked his legs out from under him. He went sprawling backward like Velna and her other cousin had. Gabe was on him, pinning him to the ground. His eyes went wide and filled with fear as he looked up at Gabe.

"You ain't gonna get away with this," he sputtered, his voice muffled by the balaclava the coward used to hide his face. Gabe ripped it off. He could see the resemblance to Velna in his eyes and hawkish nose. "We're not violating the restraining orders."

Gabe ignored his ridiculous claim. Sure, technically, they were out of the orders' ranges, but she could still see them. Everyone could. Even if they took off before she came out for recess, that sign would have been there for everyone to see. He made a mental note to check the other side of the hill for any more signs.

Shane came up to him, his knuckles bloody. "One thing I'm

never gonna understand," he said, "is why so many families don't believe their own kids, or even turn their backs on them, and then you've got a family like this one that triples down on their support of a monster."

"I don't get it either, man. But it tells me everything I need to know about them. And it makes it easier to sleep at night when I do this."

Gabe drew back his arm. Then his fist smashed into the piece-of-shit's jaw.

That was about the time the police showed up.

Velna and Michael were already gone in the car.

Gabe got up off the asshole. He shook out his fist then held up his hands to show he had no weapons. He scanned the ground but saw no sign of the phone Shane had smashed.

"Down," Shane told Valkyrie. The dog dropped to her belly beside the other man who, Gabe assumed, she'd been using as a chew toy.

If that's the case, Shane might want to wash the filth out of her mouth.

Shane turned to face the cops and raised his hands. The men on the ground sat up.

"Hands where I can see them," one of the officers said as he approached. His partner was right behind him. "What's going on, guys?"

The man Gabe punched pointed at him. "These assholes attacked us."

"That right, Plymouth?" the officer asked him.

"Your name is Plymouth?" Shane asked. "Like the car or the rock?"

"My guess is the rock," Gabe said. "His mama took one look at him and decided he was as dumb as a box of them."

"Or maybe it is after the car. Maybe he was conceived in the back of a Plymouth."

"Quiet," the second officer said. "You two, stand up slowly, hands where we can see them. Then we're going to talk."

"Nothing to talk about, officer," Plymouth said. He stood and wiped the blood from his split lip. "Like I said, these assholes attacked us unprovoked."

"Really?" The officer said. Gabe read the name on his jacket. Caldwell. "Pretty sure you and Alphie—that's you under the mask, right, Alphie? Take that thing off—have restraining orders and you don't belong here."

"We are not near the school, as you can see, officer," Plymouth said while Alphie took off the balaclava. He was a thinner, younger version of Plymouth.

"Officer Caldwell, if I may," Shane started. "These two along with Velna Tobison were on the other side of the hill in full view of the school. They had that," he pointed to the torn-up sign.

"Might want to check for others," Gabe added.

Caldwell nodded and looked at his partner, Dowd, who marched up the hill and over the top. Then he looked at the dog, still on her belly.

"He gonna bite me?"

"She," Shane said. "Valkyrie. And no. She's a highly trained professional."

Valkyrie dropped her chin onto her front paws and looked at Caldwell with big, innocent puppy dog eyes as if she hadn't just taken a few bites out of Michael before he ran away with Velna.

The other officer reappeared at the top of the hill just as a bell rang at the school. He was carrying two more signs under his arm. The sounds of children breaking free for recess rose behind him.

"Found these stuck in the ground," he said as he dropped

the signs one at a time at their feet. The first read *Lying Laurie* and the second said *Dirty Hore Laurie.*

"Nice spelling," Shane said.

"I took photos and marked where they were," Dowd continued. "Positive they violated the restraining order."

"Those ain't ours," Plymouth said, his eyes shifting to Alphie, who nodded.

"Definitely named for a box of rocks," Gabe said as he looked pointedly at the other sign.

"Well, that's yours," Plymouth said. He looked at Caldwell. "Dust it for this asshole's prints and you'll find 'em."

"Will I find yours, too, Plymouth?" Caldwell asked dryly.

"I want my lawyer," Plymouth said, looking away.

"You can call him down at the station," Caldwell said. He looked at Shane and Gabe. "You fellas too. Let's go."

GABE AND SHANE sat across from each other in a cell across from Plymouth and Alphie. If the looks they shot across the hall at each other could kill, the jail would have a quadruple homicide on its hands.

"How much longer?" Gabe asked Shane.

"They have forty-eight hours max they can hold us before the bond hearing. So get comfy."

"Fuck," Gabe muttered. They'd already been there for hours. He hadn't called anyone. Not Rochelle, obviously. Not Stephanie, though if they held him overnight, he'd have to call in sick to the rec center. No way in hell was he going to explain the situation over the phone—he'd save that for the in-person meeting with his boss and hope he wasn't fired.

Shane had called Kyle first thing. Not for his own benefit so much as for the dogs. Gabe couldn't imagine Kyle was too thrilled with having to rescue the pups. Gabe hoped it wouldn't be the end of Kyle's support for Laurie.

Gabe closed his eyes and leaned back against the concrete wall. He pictured Rochelle in her seat at Riversong, snow softly falling outside the glass as if she were safe in a snow globe. His sanctuary. His peace.

How could he ever explain to her what happened? God, it had killed him to see the scared look on her face when he got the message from Shane. They'd made such progress, and at that moment he felt like he was back at zero.

But then again, she'd known where he was going, had some idea of what he was doing. She'd kissed him. She'd told him to be careful. But did she really, truly understand what he was doing? The risks he took? Mountain Division worked outside the law to protect the innocent, and that hadn't bothered him, not after the injustices he'd seen. It didn't bother him at all. Up until now. Now that he had something to lose.

Ah, Rochelle.

Knowing that he was going off to protect a girl was one thing. What would she do if she found out there were assault charges against him?

Lost her before I even had her.

He ran his hands through his hair for the hundredth time and looked over at Plymouth, who gave him the middle finger. Fuckers had probably called Jesse's fancy lawyer and would be sprung here momentarily. He was surprised the man hadn't come to get them out yet.

Probably busy in court defending other monsters.

The metal door at the end of the hall opened and Gabe figured that was him, summoned by his thoughts like the devil he was. Instead, it was Officer Caldwell. Plymouth and Alphie stood up grinning.

"Not you two," Caldwell told them as he turned and unlocked Gabe and Shane's cell.

"What the hell?" Plymouth said.

"None of your business," Caldwell said. "Gentlemen." He slid the door open and swept his arm back, an invitation for Gabe and Shane to exit their cell.

"This isn't over," Plymouth said as they stepped into the hall.

"I suggest you shut up," Caldwell said.

Plymouth stood and grasped the bars of his cell. "Where's my lawyer?" he demanded as they walked away.

"Beats me," Caldwell said. "Can't imagine why he'd keep a fine, upstanding citizen like yourself waiting."

Shane turned and smiled at Plymouth just before they stepped out of the room. Gabe echoed his expression.

Neither smile was friendly.

Caldwell led them into an interrogation room. Gabe almost laughed. It was nothing compared to what he'd been taught to survive in the Rangers.

"Have a seat," Caldwell said. Officer Dowd was already in the room. "Coffee?"

"Is that part of the torture?" Shane asked.

"This time of day out of the communal pot, yeah," Caldwell said with a smile. "Getcha a soda instead?"

"Sounds good," Shane said as he took a seat.

"Same," Gabe said, sitting beside him across from Caldwell. Dowd left the room and returned a minute later with two cans of soda. Gabe picked his up and wiped the rim on his shirt before opening it. It was good and sweet and cold.

"You boys are free to go," Caldwell said. "But I just want to have a little chit-chat with you first."

Gabe and Shane exchanged looks.

"Why are you letting us go?" Shane asked. He took a sip of his soda.

Caldwell leaned forward and lowered his voice. "I'm not the one responsible for getting you out of here. But, that said, let me tell you this. We obviously know what's going on here. They are in violation of their restraining orders. Add to that trespassing, littering, harassment," he looked at Gabe's bruised jaw, "assault. And they weren't choir boys before this, as you can imagine. We know about Velna, Michael, and Jesse, too." Caldwell's mouth twisted like the name Jesse was a bitter lemon rind in his mouth. "So, I personally am not broken-hearted about what happened among you all today. However, I can't have you playing vigilante, all right? I'm telling you to stay out of the way. And you can pass that message on to your friends. Showing up in court down in Denver to support that girl is one thing, and I applaud that."

Caldwell slid his business card across the battered table. "But next time you see those yahoos up to something here, you don't go in swinging—you call us instead and we handle it. Got it?"

Shane set his soda down, leaned back, and crossed his arms. "And if we don't?"

"Then Velna Tobison will call us again like she did today, and boys, I'm gonna be cranky if I have to do Velna's bidding."

"So that bitch did set us up," Gabe said.

Caldwell shrugged. "Not for me to say. So, you gonna listen to me, or are we going to talk in here again on a different day when I'm cranky?"

Shane and Gabe exchanged looks. Finally, Gabe said, "Yeah, we'll tell 'em."

Caldwell slapped the table and stood. "Hooray. Then you're free to go, gentlemen. I'll even let you take your beverages. On the house."

"Thanks." They stood.

"You can collect your things at the desk and your ride is waiting. Just don't be a pain in my ass after this."

"No, sir," Shane said. "Have a nice day, officers."

They all left the room and followed the signs to the desk. Gabe wondered who their ride was. Maybe Elias since he was on the scene. Maybe Kyle, in which case Gabe was sure he'd be treated to hearing the man chew Shane out all the way back to his truck, if Kyle was kind enough to take him back to the school where he'd left it.

They stepped outside and Gabe realized he'd guessed wrong about their ride. When he saw the woman with the auburn hair standing beside the SUV he understood why they'd been sprung without a hassle.

"Let's go, guys," she said.

Gabe and Shane both grinned.

"Good to see you, too, Gina," Gabe said.

———

GINA SMITH PACED behind Lachlan Campbell, who sat with Kyle, Shane, Gabe, Ben, Waylon, and Bear around a conference table at Watchdog. Gina and Lachlan had started Watchdog Security in Los Angeles a few years ago. Kyle's security company was an offshoot from the original office, where he'd been the dog handler before meeting Arden and settling in Colorado. Mountain Division had worked with Gina once to save a woman named Sylvie, a police officer who'd gotten in over her head and pissed off the wrong people.

Gina was still a bit of a mystery. Gabe wasn't sure if she was CIA, FBI, NSA, or something else entirely. None of Mountain Division had met Lachlan, but Kyle always spoke highly of him. Looking at Lachlan now, Gabe could see why.

The man exuded both warmth and strength, especially when he looked at Gina. Gabe didn't know all of the details about the couple, but he'd heard that Gina and Lachlan were retired now and traveling the country with their dogs, looking for a new home. They were thinking of settling in Colorado, and if Kyle and Arden had their way, that was sure to happen.

One thing was for sure—Gabe was grateful they were here now.

"Thanks again for bailing us out," Gabe told Gina.

"Thank Kyle for telling me about this situation," Gina said with a smile. "I may be retired, but I still have a few contacts here and there." She bent to pet Fleur, her golden-eyed dog who paced alongside Gina like a ginger-colored shadow. Lachlan's dog Sam was older and lay at the man's feet beneath the table beside Camo, Kyle's gold-and-black-patterned Lab.

Kyle rolled his shoulders, his spine popping like a string of firecrackers. "Not happy about having to pick up my dogs like that, but this situation with a bunch of assholes harassing a little girl is bullshit." He looked from Shane to Gina. "What can we do?" he asked her.

"Well, we could have the family killed, but if you all want to keep flying under the radar that might cause more problems down the road," she said, her expression totally serious. "I'm looking into their finances right now to see if anything stinks there. Considering how much they're paying that lawyer, especially now that the daycare centers are under scrutiny and parents have pulled their kids out of their care, they have to be running low on funds. Or, their source of income is not entirely above board."

"Plymouth and Alphie were surprised Jesse's lawyer hadn't bailed them out yet," Gabe said. "Might be a sign that the gravy train is about to chug off into the sunset without them."

"That's good news," Lachlan said.

Ben cleared his throat. "It won't stop them from harassing Laurie. I think they could be dead broke and half in their graves and they'd still fling shit at her."

Gina made a face. "I hope you don't mean that literally."

Ben just looked at her, sending a clear message without saying a word.

"Wow," was all Gina said. "Even if their funding is solid, it won't be after today. I'll make sure of it."

"Appreciate it," Kyle said. "Now," he turned to Ben. "What else can we do to support you?"

Ben shook his head. "You've done so much already. We're good."

"Yeah," Shane said, his head hanging down. "Sorry for the fuckup today. I don't wanna see anyone fling shit at Watchdog literally or figuratively because I went and got stupid—"

Kyle held up a hand. "Stop right there. You should know by now how I operate. We've handled bigger problems and we're still standing. This isn't going to affect our rep, or our business. Hell, with some clients, it might help." His ice-blue eyes flashed. "Besides, you think I could sleep knowing Laurie's made it through hell only to get plunged back in, thanks to a damn mistrial? You think Arden, whose mission in life is to help kids with PTSD, would *let* me sleep if I stood by and let a little girl suffer because I was worried about Watchdog's reputation? Fuck that noise, brother. Just fuck it."

Shane smiled gratefully. "Thanks."

"Have we heard anything from Elias?" Gina asked.

Ben nodded. "Officer Dowd grabbed all the signs they put up just before recess. No one saw them, so Laurie has no idea that they were even there. Elias says there was no activity around her house, either. He's spending the night, just in case."

"He need backup?" Waylon asked.

"I'm seeing to it myself," Ben answered. "I'll head over

there right after this. I think with Plymouth and Alphie in jail, they might cool off until they're back out, but God knows. What that family lacks in brains they make up for with tenacity."

"What about Caldwell?" Gabe asked. He tapped the officer's business card on the table. "Something happens again, do we call him?"

"Mmm." Ben shifted in his chair. "Sure. Eventually. Get my meaning?"

Each man at the table nodded.

"In the meantime, watch your backs. These people are unhinged."

Gabe's stomach clenched. *Maybe I should skip going to Riversong for a few days*. He dreaded trying to figure out how to tell Rochelle he needed to lay low without making her think he was avoiding her. But no way in hell was he not taking her to the party.

Ben turned to Gina. "Thanks again." He lifted his chin at Kyle. "You, too."

"My pleasure," Gina said. "So, lighter note, will we be seeing all of you at Bear and Ellie's cabin?"

"Count on it," Shane said.

Bear grunted. "I'll knock heads otherwise. Ellie'd be real disappointed if she didn't see everyone there. Nobody disappoints my Ellie."

It was a toothless threat and everyone knew it. No one would in that room would ever want to disappoint that sweet woman.

Gabe lifted a finger to get his attention. "Mind if there's one extra to the party?"

Bear grinned. "There'd better be."

THIRTEEN

Rochelle returned to her house after watching Gabe drive away from the restaurant. Her insides felt light and fizzy from being brave enough to kiss him as hard as she did. It wasn't like her to take what she wanted like that. But, since spending time with Gabe, she'd felt braver and surer of herself. The sting of the texts from her mother that morning faded. They could have their lives; her life here was just as good, just as important. All she had to do was reach for it. Claim it. If she was brave enough, happiness would be hers, and so would Gabe.

In the meantime, she worried about him. What if the people he was protecting that little girl from were dangerous enough to attack him? Then she laughed to herself. Gabe was a Ranger. All his friends were former military, and if they were anything like Gabe, they were pissed off, too. If anyone was going to get hurt, it was the bad guys.

Rochelle's cat met her at the door. Greg acted nonchalant, rubbing against her legs to greet her even though he wasn't used to her coming home so soon during the week. She bent to pet him and he sniffed around her face, his whiskers tickling her.

"That's Gabe," she told the cat. "You'll get to meet him soon." Gabe was planning on picking her up at her place on Saturday for the party. And Rochelle was planning on inviting him in when he dropped her off.

The idea made her giggle. She'd never in her life invited a man in after knowing him such a short time. She didn't think months of—how did April put it? Oh, right—'making googly eyes at him' counted as knowing Gabe. Most of that time was taken up with fantasizing about him as a book boyfriend.

Then again, the reality was certainly matching up with her fantasies.

Gabe was not only gorgeous, but smart, kind, understanding, and protective.

Her phone buzzed in her tote and she quickly took it out to see if Gabe was texting her. Nope, this was a shock. Sandra's name appeared at the top of the screen. Rochelle's sister almost never reached out to her. Rochelle stood up and carried her tote to the kitchen counter and set it down. She unlocked her phone and looked at her texts.

> Hey, Bookworm! How's it going?

A simple question on the surface, but what did Sandra want? Was she upset that Rochelle hadn't responded with ten thumbs up on her latest photo? Rochelle did a quick mental calculation. It was five fifty-five in the morning in Kyoto and Sandra was definitely not a morning person. Maybe she was only now coming in from a bar and going to bed. Their parents let her do whatever she wanted without judgment. If Rochelle had tried to get away with staying out all night, she wouldn't have lived to see the next night.

She leaned on the counter and texted back:

> Hey, Luggage! What are you doing up so
> early?

Rochelle expected Sandra to send her a photo of herself at a club, laughing and drinking with 'friends' she'd just met and would never see again when the night was over. Sandra just texted instead.

> Can't sleep. Serious jetlag. I'm exhausted.
> This tour actually sucks.

"Sucks? Is she serious?" Rochelle said aloud. Greg had jumped onto the counter—naughty kitty—and bumped her arm, purring. She picked him up and set him on the floor while she thought about how to respond. Her first impulse was a snotty one—*Sucks to dress up and have people tell you how beautiful you are?*—and she took a deep breath. Her sister's tone was different. Her text didn't feel like a humble-brag. She truly sounded tired.

> Sorry to hear that. I saw your

She deleted and started over.

> Sorry you can't sleep. Is everything else
> okay?

Rochelle waited. At the edge of her attention, she heard one of her neighbors get off the elevator and walk down the hall.

Sandra finally texted back.

> No, actually. I'd say that I want to come
> home, but I don't really have one.

"Wow." Rochelle frowned. Sandra was never this blunt.

What's wrong? Talk to me.

> I'd just like a break, you know? I do literally
> feel like a piece of Maman and Dad's
> luggage.

Rochelle grinned. Yeah, she could relate. That's how the first part of her life had felt. Now she felt like a bag that had gotten lost and never reclaimed, left behind while her parents continued on their adventure without her. That's when she'd started calling her sister Luggage.

On impulse, she typed:

> You know, if you ever wanted a break you
> could always come and visit me.

As if Sandra would say yes.

Rochelle had dropped the hint enough—and more than just hinted—outright asked her parents if they would all come and visit her over some holiday. Any holiday. Or anytime, really. And the answer was always that they were too busy, that they had another tour coming up, they couldn't possibly take the time. Rochelle had never asked her sister directly, but imagined the answer would be the same since she never took her up on it. Rochelle almost put her phone away, not expecting to get a reply when it buzzed.

Are you serious?!? I would LOVE that!!

Um. So where do you live now?

"*What?*" Rochelle's thumbs flew over the phone screen.

> You don't know where I live?

Why would I? Never got an invite before now.

Confusion made her brow furrow. Then Rochelle blew out an angry breath.

Maman and Dad know EXACTLY where I live because I INVITED all of you to come see me when I moved to Colorado! Several times actually.

> That's all news to me, Bookworm.

Gut. Punch. Rochelle leaned against the counter to keep from sliding to the floor. The apartment felt extra quiet around her. Lonely. Their parents hadn't even told Sandra where she lived? She'd been in Colorado now for the better part of a year.

In the quiet, Rochelle heard a sound right outside her door. Someone shuffling their feet.

Wait. Someone walked by a minute ago. Didn't they?

Maybe it was somebody looking for a different apartment. The elevator had a mind of its own and sometimes took people to the wrong floor. Even she'd stepped off not paying attention only to find she was a floor up from her apartment. The halls all looked alike.

Rochelle quickly texted her address back to Sandra, then added:

> Come see me anytime.

She walked from her kitchen to the front door. "Hello? Can I help you?" she called.

Someone was definitely outside her door because as soon as they heard her voice, they took off down the hall. Rochelle got to her door in time to look out the peephole at the elevator doors closing behind someone.

Rochelle's phone buzzed and she absently glanced at the screen.

> And yeah, something else happened. Some total rando guy Dad's age grabbed my ass yesterday while I was dressed up. I hate this.

All of Rochelle's focus went straight back to the phone. Rochelle fumed. *How dare anyone violate my baby sister!*

> Asshole! Did you tell Maman and Dad?

> Yeah. Later. They said well you're ok and that's what you get for looking so pretty.

> Kinda laughed it off.

> You know how they are sometimes.

Rochelle closed her eyes and leaned her forehead against the wall. Yes. Yes, she did know how they were sometimes.

> Look, I mean it. Come see me. Anytime. Ok?
> Fly into Denver and I'll pick you up.

She walked back to her kitchen where Greg had jumped back onto the counter. She dumped him on the floor again and waited for a response. After a couple minutes, she typed:

> It's not your fault what happened to you and it's not ok that they didn't take it seriously.

Finally another text came through; a sparkly heart emoji. And then the phone rang.

"Sandra?"

"Could you just maybe read to me, Bookworm?" her sister asked in a tiny voice. "Like you did when we were kids?"

Rochelle felt her heart break right down the middle.

"Of course." She scanned the bookshelf across the room,

thinking *maybe not the spicy romance for my kid sister* before another choice hit her, one that always made her feel better.

Huey's first book of poetry. The one that always made me feel better as a kid.

"How about some poetry?"

"Perfect. Thank you."

———

ROCHELLE READ to Sandra until she fell asleep, then disconnected and got some more work done. She fed Greg his dinner but skipped her own since she was still full from lunch and from worry, both about her sister and about Gabe. Was he okay, or was he in trouble? Why hadn't he texted her to say he was fine?

A couple of kisses doesn't mean he has to check in with you all the time.

She debated sending him a text asking how he was.

Stop being so clingy, Rochelle!

Maman's voice echoed in her mind, probably because she'd just talked to her sister. One after another, her memories of Maman telling her to stop clinging to her surfaced. Boy, she was angry at them! She turned on the TV to distract herself. By ten o'clock, she'd given up on hearing from Gabe and decided to turn in. She picked up the half-empty bowl of popcorn that substituted for dinner off the coffee table in front of the TV and dumped the rest into the garbage. She rinsed the bowl and started the dishwasher. Greg meowed, telling her it was time for bed. She plugged her phone into the charger on the counter, turned, and that's when it buzzed.

Rochelle turned back, grabbed it, and read the text from Gabe.

> Hey, sorry. I'm an asshole for not texting before now. Just letting you know I'm okay but the day was kind of crappy.
>
> Well, crappy after leaving you. The part of my day with you was great.

> You're great.

> I can't wait to take you to the party, beautiful.

Zing! Her bad mood immediately lifted. Rochelle typed back:

> Thanks for letting me know! I was worried. You're okay though?

> Yeah, I'm fine.

She hesitated then typed:

> Will I see you tomorrow?

A pause, then:

> Not tomorrow, sweetness. Sorry. I'll text you though. Or call. And I'll see you Saturday.

Saturday was four days away. He wasn't coming to River-song at all before then?

> You sure you're okay?

> Yeah, promise I'm fine!

It took everything she had not to ask *Are we okay?* Of course they were. He'd said so. She had to learn to trust someone, and Gabe so far had been nothing but honest and sincere. Then, something occurred to her.

> Are you maybe covered in bruises? And you don't want me to see them?

He quickly sent back a laughing emoji and then:

> Yes, okay, I have a bruise from a left hook. It's nothing. It looks worse than it is. And I didn't want you to see it and upset you.

> Or make you feel uncomfortable sitting in public with a guy who's all banged up.

Rochelle grinned.

> I don't care what anyone else thinks. I'm just glad you're ok.

Then she got an idea.

> We could go for a walk under the stars by the St. Vrain if you really don't want me to see the bruising.

She watched the three dots bounce, then disappear, then reappear.

> I'd like that. A lot. But maybe we should wait on it.

Her heart dropped down into her stomach. But he wasn't done typing.

> It's not you. I don't want to scare you but I need to lie low for a couple of days. If there's any retaliation, I don't want them seeing you with me.

So should I be worried about YOU?

> Nope. My brothers and I can handle this. I
> just want to keep you safe.

Then he added:

> You mean the world to me, Rochelle.

So do you, Gabe.

> Goodnight.

Goodnight.

She smiled, held the phone to her chest, then plugged it into its charger.

As she was drifting off to sleep, Rochelle briefly remembered the person in the elevator, but by morning she had forgotten again.

THEY MAY NOT HAVE GOTTEN TOGETHER, but Gabe texted regularly and called her every night after that. And he insisted on paying for her a latte every day—which, by the dreamy look on Aprils face, made April just as happy as it did Rochelle, she thought. But by Friday morning, Rochelle was despairing.

She had no idea what she was going to wear to the party.

"What's wrong?" April asked her when she came in to Riversong.

"My closet is full of clothes and I still have nothing to wear."

April already knew all about the party. "Nothing?" she asked. "No cute dress slacks? Some sexy, low-cut blouse?"

"Do I look like the type of person who wears sexy, low-cut blouses?"

April just grinned. "You will once I get done with you. Hey, Dad. Hannah," she shouted over her shoulder. "Take over for me. I have an emergency."

"Emergency?" Sonny looked at his daughter, alarm on his face.

"I'm just helping my friend here with a wardrobe emergency, so calm down, please, alright?" April took off her apron, wadded it up, and tossed it into a hamper beside the espresso machine. She came around the counter, approached Rochelle, and said, "Alright, let's go."

"Really. Are you sure?"

Of course I'm sure," April said, laughing. "I can use an excuse to get out of here anyway. Twist my arm to go shopping."

"Just be careful," Sonny said.

"Yes, Dad." April didn't literally roll her eyes, but the sentiment was certainly in her voice.

"Where are we going?" Rochelle asked as April led the way out the door.

"Well, that's up to you. We could go to Cherry Creek down in Denver, but I'd have to cut it short to come back and get Kevin from school. Or, I know of a fun little boutique that's much closer. What do you say?"

"Not Denver, please. How about the boutique?"

"Sounds great," April said. "I'll drive."

They spent the entire morning picking out something for Rochelle to wear. April let Rochelle grab some clothes and try them on before they realized April's idea of sexy was different from Rochelle's. She kept nixing Rochelle's chosen outfits until they went back to the racks.

"How about this?" Rochelle held up a dress she thought would make her look good.

"Sure...if you've got a meeting with your pastor. What's up with that floppy bow? Okay, we're getting nowhere so it's time for me to drive. Here." She rummaged through the same clothing rack that Rochelle had gone through and picked out a sweater dress with a V-neck. "So cute, and you can wear some patterned tights under it. Go try it on." She thrust it at Rochelle.

"Patterned tights?" She looked around. "I don't see any here..."

"Nope. But they have plenty next door."

"Oh? Ooohhh." Rochelle felt her cheeks pinken up. The shop next door sold lingerie.

"Can't let you wear white granny panties under that dress," April said. "Now scoot." She shooed her toward the dressing room.

"Who says I'm wearing white granny panties?" Rochelle protested.

"Are you saying you aren't?" April folded her arms.

"I'm...not saying a word. Except to say my underwear is just fine *and* comfortable." She ducked into the dressing room and changed, deliberately *not* looking at her underwear in the mirror.

But she couldn't look away once she had the cream-colored dress on.

It looked a bit baggy on the hanger, but wearing it, the dress hugged Rochelle's every curve—curves she never realized she had. She turned slowly, craning her head over her shoulder to get a look at herself from every angle.

"You've been in there forever. Lemme see," April called.

"Yeah, hang on." Rochelle pulled the curtain back and stepped out. April dropped her arms to her sides and her grin turned to a full-on smile.

"Perfect. Perfect. Perfect. If I do say so myself."

"Really?" Rochelle turned. "It's not too much?"

"Nope. You look lovely. He's going to die." She smirked. "Still think your underwear's just fine?"

Rochelle laughed. "Maybe not?"

"Right answer. Get changed and we'll head next door."

Fifteen minutes later, they were looking through much smaller, much brighter, much frillier clothing.

"So cute!" April held up a matching bra and panties in peacock-blue silk and toffee-colored lace.

"Won't they show through the dress?"

"Take it out and we'll check, but I think the material is thick enough."

"Oh, those *are* cute," a woman behind Rochelle said. She turned to see an older woman with white hair smiling at her. She was holding a pair of red panties with black lace. "Hot date?"

"Her first night out with him," April answered before Rochelle could speak.

"That'll do it." The woman winked. "Where is he taking you?"

"Oh, it's a party, actually. A friend's cabin in the mountains."

The woman grinned as if she knew a secret. "You don't say?" She studied the lingerie again. "I hope the two of you have a wonderful time."

"Thanks," Rochelle said. She looked at the other woman's lingerie. "I hope you do, too."

She laughed lightly. "My boyfriend's getting back to town

and he figured out I was telling him a little white lie about how many laps I was swimming."

April whistled. "If he doesn't forgive you, dump him."

She laughed. "Oh, this isn't about asking forgiveness, sweetie. I told him he was being a control freak and he admitted that he was and that he'd do better. This is his reward." She set the panties aside and offered her hand. "I'm Stephanie."

"Rochelle."

"April. I'm over at Riversong."

They shook hands.

"Riversong." She nodded. "I haven't been in yet, but I've heard great things," Stephanie said. "Rochelle, good luck and I hope to see you again." She winked, then picked up the panties along with several other pairs and headed for the checkout counter, looking like the cat that caught the canary.

"I want to be her when I grow up," April said.

"Me too," Rochelle agreed.

FOURTEEN

"You look like the cat that caught the canary," Gabe said when Stephanie got back from lunch. He stood up from behind the front desk, took one look at the bright fuchsia bag with the name of the lingerie shop printed across it, and raised his eyebrows.

"MYOB, mister." Stephanie stashed the bag behind her back.

"Doctor Boyfriend found out, didn't he?"

Stephane plunked down in her chair. "Poor man. My watch slipped off the boat into the middle of the pool and died. By the time I got it fished out, he thought I had, too."

Gabe laughed. "Serves you right, Steph."

"Well, if he hadn't been so pushy about my knees, we wouldn't be in this pickle."

"You got a shopping trip out of it."

And there was that cat-with-the-canary smile again. "Sure did."

"What?" Gabe narrowed his eyes at her.

"Nothing, nothing." She waved him away. "Are you looking forward to your party tomorrow night?"

Gabe couldn't help his grin. He'd both texted and called Rochelle every day, wishing he could see her instead. With Velna's family pissed at him, he didn't dare chance it. But, they'd stayed quiet all week, and he was feeling confident that they'd backed off for good, especially since Gina had made good on her word and cut off their funding. She'd been closed-lipped about it, but promised to give them details after the party.

"You know I'm looking forward to it."

"Excellent," Stephanie said, rubbing her palms together like some sort of villain. "As well you should be."

"What?" Gabe repeated.

"Nothing." The phone rang and she picked it up quickly, dismissing him. He started to walk away but then she held up a finger signaling him to wait.

"That's wonderful news," Stephanie said, suddenly beaming. "Yes, thank you. I'll let everyone know. Thanks again. Have a wonderful day and bless you for all you do."

She hung up the phone and looked at Gabe. "That man who collapsed the other day at the clinic? He made it through surgery in Longmont but now they transferred him to that new hospital down in Denver. He's still in the ICU but he's doing well. Looks like he's going to make a full recovery."

Gabe felt a weight he didn't know was there lift off his chest. He sent up a quick prayer of gratitude.

"Fantastic. Thanks, Steph. I'll let Elias and Waylon know if you'll call Sue and Fran."

"Done and done, boss. Tell the boys I said hi at the party." Stephanie picked up the receiver and dialed, cat-with-the-canary smile replaced with a grateful one.

SATURDAY, Gabe knocked on Rochelle's apartment door. Even though he'd taken a route that made him double back and forth to flush out anyone who might be following him, he still showed up half an hour early. He knew it was rude to be there before she expected him, but he just couldn't wait to see her again.

A moment later, he felt her footsteps approach the door and stop. He hoped she was looking out the peephole instead of just opening the door. He waved at the little round window and the door opened.

Oh, wow. Oh damn. *I've never been jealous of a dress before.*

Rochelle wore a dress that caressed her breasts, waist, and hips the way that he wanted to.

Lucky dress.

But the beauty didn't stop there. Her dark hair cascaded over her left shoulder in glossy waves. She was wearing herringbone-patterned tights that disappeared into off-white, high-heeled boots that hugged her calves and ankles. She looked amazing.

No. Stunning. Breathtaking.

Rochelle looked anxious. "Is everything okay?" she signed, and Gabe realized he was just standing there like an idiot, taking her in.

"Everything is wonderful," he signed back. "You are so beautiful right now, I lost myself for a moment."

Her anxious expression melted into sparkling eyes and a radiant smile. "Come in."

Gabe followed her into her apartment, closing the door behind him and locking it. "Sorry I'm so early," he said. "I guess I couldn't wait to see you."

"I got ready early, too. I couldn't wait to see you, either."

Gabe looked around at the simply furnished space. A few pops of color were scattered here and there—an Oriental carpet, some brightly patterned throw pillows, a tapestry—but her home was dominated by her bookshelves. His woman was a reader.

My woman?

Yeah. My woman.

That felt good. Right.

Movement on the floor caught his eye and Gabe blinked at the streak of brown and black fur, thinking he'd just seen a raccoon dart down the hall.

"What—?"

Rochelle looked at the surprise in his eyes. "Oh! I should have warned you I have a pet."

"A pet raccoon?"

She laughed. "Oh, gosh, no! That's Greg, my Norwegian Forest Cat. But he does look like a raccoon, and he's about as big. Come here, Greg," she called. "He's very friendly, but he's not used to people coming over. He'll come out when he's ready."

That made Gabe sad, the idea that no one ever visited Rochelle. Well, that was about to change, once she met his friends, especially the women. He just knew they'd love her on sight and fold her into the pack. He hoped she would want that.

"If Greg were a raccoon, you wouldn't be the first wild animal owner I've known. Actually, Bear and Ellie have a pet skunk named Spot."

She covered her mouth. "In their house?"

Gabe laughed. "No. Maybe if Bear were living alone though. He's a regular St. Francis. But no way Ellie would let Spot live inside. The little guy lives under their porch."

"Does he...smell?"

Gabe laughed again. "Nope, not that I've smelled."

Greg chose that moment to saunter into the room. He really did look like a raccoon in cat-form. He looked at Gabe, sized him up, then his tail curved into a shepherd's crook and he approached. Gabe squatted down and held out his hand for the cat, who rubbed his soft head against Gabe's fingers. He scratched the cat behind the ears and was rewarded with a purr.

"He likes you," Rochelle said, smiling.

"Guess I've passed the audition."

She grinned, her eyes crinkling. "You did, but I would have overruled him. I own my cat, my cat does not own me. Usually."

Gabe stood back up and Greg retreated to a cat bed beside the couch. He looked at Rochelle, then spread his arms out.

"I haven't done this yet and I've been waiting all week."

She stepped into his arms, looked up into his face and kissed him. She touched his jaw where he'd been punched.

"I can see why you stayed away. This looks faded, but I bet it wasn't pretty a couple of days ago."

"No, it wasn't."

"You don't have to hide stuff like this from me, Gabe. April told me a little about you and your friends. And you told me you were protecting a little girl. I think that's wonderful. Even if I have to worry about you from time to time." Her eyes darkened. "There are bad men out there, and they don't care about who they hurt."

Gabe's heart raced. "Baby? Anyone hurting you?" He cupped her face and she pressed her cheek against his palm.

"No, not me." She sighed. "My sister."

"What? I can help. We can—"

She smiled sadly and shook her head. "Not unless you're willing to jump on a plane and fly to Japan. Or wherever they are by now."

"I'll do it," Gabe said without hesitation. "What kind of danger is she in?"

Rochelle's mouth dropped open. "You don't even know her."

"It doesn't matter that I don't know her. She's your sister."

"You barely know *me*," Rochelle said, her voice full of wonder.

"Rochelle." He ran his hand through her hair. The smell of her skin—vanilla, paper, a quiet and peaceful library—rose under his fingertips. "We've talked and texted all week. We kept the topics light. I know all your favorite books. Your favorite flavor of ice cream. I know that you love watching the morning sun hit the red sandstone around Lyons when you go to Riversong. I just realized you never once brought your sister up in conversation. You didn't talk about your family at all. Is it because you don't see this going anywhere?"

He shook his head. "No, don't answer that. That's an unfair question. That speaks to my own insecurities." Gabe growled. "I'm saying this all wrong, dammit. I'm trying to say that I care deeply about you, Rochelle, and I want to give you anything and everything you need. If you need me to get your sister out of danger, it's done."

"Gabe. That's amazing. I've never... No one has ever said anything like that to me. My sister is fine, I promise. She's traveling with my parents, got dressed up as a geisha in Japan, and some jerk grabbed her butt, that's all. They aren't even in Kyoto now. He was just some rando, like she said."

"It's never okay for a man to do that. I don't care what your sister was wearing or how she looked. It isn't right, and never will be. Is she alright?" He pointed to his head. "Up here, I mean. I don't have to tell you that kind of thing can mess with your head."

"She was upset enough to call me, but she's better now. She's just tired of traveling."

Gabe saw in Rochelle's eyes that there was more to it and he desperately wanted to know what it was. He wanted Rochelle to feel comfortable sharing her life with him.

"I want to know you better. I want to learn everything about you. Tell me about your sister. Are you two close? Estranged?"

Rochelle shrugged. "What can I say? She's my sister. We're two very different people but I love her. I told her to come visit me."

Gabe smiled and relaxed. "So, is she coming?"

"Maybe. We'll see." Rochelle smiled again in a way that told Gabe she was done talking about her family. He noted it as a sore spot, not that she was shutting him out necessarily, or that she didn't think they had something here.

"What about you?" she asked, running her fingertips over his cheek and raising goose bumps along his arms. "You said you had insecurities? You can't possibly be insecure about anything. Look at you," she whispered. "You're perfect."

"What about these?" He touched the hearing aid in his right ear. "Hardly perfect."

He'd been in to see the doctor who'd done some tests and made some adjustments, plus Gabe's brain was finally getting used to the new hearing aids. He had no problem hearing Rochelle's whisper in the quiet apartment. All the same, his hearing was far from perfect. Gabe's mind strayed to the night at Cocks and Strippers and to other nights when a woman realized he was hearing-impaired and decided to keep looking.

"You think *that* bothers me?" Rochelle retorted. "Gabe, your hearing may not be perfect, but you *listen* to me more than anyone I've ever known. You hear me, even when my words aren't there." She looked down. Her eyes watered and she blinked back tears.

"I hear you because I care so much about you, Rochelle. And you hear *me*."

Gabe cupped her face and tilted her chin up. He leaned in for a kiss and she met him eagerly. She pressed her body against his and he felt his shoulders ease, felt his whole body pulse with need. If he didn't stop now, they'd miss the party because he would pick her up and carry her into the bedroom. As much as he wanted that, as much as his body ached to touch her naked skin, feel her softness under his hands, cup her breasts and hold their weight in his palms as he took turns sucking each nipple, she wasn't ready. He wasn't ready, either. He wanted more than a physical relationship with her, one that was fated to end in a month or two. He wanted her. Her smile. Her kindness. Her shyness. Her love of books, of language.

All of it.

Gabe broke the kiss and looked into Rochelle's face. She kept her eyes closed and her lips parted as if still savoring the taste of his lips. It made Gabe hard just watching her barest pleasure, knowing he could give her so much more than that. How he could tease her right to the edge of ecstasy then pull her back only to bring her there again.

Her eyelids fluttered and she looked deeply into his eyes. Her gaze looked fuzzy and her lips curved into a dreamy smile.

"Wow," she mouthed. "What were we supposed to do tonight? That kiss erased my brain."

Gabe chuckled softly. "I think we're going somewhere in the mountains. Something like that. Can't really remember either."

Her eyebrows rose and a glint of mischievousness flickered in her gaze.

Uh-oh. Does she want...

"Nope," he said out loud. "Time to go."

"But we're running early. We could keep doing a little more of this for a while."

Gabe closed his eyes and groaned. He had a hard time believing this was the same woman who was so shy she ran out of Riversong just over a week ago.

It became even harder for him to remember that when she led him to the couch.

They showed up late.

AS THEY LEFT the parking lot in front of her apartment building, Gabe once again looked around for any sign of Verna, Alphie, Plymouth, or anyone else from Jesse's family. He didn't see them or any suspicious vehicles.

"Everything okay?" Rochelle asked. Her face was still flushed from their heavy make-out session.

"Just fine, beautiful." He turned onto the street. No cars pulled out to follow. So far, so good. From Rochelle's apartment, they had a forty-five minute drive to the cabin. The closer they got, the less traffic and the easier to spot a tail, but first they had to get through Longmont and Lyons.

"So, tell me about your family," Gabe ventured. "They took a trip of a lifetime, but you decided not to go with them?"

Rochelle hesitated and Gabe knew he'd asked the wrong thing. Then, she relaxed.

"No, it's not a vacation. They travel for work. My parents have always had the travel bug and found creative ways to not pay for it."

Gabe jerked his head back. "How so?"

"They met doing overseas missionary work."

"What? Seriously? Your parents are missionaries?"

Rochelle practically snorted. "Oh, God no. No. They had a falling out with the pastor at the church that sponsored their trips years ago, back when they got chased out of China."

"Hang on, what?" Gabe looked at her when he stopped at a light.

"Yup. We were spied on constantly. The government didn't like foreigners coming in to spread the word of God. They barely tolerated it in their own people. I remember we had to be careful at house churches. That's where people held services, in someone's house. I'm not sure what happened, if the authorities threatened my parents directly or if things just got too scary. They didn't just preach, they sometimes sent things home they shouldn't have."

"Damn."

"Yeah. So I don't know if it was the missionary work or if they got caught exporting things illegally. But one night, we just left everything and flew back to America."

"Damn! That must have been scary and confusing as a kid. How old were you and your sister?"

"It was just me. My Maman was newly pregnant with Sandra and that was further incentive for them to get out. My sister was a surprise. We're eleven years apart. Maman's miracle baby."

"Eleven years. I bet you were a protective big sister."

"Mmm. Sometimes. Sometimes, I..." Rochelle mumbled something and Gabe didn't hear.

"Say again, I missed that. Your voice got quiet."

"Oh, sorry, I didn't realize. Probably because I'm embarrassed to say that sometimes I was just jealous of her."

"Ah." Gabe reached over and grabbed Rochelle's hand. *There's that sore spot and I brought her straight into it.* "Is that why you aren't traveling with them now?"

"More like they never ask if I'd like to go." Gabe glanced at her and she smiled sadly. "They say that I got to travel the world with them first, now it's her turn."

"Wow, that's harsh. Rochelle, I don't blame you for being jealous."

She shrugged. "Sandra doesn't deserve my jealousy. She didn't ask to be carted all over the world any more than I did." She grinned. "I have a nickname for her. Luggage."

"Ha! So what does she call you?"

"What else? Bookworm."

Gabe laughed again. "So what do your parents do now? Import-export business?"

Rochelle shook her head vehemently. "Oh no. After they got back home, the church they belonged to basically kicked them out for their extra activities. So my mother started a blog, first to raise money to continue missionary work, but it eventually evolved into a travel blog. A popular one, actually. She moved it onto another platform, took a ton of photos, and all sorts of companies started sending her their travel gear to use and review. Pillows, water bottles, luggage, you name it. She did the reviews, then sold the stuff for extra money. She figured out she could get bigger sponsorships if she promised to keep promoting companies."

"So you're telling me your parents went from being missionaries to influencers?"

"Yup, and my sister is an influencer, too. Once Maman learned how to monetize videos, and that there was a market for advice on how to travel with a baby, my sister basically became an internet star before she could talk."

"So what about you?"

She turned and gave him a confused look. "What about me?"

"There was no market for how to travel with a pre-teen?"

She smiled sadly before facing the window. "Not for a

quiet, awkward pre-teen who pretty much packed her own stuff, looked after her little sister off-camera, and tried to stay out of the way the rest of the time."

Damn. "So you weren't in any of the videos?"

"No. I was the one behind the camera recording the three of them."

"That was by choice?"

She shrugged a shoulder. "After a while, sure. It was just easier that way."

"And they all still travel together? Your sister's not a baby anymore," Gabe said.

"She's not, but she's gorgeous so they still make videos of her. They also lead tours now. High-end, themed ones. Things like, eat your way through Italy with some popular chef or food writer, or spend a week in Sonoma Valley glamping in the vineyards. They're touring heritage sites all over Asia right now."

"And your sister still goes along?"

"She does. Now that she's an adult, she can set off on her own, but I think she's scared. She's still young and doesn't know anything else. Any other life."

"But you're going to give her that chance to figure it out when she stays with you."

Rochelle tilted her head. "Yeah... I guess I am."

"You never thought of it that way."

"No. I just wanted her safe."

"I don't see a speck of jealousy there. I see a loving sister still looking out for her. Doing what's right for her."

Rochelle looked at Gabe and her smile lit the cab. "Thank you."

"For what? Pointing out the truth?"

"You know it's more than that." She smiled to herself for a few minutes before adding, "One other thing."

"What's that, baby?"

"Thanks for not asking who she is or who they are so you can look them up and see the posts."

"Why would I do that?" He squeezed her hand. "When I already know I have the most interesting, most beautiful member of the family right next to me."

The truck rose into the mountains in time to catch the last of the setting sun. Gabe turned up the heat in the cab and rolled down a window. The mountain air was crisp through the half-open window, carrying with it the scent of pine, snow, and wet earth. Gabe glanced at Rochelle's silhouetted form against the backdrop of the sun's golden light over the Rockies. Her fingers traced an invisible line over the glass as if she could feel the texture of the sharp peaks in the distance.

He brushed his fingertips against her cheek—a silent beckoning. Her gaze shifted from the grandeur outside to the quiet question of his touch.

"You like the mountains?" he asked.

"It's like poetry," Rochelle replied. The corners of her mouth curled into a smile that reached her eyes, lighting them up with the same intensity as the evening sunlight breaking through gaps in the trees now lining the road to the west. He gave her a smile that mirrored hers. Gabe's heart stirred within his chest, a gentle acknowledgement of connection, knowing that the mountains he so loved were finding a kindred spirit in Rochelle.

They continued into the mountains as the light turned soft and glowing. Beside him, Rochelle sat quietly, her gaze fixed on the passing scenery. The tranquility of the mountains seemed to envelop her, smoothing away the creases of everyday worries from her forehead. Gabe found himself stealing glances, admiring the way the soft light played across her features.

"Almost there."

She nodded absently, still absorbed by the beauty of the

scenery around them. Gabe wondered how it compared to all the landscapes she'd visited around the world. He wondered if his home would measure up to the places where she'd stayed. He hoped too that she would like his friends, his brothers. He had no doubt they would adore her.

"How do the Rockies compare to the places you've been?" he asked, his voice cutting through the quiet between them.

"They look very different from the mountains in China, but they have the same effect on me. They make me feel peaceful."

"Did you go into the mountains often when you were there?"

"A few times, yes. But mostly, I looked at paintings of mountains. Landscapes. And I loved reading the poetry that went with them."

Gabe chuckled. "Of course you did."

"There is an exhibition at the Denver Art Museum on Chinese landscape paintings coming next month. My favorite painting is in it, mountains painted by an artist named Qu Ding. I'm not a fan of going to Denver alone. Would...would you like to go with me? I know you hate big cities, so it's okay if you don't."

He shook his head. "I'd love to," he said. "Museums are quiet and peaceful. And I want to see the paintings that inspired you."

That did it. She gave him that little grin he so loved as she looked down. "Okay," she signed, then looked up at him through her lashes. "It's a date."

Gabe turned onto the newly paved road leading to Ellie's property. Other roads branched off to her neighbors, though their houses were impossible to see through the trees. A sign marked the boundary of Ellie's land and the road turned private after that. At the end of the private road was a wide apron to park on. A gravel path led through an aspen grove that circled the cabin. Gabe was looking forward to introducing Rochelle to everyone. Diane had taken Laurie out of town for the weekend to visit family, so everyone would be at the party.

Gabe had texted ahead to let Ellie know they were on their way. He wanted to make sure Rochelle could meet Ellie first. He thought that Rochelle would be more comfortable that way. Both of the women were on the quiet side and both of them were very sweet. He also worried that Rochelle would feel overwhelmed walking straight into a room full of people. Maybe he was being too cautious, but he wanted everything to be perfect.

Gabe exited the SUV and opened Rochelle's door for her. Then he locked the vehicle with a beep that echoed off the trees. Stepping out into the cooling mountain air, Rochelle took in the sprawling property. Gabe had told her about Ellie's efforts to restore the cabin, how Bear helped her, and now, they were planning on hosting a herd of bison, stocking the lake, and eventually building little cabins along the water to rent out for fishing or for retreats. He sensed Rochelle's hesitance, the slight tensing of her shoulders as she surveyed the new environment, and he moved closer, an unspoken vow to be her anchor.

"Ready to meet Ellie?" he asked.

"Ready." She nodded, showing him a subtle firming of resolve that he'd come to admire in her. Her gaze locked onto his with a bravery that hid her nervousness.

"Just let me know if it gets to be too much, and we can duck out. My friends are great, but they can also get—"

"Gabe. It's going to be okay." She smiled bravely into his eyes. "If they are anything at all like you, it's going to be great."

Gabe smiled back. "Even Shane?"

Rochelle laughed. "Yes, even Shane. He's not so bad." She looked toward the cabin. "Let's go." She took a deep breath, squared her shoulders, and gave a small, yet determined nod. Gabe's heart swelled with pride; here was a woman as brave as she was gentle, ready to step into a house full of strangers with a quiet confidence that matched her unassuming grace.

Gabe offered Rochelle his arm, an unspoken promise of support. As they approached the cabin, the door opened and the sound of laughter and soft music spilled out from inside, mingling with the crackling of an outdoor fire pit. Ellie appeared on the porch, her presence like the first star in the night sky. She caught sight of them and the corners of her eyes crinkled with genuine delight. She stepped off the porch and walked toward them.

"I saw you pull up on the cameras. Hi, Gabe. And you must be Rochelle." Ellie's voice was a soft melody. "I'm so glad you could make it." She took Rochelle's hand in hers and the two women smiled at each other.

"Thank you, Ellie," Rochelle replied, her voice steady. "This is for you." She took out a bottle of wine from her tote. "And your cabin is so cute."

"Thanks! I couldn't have done it without Bear and his friends, including this guy." She smiled at Gabe. Ellie gestured towards the cabin with an inviting sweep of her arm. "Come on in. Make yourself at home. Everyone's eager to meet you." She looked over her shoulder. "Or if you'd like, we have the grill and the fire pit going just on the other side of the cabin. Bear's over there right now getting ready to cook up some steaks."

Rochelle glanced at Gabe, then at the cabin just as they heard a sudden burst of laughter. "Sure," she said. "I'd love to meet Bear first, where it's a little quieter."

Ellie led them around the cabin and Rochelle's eyes widened when she got a good look at the lake with the cliffs and mountains rising behind it in the day's last light.

"So beautiful," she signed to him. Gabe nodded, then

watched as her attention went to the big man squatting beside the fire pit, but he wasn't facing it. All of his attention was focused on a fluffy little shadow trundling toward him from the cabin. Rochelle froze.

Ellie laughed. "Don't worry, that's just Spot."

"Your pet skunk," Rochelle said, relaxing. "Gabe told me about him. I thought he'd be hibernating."

Bear looked up. "Skunks don't hibernate. They go into torpor. Drop their body temp to save energy, then come out once a day to forage." He turned his attention back to the skunk and held out his hand. Spot went straight to it and the food there. "Usually feed him earlier but the party was gonna wake him up anyway."

"He's cute." Rochelle stepped forward slowly and dropped down in front of them. "And he never stinks?"

Bear smiled. "Naw. He feels safe here." He ran one large finger over the skunk's head as Spot ate peanuts out of his palm.

"I can see why," Rochelle said softly. She started to get up and Gabe offered her his arm. She beamed at him and his heart lifted.

"Thanks," Bear said. "Gabe's place is like this. Quiet. Peaceful. You'd like it there, too."

Gabe just smiled at Bear's not-so-subtle wingman attempt.

Spot finished the last of the peanuts. He twitched his nose, looking for more. Bear picked up a plastic food container beside him. He walked back toward the side of the porch, Spot following like a faithful dog, and opened the container. Vegetables, scraps of meat, and more nuts filled the container. Bear emptied it on the ground beside the porch and Spot went back to work.

Bear smiled at Spot before turning and walking back to them. Then he stopped and did something that shocked Gabe.

Bear lifted his arm, palm up, and swept it back toward his body —the ASL word for *welcome*.

Gabe looked Bear straight in the eye. He touched his fingers to his chin then moved his hand away from his body. "Thank you," he told his brother and best friend.

"I'm Bear." He held out his hand for Rochelle to shake. "We're happy you're here." He put his arm around Ellie. "We can all stay out here, watch the stars come out." He glanced down at Ellie, who gave him a radiant smile. "Or go on inside. Meet the rest. Your choice, Rochelle."

"Let's go inside," Rochelle said. Gabe was proud of her for wanting to rip off the Band-Aid.

As they stepped inside, the cabin embraced them in its warm glow. Gabe felt Rochelle relax by his side, the tension melting away like snow in sunlight. In this place, among his friends, Gabe was sure Rochelle could be herself. A gentle squeeze of Rochelle's hand was all it took for Gabe to convey his thoughts—*you're safe. You're welcome. You're with friends.*

FIFTEEN

Rochelle hadn't quite known what to expect at the party, but the moment she saw Ellie, her anxiety disappeared. She'd heard other people talk about seeing someone for the first time and just knowing right off the bat that they were destined to be good friends. She'd never had that happen until now. Ellie radiated friendliness, putting Rochelle at ease. But there was more to it. Rochelle had an immediate *There you are* moment, like Ellie was already an old friend she was seeing again after a long time.

Thank you, Gabe.

She liked Bear too. The man was a walking contradiction—a big, hulking guy, but gentle and quiet. Rochelle also liked his not-so-subtle suggestion to go home with Gabe.

A great idea. And judging by Gabe's smile, it looked like he agreed. Rochelle felt like she was floating a few inches off the ground.

The woman Rochelle had been a little more than a week before might have taken up Bear's suggestion that they all stay outside and watch the stars. No—that woman would probably be home alone right now. She wouldn't have dreamed of going to a party full of strangers.

But that's not who Rochelle was tonight. Not after meeting Ellie and Bear. Not after spending time with Gabe. She was a woman who'd made a new friend, just like that. She was a woman who spoke and laughed without hesitation. She was a woman who wore a sexy dress and was late to a party because she was busy getting busy with her book boyfriend on her couch.

She liked being this confident woman. Liked it a lot.

And so she was more than ready to go inside and meet more of Gabe's friends.

When Shane saw them, he waved from where he sat beside a man with stunning ice-blue eyes. Rochelle braced for some sort of wisecrack about how they were late, but instead, Shane said, "Glad you could make it." And left it at that.

Ellie took Rochelle's arm. "Come on, you've got to meet my friends Arden and Gina first." With Bear following in their wake, she directed Rochelle to a chair close to a roaring fireplace across from a loveseat where two women sat, engrossed in a conversation. One had shiny, golden hair and sharp grey eyes. The other was auburn-haired, with golden eyes—the most interesting eye color Rochelle had ever seen. A ginger-colored dog lay curled up at her feet and when she lifted her head, Rochelle noticed her eyes almost matched the woman's.

The grey-eyed woman said hello first. "I'm Arden. It's nice to meet you."

"I'm Gina." The woman with the golden eyes stood and shook her hand.

"Hi, I'm Rochelle," she answered, her voice steady. She took an empty seat and Gabe was right there with a glass of wine for her. He quickly signed, asking if she'd like him to stay close, and she nodded. Not because she was feeling intimidated, but because she wanted him near. He pulled up a stool and set his beer on the little table beside her chair.

In the meantime, the man with the ice-blue eyes came and stood behind Arden, then placed his hands on her shoulders. She covered his hands with hers.

"I'm Kyle," he said, and gave Rochelle a dazzling smile that thawed the ice from his eyes and turned them into warm pools.

"Good to meet you."

Rochelle turned her attention back to Gina. "I've lived all over, but I just moved here from the East Coast last spring. Gabe mentioned your plans to move to Colorado."

"Oh, yes, it's a possibility," Gina replied, her voice tinged with the faintest hint of nostalgia. She looked over at a man with auburn hair that was just going white at his temples. Rochelle assumed he must be Lachlan. He came over at Gina's unspoken invitation. "But we're coming from the opposite coast, Los Angeles. We're looking for a change of pace, something much quieter," she continued. "The mountains are quite persuasive." She smiled at Arden. "Plus, my friend here is unfairly using psychological tactics against us."

Arden's grey eyes turned silver as she laughed. "Is *that* what you call my cookies?"

"*And* your homemade jam, *and* the gorgeous hiking trails, *and* the incredible views from your deck, and, and, and..."

Arden laughed harder. "You're seeing through all of it, aren't you?"

Gina laughed with her and Rochelle felt the easy warmth between the friends. "It's pretty damn obvious." Gina nudged Arden's shoulder with hers. "But the truth is, I've loved it here since my first visit."

Lachlan sat down on the rug between the fire and Gina's end of the loveseat. His eyes sparkled with humor. "Arden, I say this with the utmost affection for you, but your motives are as transparent as the ghost you claim haunts your house." Yup—with the faint Scottish lilt to his voice, this *had* to be Lachlan.

"Come on, Boss," Kyle said, "you've been staying with us for how long, and you're telling me you still don't believe in Nancy?"

Arden leaned across Gina to look Lachlan squarely in the eye. "The ghost of my great-great grandmother is totally real and sticking around."

"All right, lass," Lachlan said, laughing and holding up his hands. "If she's had a taste of your cooking, I believe she'd stay."

"That's better." Arden sat back, arms crossed, smile on her face.

"If ghosts were real," he added, yanking her chain.

Gina scoffed. "I believe in Nancy."

Lachlan's eyebrows rose. "You? Really? You need proof for everything."

Gina crossed her arms. "And I have it. I *saw* her, Lach."

"Oh my gosh, I think I think I saw her, too!" Ellie said. "While I was staying with you Monday night. Just out of the corner of my eye in the great room."

"In front of the fireplace?" Kyle asked, leaning forward.

"Yes! I thought it was a trick of the light."

"That's where I saw her, too," Gina added. "Just for a moment though. I couldn't sleep so I got up and I swear I saw a woman standing perfectly—and I mean *perfectly*—still." She turned back to Arden. "I thought it was you because of the long, blond hair, and I started to say your name, ask you if you couldn't sleep, either." Gina shivered. "She turned and I realized it wasn't you, and then she was just…gone."

"That's her favorite spot," Kyle confirmed. "I first encountered her there, back when I met Arden. I couldn't sleep, either."

"Now he calls her the Christmas Ghost," Arden said.

Gina looked back at Kyle. "I thought she looked very... happy. Content."

"I think she is." Kyle smiled warmly at Arden and she reached out and took his hand. Rochelle's heart skipped a beat watching them. If Kyle wasn't a real-life book boyfriend like Gabe, she'd eat every paperback romance at Riversong.

Lach shook his head. "Eh, you were sleepwalking, the both of you."

Ellie craned her neck up to look at Bear standing behind her chair. "Have you ever seen any ghosts in our cabin?"

"Not a one, honey," he answered.

She looked crestfallen. "Yeah, I didn't think so."

Rochelle looked at Ellie. "You *want* a ghost here?"

"Well, not just *any* ghost. I want one that looks out for us like Nancy does for Arden." Her expression turned wistful. "This cabin belonged to my uncle and he left it to me in his will when I needed it the most. I'd like to somehow tell him thank you."

"I don't think you need a ghost to do that," Rochelle said. "Just by loving this place, sharing it with your friends, and a relative stranger,"—she pointed at herself—"tells him thank you every day."

Ellie grinned. "I never thought of it that way." Then she frowned. "But, let's get one thing straight. You're not a stranger, not once you've come through my door. You're a friend."

Rochelle basked in the warmth of Ellie's words.

"Maybe your Uncle Walter's ghost could keep you out of trouble," Kyle joked. "This one," he pointed at Ellie, "sneaked onto Watchdog property past all my security when we first met."

Rochelle laughed. "What? How did you do that?"

Ellie covered her face as she laughed. "I have no idea. I was just pushing my bike through the woods for what seemed like forever, and suddenly, I was in trouble."

"Oh, she knows, she knows how," Kyle kept joking. "And she refuses to let me hire her as my security system troubleshooter."

"I've got enough going on right here, with the bison herd and the fishing cabins going up soon."

"And, she's still recovering." Bear leaned way down and kissed her on the forehead. Rochelle felt Gabe squeeze her shoulder and she reached up to lace her fingers in his as if they'd been together forever.

That warmth kept growing throughout the evening as she got to know every one of Gabe's friends. Kyle had seemed intense at first, but he had a great sense of humor. Arden helped people with PTSD get better by working with horses, alpacas, and goats. Elias and Waylon talked about their jobs as paramedics and some of the crazier things they'd seen. Shane was Shane—cocky and confident. Ben reminded Rochelle of Bear—big, quiet, thoughtful. From what Rochelle gathered, Lachlan was a former SEAL and Gina had something to do with the CIA or FBI, or...something. They gave Rochelle the impression of two people who had gained wisdom through hard trials. She hoped that they would stay here, and find peace.

The party went on into the night. Then in ones and twos, people left until it was just Gabe and Rochelle, who offered to help clean up the last of the dishes. Ellie waved her off like she had the other guests, but Rochelle stuck to her guns, stealing the dishwashing soap and threatening not to give it back unless she could help worked wonders.

"Now we'll get out of your hair," Rochelle said as she dried the last dish. Ellie had washed dishes beside Rochelle while the guys moved furniture back where it belonged and put the extra chairs away.

"Aw, don't say it like that. You could stay all night if you wanted and that would be fine by me." She leaned in closer to Rochelle. "But I'd totally understand if you had other plans."

Rochelle stifled a giggle. "I *hope* I have other plans."

Ellie surprised Rochelle with a hug. "He adores you, you know. And I can see why."

"I adore him." The words were out of her mouth before she could stop them, but she realized they were true. She adored Gabe. Not just as an idealized crush anymore, but for who he really was. And for the joy he'd already brought into her life.

ROCHELLE AND GABE talked about the party all the way back to Rochelle's apartment.

"You promise you had a good time?" Gabe asked.

"Are you kidding? My face hurts from smiling so much. I can't remember the last time I had that much fun."

Gabe grabbed Rochelle's hand and kissed it. "I love that you got to meet everyone."

"Me too." She sighed happily. "I've lived here for almost a year, and up until now, it only felt like an extended visit. Tonight, it started to feel like a home. A real home. Something I've never really had."

Gabe made a soft, contented sound. "That means everything to me, Rochelle."

When they got to her apartment, Gabe walked her to the door. Rochelle was afraid her knees would give out on her the entire way.

Not trusting her voice, she signed, "Come in?"

Gabe's eyes flashed. He looked her over from head to toe and back again. "You want me to?"

She nodded, then unlocked and opened the door.

The moment they were inside, Gabe caught her up in his arms, picking right up where they'd left off on the couch. He alternated between hard kisses and soft brushes of his lips over her jaw, her throat, her collarbone.

"You look so incredibly sexy in that dress," he growled into her ear. "I couldn't keep my eyes off you all night."

She waited for him to sweep her up and carry her into the bedroom—it's what she'd been fantasizing about all night. Oh, who was she kidding—she'd had that dream all her life. To have a man focus solely on her, to lose his mind at the thought of making love with her. Great dress or not, she could forgive Gabe for tearing it off her.

Isn't that what book boyfriends did?

"Bedroom's that way," she said. "End of the hall."

Gabe groaned. "Rochelle, I've never felt this way about any woman. I was always quick to rush into a relationship, because deep down, I knew it wouldn't last. It was never right. "This," he gestured between them, "feels absolutely right." He grinned. "Believe me when I say I want to sleep with you. God, how I want to see which words you've learned in ASL," he added, his grin turning lascivious as his gaze heated. "But I want to make sure you're ready. Because once I start down this road, I'm not turning back. I want everything with you."

"I want that, too. I'm not afraid if that's what's stopping you," she said.

He clasped her hand in his, brought it to his lips, and kissed her knuckles.

"I know. It's not that. I'm not making excuses, it's exactly what I said. I guess what I'm saying is that I want to build a relationship with you, as old-fashioned as that is. I've never had that chance. I went into the military straight out of high school, and then into the Rangers as soon as I could. That didn't allow for much in the way of real relationships, just hookups that turned convenient. Things are different now."

He brushed his thumb across her cheek. "But it doesn't mean I know what I'm doing. I want to get this right, Rochelle. You're worth it."

Her breath hitched. No one had ever told her she was worth it. All her life, she'd been anything but worth it. She'd never measured up to expectations. And now, to have this amazing man tell her he thought she was worth taking his time, worth getting to know before sleeping with her, it took her breath away.

"I've never been in a serious relationship either, Gabe. Not really. I want it to be right, too." Rochelle gave him her most devious grin. "And I want it to start tonight."

He took her face in his hands and leaned down. He stopped just millimeters away from her lips and breathed her in. Then he closed the gap and kissed her hard and long, until her head spun.

SIXTEEN

Message received loud and clear.

Rochelle wanted him.

Gabe didn't hesitate to pick her up and carry her to her room.

A small lamp on her bedside table provided the only light in the room. Gabe set Rochelle on the white muslin comforter and sat beside her, resisting his urge to rip right through her sexy dress and claim her. Rochelle deserved more. She deserved tenderness, a slow buildup until she couldn't take any more. He wanted their first time together to be special, to communicate to her that she would always be safe with him. That he would do anything to keep her in his life.

Gabe lifted his hand and let it hover just to the side of her face. His fingertips barely brushed Rochelle's cheek, a touch he kept feather light as if she might disappear under too much pressure. Instead, she tilted her face into his palm. Her eyes closed for the briefest moment as if to savor the warmth of his palm against her face. When she opened her eyes, an unspoken question filled them as color flooded her face.

Gabe leaned his head closer until his breath mingled with hers. His lips brushed hers as softly as his fingers had touched her cheek, telling her without words that she was safe with him.

Rochelle's breath caught, a quiet gasp that he felt ripple through her. She kissed him back eagerly. Her response to his kiss made his heart race. This kiss was the twin to the one she gave him at the restaurant. But there was nowhere he needed to be this time except here with her. All the same, Gabe pulled back just enough to search her face, asking for permission one last time without uttering a word.

She smiled and signed with deliberate clarity, "Yes." Her hands moved with confidence, shaping the words, "Don't stop," as she said them. Her gestures and her voice were both bold, more assertive than he'd ever seen her.

A mixture of relief and desire flooded his veins. He kissed her again, this time with a certainty that told her how much he wanted her. Rochelle's fingers found their way under his shirt. Her fingertips grazed over the scars from the explosion that took away his life with the Rangers but ultimately brought her to him. They communicated in the language of touch, each brush of their lips and fingers a new word to add to their vocabulary, creating a new language—one with no hesitation, no fear, only love and understanding between them.

A soft moan escaped Rochelle's lips as Gabe's mouth trailed down her neck, laying kisses on her sensitive skin, making his way along her collarbone, dipping into the hollow of her throat. She threw her head back and whispered a shaky "Mmm" that he felt more than heard as his lips grazed her throat.

He gripped her waist and settled her on his lap so that she was facing him. Her skirt hitched up almost to her waist and revealed her smooth, rounded thighs. As he continued his exploration—kissing, licking, tasting her skin—Rochelle writhed on his lap until his erection threatened to tear through his pants.

"Sorry," he whispered as he tried to shift her away.

"Sorry about what?" she said boldly. "About this?" She deliberately ground down on his hard cock and he groaned. He'd never seen this side of her. So hungry, so certain of what she wanted. His hands moved up to cup her breasts through her dress. He tweaked her nipples ever so gently, teasing her. She pressed into his touch. A whimper escaped from her lips and sent shockwaves straight to his cock.

Gabe grabbed the bottom hem of her dress and slowly pulled it up. Rochelle smiled and raised her arms. Her gaze only broke from his when he lifted the dress over her head. She was sexier than he'd even imagined. He feasted on the sight of her wearing only lacy lingerie and her—

"Boots on or off?" she asked with a playful grin.

Holy shit.

"On. For now."

"Okay. But I think you're overdressed."

"You do?" He looked himself over. "Maybe."

"Definitely." Rochelle got off his lap and scooted back onto the bed. She stretched out onto her back, crossed her legs, and propped herself up on her elbows. "These legs aren't uncrossing until I see some clothes hit the floor, mister."

Knock me over with a feather. Laughter practically exploded from Gabe. *Yup. Never, ever in a million years would I have pictured this scenario after Rochelle ran from the coffee shop.*

"You want a show?" he said once he got his laughter under control.

"I do," she said. "Hurry up."

Gabe caught his breath at how good she made him feel in this moment. How wanted—something he'd been afraid no woman would ever make him feel again. How was it that they'd only known each other for a handful of days, and yet he felt like he could reveal anything to her and she'd accept him?

He bent and took off his shoes and socks. Then Gabe stood up and faced Rochelle. He slowly unbuttoned his shirt over his cotton tee, watching her eyes. He let his button-down shirt fall to the floor then grabbed his tee between his shoulder blades and pulled it off over his head. Rochelle's eyes widened and her lips parted as she studied his bare chest. His cock swelled at her reaction and she noticed that, too. Rochelle's gaze lingered there.

Her eyes roamed back up his body and he swore he felt her gaze like a feather stroking over his belly, his abs, his chest. Gabe shivered. *Unbelievable.* She wasn't even touching him yet and she was already heating him up.

And she *knew* it. Reveled in it, from the look on her face.

As payback, Gabe took his time taking off his jeans. He took out his wallet, fished out a couple of condoms, and tossed them onto the bed. He undid his jeans and pushed them down over his hips. Rochelle appraised him again and from the way her chest and cheeks blushed, she liked what she saw.

Cock pressing against his boxer briefs, Gabe climbed onto the bed.

"Now we're even," he said as he covered her body with his.

He held himself up over her, lifting when she rose to press herself against him, loving the way she pouted each time. Then like a hawk, his head dove and he claimed her lips. Gabe clasped her lower lip in his teeth, biting gently until she moaned. This time, he lowered his body and let her press against him, loving the heat building between them. Her legs encircled him and he felt the scrape of her bootheels against the backs of his legs.

Rochelle tried to reach for his boxer briefs but he pinned her hands.

"So naughty," he breathed, and she gasped. "What? No one's ever called you that before?"

She shook her head, her eyes growing darker and heavier with desire.

"Well, you are. Naughty in all the best ways. So damn sexy, I can't believe it. Can't believe I'm here with you." Gabe kissed her hard. "I'm going to make you feel so damn good, Rochelle." Gabe took a gamble when he added, "But I want you to tell me what you want."

"Tell you?"

"Yup. Tell me. *Make* me do what you want, naughty girl."

Gabe's gamble paid off. Rochelle's eyelids fluttered shut and she took in a deep breath. Then she whispered something.

"What was that?" Gabe grinned. "Maybe you'd like to sign it instead? Like I told you, I'm very curious about what ASL signs you learned."

Her eyes got wide.

"Did you just remember you told me that? Because I haven't forgotten. It's been in my dreams ever since." He nipped at her shoulder. "And in my waking thoughts."

Rochelle pushed against him and he gave her room to sign.

And sign she did. The first thing she told Gabe to do was to kiss her, so he did.

"Very cute," Gabe growled. "What else you got?"

She smirked. Then she told him to play with her tits.

"Mmm. Now we're getting somewhere."

Gabe pushed her bra straps down until the tops of the cups folded down with them. He noticed the front closure and smiled wickedly. Rochelle didn't stop him when he undid the clasp and parted her open bra. Her nipples were small and standing up for him. He ran his fingers over the right one and Rochelle dropped her head back. Gabe bent and took her nipple into his mouth, sucking hard until she whimpered. When he started to let up, she pushed his head back down. He chuckled against her skin and punished her some more, until she begged him to give the other one equal attention.

"What now, Rochelle? What else have you learned that you want to tell me to do to you?"

Rochelle licked her lips and gave him a wicked grin he never knew she was capable of.

Oh. My. God.

"Go down on me," she signed.

Message received.

Gabe kissed his way down her middle, over her rounded belly to her panties. He ran one finger straight down the middle, pressing in and watching the silk darken with her wetness.

"Just as I thought. You are soaked under your panties."

He grabbed the lace hem and Rochelle lifted her ass so he could slide her panties off. He carefully parted her folds and found her clit, already slick and ready for his tongue. Gabe breathed on her mound, then blew on the sensitive nubbin, and Rochelle arched her back.

"Please," she begged.

Gabe flicked his tongue over her clit and she gasped. She tasted so good. Gabe couldn't restrain himself. He dove in and licked and sucked and swirled his tongue around until Rochelle clutched the comforter and bucked her hips. He loved this wild, untamed side of Rochelle, a side he never suspected. Her boots scraped against his back and he didn't care. The roughness spurred him on until he'd sent his woman over the edge, screaming his name.

Rock hard, aching with need, Gabe got to his knees on the

bed, straddling Rochelle. She opened her eyes and gave him a smile like the cat who stole the cream.

"Your turn," she signed. "I want you inside me." She pointed to his boxer briefs. "Off, now."

She didn't have to tell Gabe twice. He backed off of her, stood up, and removed his boxer briefs. His cock curved up, the tip touching his belly and Rochelle stared.

"Touch yourself," she signed, her eyes never leaving his cock. Her face was bright red. She knew what she wanted, but Gabe had a feeling this was the first time she'd ever been brave enough to ask for it from a man.

"Whatever you wish," Gabe said. He gripped the base of his shaft and squeezed. He stroked himself while Rochelle watched his hand move up and down. She licked her lips again —Gabe was pretty sure it was unconscious. All her attention was on his hand pleasuring himself for her.

"Stop," she signed. And not a moment too soon—if Gabe kept at it, he'd spill himself across her belly.

Gabe dropped his hand, his cock throbbing, aching for her.

Rochelle nodded. She stared into his eyes, making it perfectly clear what she wanted.

Gabe tore open one of the condom wrappers and rolled it on. Then he crawled back onto the bed and covered her again.

"You're in control," he said. Guide me in, baby. Take me home."

Rochelle reached between their bodies and gripped Gabe's cock. She stroked it and he hissed, straining not to come before he could feel her pussy massaging him. She gave him one more torturous stroke before lining his tip up with her lips.

Sweet, soft, teasing warmth, then he was inside her.

God, she feels incredible. So tight, so soft and hot. Gabe squeezed his eyes shut and held perfectly still, fighting the urge to pound into her, wanting to make this moment last.

Rochelle decided for him. She gripped his back and thrust her hips up into his.

"So hungry, aren't you?" Gabe groaned. He pushed back, sinking into her up to his balls. She squeezed her walls around his cock. When she released, he pulled back quickly, then plunged slowly. Stroke by stroke, he built Rochelle's desire back up along with his own. By the time he was ready to come, she was gasping and moaning, incoherent.

"For you, baby," he told Rochelle. "All...for...you."

Gabe's balls tightened, his cock throbbed, and he came harder than he ever had as his groans echoed off the walls of her bedroom.

Rochelle was his.

And he was thoroughly hers.

SEVENTEEN

Rochelle lay in Gabe's arms, completely spent. She couldn't believe what just happened or how incredible she felt.

Was that me? Was I really telling Gabe how to please me?

She'd never been aggressive in bed—even though her wildest book boyfriend fantasies always included just that— telling a hot man who wanted her exactly what she wanted him to do to her body. In her fantasies, she was always safe; her book boyfriend always understood what she needed, and would never do anything to hurt her—only make sure she had a toe-curling orgasm or two.

Just like Gabe did.

Now she realized that she'd never had good sex before tonight. She'd never been hurt or afraid, it was just...*bad*. Boring. Selfish on the guys' part, usually. Men who never asked if she'd orgasmed, just assumed she had if *they* felt good. And she'd never been confident enough to tell them that no, it wasn't good, that she would have preferred staying in with her vibrator over what they thought had been a great night.

As Rochelle snuggled into Gabe, feeling his heart pounding, his body lightly slick with sweat, she knew.

I can never go back. He's ruined me.

When she awoke still in his arms the next morning, she knew something else.

Gabe was the one she'd waited for. Her one, true book boyfriend come to life.

"Good morning, gorgeous," he said as he stroked her cheek and looked into her eyes. "Thank you for last night."

He sat up and Rochelle's heart fell. She'd been wrong. He was leaving. Of course he was leaving. She needed to face reality—no one was book-boyfriend-level good. She started to sit up, pulling the sheets up to cover her body.

"Nope," Gabe said. "Stay right there and sleep. First, I'm going to get coffee going, then I'm going to make you breakfast. I'll bring it in when I'm done." Gabe stretched. "Sound good?"

She was wrong again.

Gabe *was* that good.

THEY SPENT the morning in bed—eating, talking, laughing. They made love again, twice. Rochelle never wanted the day to end. Gabe might have been perfect, but the world wasn't, and it was calling him away. He worked one weekend a month and this was his weekend. He also needed to check and make sure the little girl he helped protect was safe. They both had a busy week ahead. Rochelle had several new projects come in for a company and she also wanted to be prepared for her upcoming meeting with Huey at Riversong on Friday.

Rochelle kissed Gabe goodbye at the door. He promised to take her out after her meeting.

"I want to take you home with me after that."

"Oh, good," Rochelle teased. "I have it on good authority that it's quiet and peaceful and I'll like it there."

Gabe chuckled. "I wonder who told you that."

"Spot. It was Spot the skunk."

He laughed, which made her feel amazing. Then his smile turned sexy.

"It may not be so quiet and peaceful once I get you there." He kissed along her throat. "Once you're in my bed, it won't be quiet or peaceful at all."

ROCHELLE THREW herself into her work over the rest of the week, along with more ASL lessons, determined to become fluent as quickly as possible. She loved this new-to-her language. It was fun and interesting. And it was one more bond between herself and Gabe. Even if their relationship didn't work out—though she had no doubts, or intention of letting that happen—she wanted to master sign language.

She answered emails, worked on her other, smaller translation projects, and sent off an invoice to a customer who praised her translations. And of course she worked on her pet project. Just before their meeting, Rochelle opened up the document with the poems she'd translated for Huey. She wanted to look them over just one more time before she read them to him, making sure she had them just right. She scrolled down to the third poem, only half-translated. She had a couple of questions for Huey about the first lines:

While the fox hunts the sheep
The sunlight across the fields
claims every stray blade of grass,
Paints them red for itself.
Blades shed blood against their will.

That was her translation, but she thought she could do better if he would clarify a few points. It was that first line that puzzled her the most—a fox hunting a sheep? She didn't think a fox was big enough to hunt anything much larger than a rabbit. Did he mean wolf, or was there a deeper symbology she was missing? Was this somehow a subtle protest or a light shining on what he'd gone through in China before escaping? If so, she could go more direct for an American audience who might not understand, if he wanted that, or she could leave it subtle as it was.

If you're even reading it correctly. Her mother's voice sounded doubtful in her head. She shook it off. If she started feeling unsure of her translations she might as well hang it all up.

She made notes for the meeting on Friday.

On Wednesday, Rochelle decided to go to the rec center to surprise Gabe with lunch. They'd talked on the phone each night. He'd been busy with a new member drive and year-end meetings, resigned to desk lunches for the week.

Just as she picked up her coat, her phone buzzed. She looked at the screen and saw that Sandra had messaged her. Her phone buzzed again and she realized that her sister was sending a series of photos. The first thing she noticed was that Sandra wasn't in any of them. The next was that they were really good. There were some land-scapes, but most featured candid shots of people going about their day. One was a group of monks walking down the street, laughing. Another showed a woman at a vegetable stall arranging some brightly colored peppers. Rochelle checked her parents' account and the photos weren't posted there, just more posed shots of Sandra—the typical fare.

She messaged Sandra.

These are nice!

Thanks! I took them myself.

Rochelle smiled.

Wow! I mean it, they're great. I didn't know
you took pictures too.

Neither do Maman and Dad.

Then Sandra messaged:

Can I trust you?

OMG of course!

Rochelle waited, then Sandra messaged again with a link. Rochelle followed it to find a social media account full of photos like the ones her sister had sent her, going back almost a year. The name on the account made Rochelle laugh out loud. It was *Luggage With A Lens*.

This is you!?!?

Yup! That's me!

Love the name!

Of course you do Bookworm! lol!

And Maman and Dad have no idea you have
another account?

Rochelle went back and looked at the number of followers.

> Oh, and I see why. You have more followers than they do.

> Yup and yup. This is for ME. This IS me, not the person in front of the camera but behind it.

Rochelle looked over her sister's photos again, smiling wide enough to hurt her face. Her chest filled with pride and love for her little sister.

> I am SOOOOO proud of you!

Then she added:

> And thank you for trusting me enough to share this. That means a lot.

> Thanks for letting me trust you.

> What do you plan on doing with this, if anything?

> Weeelll…I was thinking of maybe taking some photography classes. The account's earned me enough money to do that for like a year.

Sandra added:

> Maybe there's a school somewhere in Colorado…?

Rochelle hit call on her phone.

"I will do *anything* to help you, you know that, Luggage."

Sandra laughed. "When this never-ending tour is over, I'll give you a call. You sure I can come and crash until I figure some things out?"

"God yes! I'll convert my office to a second bedroom—"

"No, I'll sleep on your couch. I don't plan on moving in."

"Eh, we'll work out the details when you're done with the tour."

"I just need to figure out how to break the news to Maman and Dad." It was the first time Rochelle heard uncertainty in Sandra's voice.

"I'll help however I can. You've got a place to land, that's the important thing."

"Yeah. Yeah, you're right. Thanks again, Bookworm."

"You're welcome." Rochelle glanced at the clock. She needed to hurry if she wanted to pick up her food order and make it to the rec center for lunchtime. "Hey, I love you, Luggage, but I've got to get going if—" She stopped. She hadn't told Sandra about Gabe.

"If what?"

Rochelle grinned to herself. Sandra was putting her trust in Rochelle—the least she could do was offer that trust right back.

"If I want to surprise my new man with lunch."

"Ooohhh! You better spill the tea next time we talk. And take a picture and send it to me."

"I'll see what I can do. Love you."

"Love you, too, Bookworm."

Rochelle disconnected. She shook her head in wonder. Sandra wasn't a little girl anymore. She'd actually taken control of her life and Rochelle would be there to see that she'd get a chance to live it on her own terms.

ROCHELLE WALKED into the rec center and stopped in shock.

The woman from the lingerie store sat behind the front desk.

"Surprise," Stephanie said. She ducked her head like she felt ashamed but the mischievous sparkle in her eye told Rochelle she felt anything except shame.

Normally, Rochelle would feel embarrassed and awkward, with no idea what to say. Instead, she found herself laughing.

"Please tell me you weren't spying on me that day in the you-know-what shop," she told Stephanie.

"No, that was pure coincidence. Or, as I like to think of it, fate." She winked at Rochelle then looked at the carryout bag she carried. "The boss is back there in his office." She pointed down a hallway. "He will be over the moon to see you."

"Thanks, Stephanie." Then feeling bold, she leaned forward and asked in a low voice, "How'd the lingerie work out for *you?*"

Stephanie chuckled. "Let's just say positive reinforcement works on Doctor Boyfriend."

Rochelle grinned.

"Now, stop talking to me and go." Stephanie shooed her away.

Rochelle started walking then stopped halfway down the hall and turned. "Good seeing you again," she called.

"*Go.*"

She laughed the rest of the way to Gabe's office.

Before she got there, the door opened and Gabe stepped out. The moment before he turned and saw her was one Rochelle would remember like a photograph. The look on his face was one of pure anticipation—his eyes wide, his lips parted. When he looked her way, he relaxed and just stared at her for a moment before smiling. Rochelle never thought she'd have someone in her life who would look at her that way, who would be so excited to see her again so quickly.

"Hello there," he said, then pointed at the bag and added, "What's that?"

"Thought you might like lunch. I was going to surprise you, but it looks like you knew I was here?"

"Stephanie buzzed me and told me there was a surprise coming my way." He took the bag from her and wrapped his other arm around her waist, drawing her close. "Best surprise ever." He leaned down and paused, his lips so close to hers they tingled. "But confession time. I was hoping it was you." Then he closed the gap with a kiss.

Gabe pulled Rochelle into his office by the waist. He closed the door, set the bag on the desk without ever breaking eye contact with her, then pressed her against the wall. The blinds to a large window that overlooked the center were already shut tight.

"Is this all right?" he breathed, studying her face. He brushed his nose against hers. "Tell me when to stop and I'll stop."

Rochelle looked up through her lashes into his dark eyes. His intense gaze pinned her in place but she didn't want to be anywhere else in the world.

She shook her head lightly. "I didn't want you to stop Saturday night, remember?"

"Mmm. Vaguely," he teased. Gabe kissed her again, his tongue teasing her lips before pulling away again.

Gabe closed his eyes and pressed his forehead against hers. He suddenly let her go and turned, and for a moment Rochelle was afraid she'd somehow offended him. Gabe studied his desk for a moment before moving everything to the side. Then he was on her again, pushing her coat off her shoulders then picking her up and setting her on the desk. He nudged her knees apart and stepped between them until he pressed against her, his hard-on obvious.

A soft moan escaped Rochelle's lips as Gabe's mouth trailed down her neck, his stubble grazing against her sensitive skin. She threw her head back, feeling the heat of his breath against her collarbone, and whispered a shaky "Mmm" into the office. As he continued his exploration, Rochelle writhed underneath him. His hands moved up to cup her breasts through her shirt, tweaking her nipples ever so gently. She arched into his touch, a whimper escaping from her lips as she felt him shudder. Their bodies spoke volumes without any words.

Gabe's fingers trailed down Rochelle's spine, stopping at the waistband of her skirt. He slowly slid his hands along her hips as he continued to kiss, nip, and lick her throat. He found the hem of her skirt and pulled back to look into her eyes.

"Do you want this?" he asked as he tugged her hem up then stopped, waiting for her answer.

Rochelle's heart pounded. They were in his office—what if someone heard? God, what if someone came in and actually caught them? She would die of embarrassment. But at the same time, the risk totally turned her on. If he stopped touching her she thought she might die anyway right there on his desk.

"Yes, I want this." She lifted herself up so that he could slide her skirt up her thighs. She watched his pupils dilate at the sight of her lacy underwear, a silent approval that sent shivers down her spine. He trailed his fingers up her inner thighs then cupped her mound through the silky fabric. He pressed the heel of his palm against the warm wetness he found there. Rochelle pressed back, needing more, needing *him*.

"Look how wet you are, just from this." There was a tinge of awe in his voice as if he couldn't believe he'd turned her on so quickly. He ran his finger over the damp silk, found her clit, and pressed. Rochelle bit her lower lip, trying not to make a sound, acutely aware of people all around them.

Gabe gave her a completely indecent smile. "They won't

hear you over the music." He brushed his lips up her throat to her ear while his thumb moved in small, hard circles. His breath was warm against her ear. "And if they did, they would just think you were getting a good workout in."

Rochelle giggled. She moved to his ear and said, "I will be, won't I?" She kissed his earlobe, then added, "And so will you."

That gave him a full-body shudder. He turned his head until their faces were centimeters apart.

"No, baby. Just you for now." His thumb moved faster, alternating between pushing hard and barely brushing her. "Just relax and let me pleasure you."

Rochelle gasped against his mouth as he pushed aside her panties to stroke her exposed heat.

"God, you're so fucking ready," he growled against her lips. In response, she bucked up against his teasing fingers.

"Please, Gabe, more," she begged.

Rochelle cried out softly when he finally slid one finger inside her. He shifted his hand, twisting it until he found a place inside that she'd never known existed. One touch and she forgot herself as her moans filled the room, bouncing off the walls as she surrendered herself completely to Gabe's expert fingers.

"That's it, Rochelle. Feel me inside you." He kissed one cheek then the other. He rubbed his stubbly chin against her throat while his finger worked its magic. "Doesn't it feel good?" He added a second finger while his thumb kept up its circles on her clit.

"Yes," she managed between gasps. "So good." Then she couldn't speak as he brought her higher. The rhythmic pleasure built in stages—every time she was sure she was about to orgasm, Gabe backed off then started again as soon as she'd caught her breath. And each time felt even more incredible.

"Please," she panted when she was sure she couldn't take it anymore.

"Almost." Gabe worked his fingers, alternating between soft touches and firm strokes, completely in tune with her body and what she needed.

"I...can't..." Rochelle threw her head back as her body jerked involuntarily against his hand.

"Yes, Rochelle, yes you can. Now. Right now."

Waves of pleasure tore through her at his command. She was helpless, floating, her body rising higher and higher as she rode her orgasm, safe in Gabe's arms.

Rochelle came back to herself leaning against Gabe's chest, her cheek pressed against his shoulder. He stroked her back and supported her as he nuzzled in her hair.

"That was beautiful," he said. "Are you happy?"

"Incredibly. But what about you?" Rochelle moved her hand between them to feel his still-hard cock under his pants.

He gently lifted her hand away from his cock and brought it to his lips. "Not today, baby. Today was for you."

"But I feel..."

"What?" He lifted her chin and looked into her eyes.

"I feel..." She couldn't get the word out. Rochelle tried to remember the ASL sign. She bent her arms across her chest and made a V with one hand then curled those fingers down and pulled her hand back along her other arm.

Gabe frowned in confusion. "Steal? Stolen?"

Oh, God, I did it wrong. She shook her head. "Sel..." She made Vs with both hands and curled her fingers, but couldn't remember from there. She started to fingerspell it, but Gabe stopped her.

"Ah." He copied her hands, making two crooked Vs, then lifted his arms and moved his hands away from his body in two rapid moves while he shook his head. *Selfish.*

"Why would you think you're being selfish?"

"Because it's not right that I..." She gestured at her lap, "...but you haven't..." she gestured at his.

He laughed as he hugged her.

"You aren't being selfish, Rochelle," he said with a gentle smile. "You being happy is never selfish. It's about time someone gave *you* what you needed."

I love you.

She couldn't say the words out loud. Her fingers fluttered, wanting to tell him. But it was too soon to feel this way, wasn't it? Even if she knew it was true deep in her heart that Gabe was the man she'd wished for every time she immersed herself in a romance, he might not be ready to hear her say it.

So she stilled her hands, tucked away those three words for another day. And smiled instead.

"Thank you," she signed, because even though she'd put *I love you* away for now, she couldn't trust that the words wouldn't push their way past anything else she had to say.

Friday night. Maybe she would tell him then.

ON FRIDAY AFTERNOON, Rochelle got to Riversong ahead of Huey. April's sister Hannah was at the counter, which meant April was picking Kevin up from school. Mid-afternoon, most customers were dashing in to pick up a to-go order and carrying their coffees back to work, leaving the place deceptively empty. A couple other regulars like herself looked up from their favorite tables as she walked to the window seat with her coffee and set up her laptop.

Huey came in and held the door for a woman holding a carrier of four drinks. Rochelle raised her hand and waved to get his attention. He looked around, a nervous expression on his face until he spotted her. He smiled at her then went to the counter to make his order. She moved her laptop to the side to give him room to set down his cup. The sweet perfume of jasmine tea wafted up in the steam. She greeted him in Chinese and he greeted her back in English.

"Please," Huey said. "I'm in America now and need to practice English more. You are a safe person for me to do that."

Rochelle covered her heart, touched at how much he trusted her. "Thank you. I'll help you learn much as I can."

Huey smiled, but it could not touch the sadness in his eyes. Rochelle wondered as she had many times while reading his new poems what he'd gone through before leaving China. He'd mentioned the daughter he'd left behind in several emails since they'd met and shown Rochelle pictures of her. Huey had lost his wife and his father, but his mother was still alive. The look in his eyes reminded her of the house services her parents had taken her to as a girl. The people gathered there had worshiped happily, but when it was time to leave, their eyes filled with the same sadness and fear Rochelle saw in Huey's eyes now.

Her first instinct was to simply dive into the poems—to talk about something happy. But maybe it was helping her sister, or maybe it was Gabe's belief that she was someone special that gave her the confidence to ask Huey how he was doing.

"You look sad. Is your daughter all right?"

A gentle smile brightened Huey's face. "She is fine. She... she is expecting a child. A boy."

"Oh, that's wonderful! Congratulations."

He bowed his head in gratitude. "Thank you. I wish I could meet him."

Ah. Now she understood. Of course—Huey had left so much of his life behind in exchange for the freedom to express himself.

"Do you think your daughter will ever come here?"

"I don't know. It is my hope that she can, and bring my grandson with her." He looked away, then into the depths of his tea. "But I don't think it will happen." Then he looked back up at Rochelle. "Perhaps I was foolish to leave. I...I can be very selfish."

Rochelle smiled remembering Gabe telling her that she wasn't selfish for wanting happiness.

"I don't think you are, Huey. Your work is very important. You have a message for the world in the poems you've written, and they wouldn't exist if you were still in China I'm guessing."

"Only here." Huey touched his temple. "Always the noise in my head. Shouting louder to be set free."

"Your poems set me free as a girl. And even more so as I grew older." She brightened. "Actually, I just read the translations of your older poems to my sister when she was sad and feeling scared. They helped calm her just like me."

Huey's eyebrows rose. "Why was your sister feeling scared?"

Rochelle took a sip of her coffee. "She was in Japan when—"

She never finished her story. An engine roared and tires squealed in the parking lot.

After that, time slowed to a horrible, painful crawl.

EIGHTEEN

Stephanie's voice came over the intercom in Gabe's office, shaky and panicked.

"Shots fired at Riversong."

Gabe stared in disbelief at the hateful phone on his desk until his body reacted before his brain could catch up. He grabbed his keys and dashed out of the office. Stephanie already had the front door open for him.

"Please be careful!" she shouted as he ran past her.

Riversong wasn't far away but today it was on the other side of the planet as he sped there, berating himself the entire way. He ignored a call from Ben as he listened to the police scanner app on his phone. Someone had called 911 reporting that a car had pulled into the parking lot and opened fire on the front window. The car tore out of the parking lot in the direction of CO-7. If it were anyone but Rochelle, he'd be picturing the route, trying to predict where the car could turn off to escape or where the police could intercept it. But all his attention stayed focused on her. He'd sent her a good luck message earlier, knowing she was meeting with her client. His gut churned as he remembered her reply:

Thank you! I'm confident in my work and besides, he's a sweetie. So I don't need luck today. It's going to be a GREAT day! I can't wait to see you tonight.

Denial crept into his skull.

She has to be okay because I just texted with her.

She has to be okay because we made plans for dinner.

She has to be okay because I'm taking her back to my house after dinner and making love with her all weekend.

She has to be okay because after that, I'm telling her again how much she means to me and that I want to keep her in my life forever.

She has to be okay because I need to tell her I love her.

She has to be okay because I will never be okay again if I lose her.

He listened as the paramedics arrived.

Elias or Waylon, maybe both. They're my brothers. They've got her. She'll be okay.

She's got to be okay. We texted. We're going out tonight. I'm taking her home with me.

I need to tell her I love her.

Injuries reported. A man and a woman.

It's all my fault.

This is Jesse's family getting their revenge.

They'd been so quiet. So fucking quiet. Jesse was lying low. Plymouth and Alphie were out and awaiting trial, and Gabe and his brothers had thought either they didn't want to fuck themselves by harassing Laurie or that they'd finally given up. Gina saw to it that Velna and her brother were out of money—funds they'd borrowed from a loan shark out of Vegas, the morons.

But he was wrong. He'd been complacent and now it cost Rochelle. The woman he loved was possibly de—

Don't think it. Don't even think it. Just drive. Just get to her.

When he got to Riversong, two squad cars and an ambulance were already on the scene. One officer was keeping the parking lot clear as a crowd gathered while another was examining the ground. Gabe got out of his truck with one goal in mind—get into the coffee shop. The police officer doing crowd control started jogging over, shouting at him. But that wasn't his problem. His problem was the gaping hole where the window had been. Where he knew Rochelle —his sweet, beautiful woman in the window—worked every day.

When the police officer reached Gabe she stood between him and the entrance to the parking lot. He glanced at her badge. *Officer Carla DeVivo.*

"Sir! Stop where you are," she said. "This is a crime scene."

"Officer DeVivo, I need to get in there."

"No one is allowed inside right now. I'm gonna need you to step back." She looked over at another officer unrolling yellow tape.

"Look, my fiancée is in there." The word fiancée flowed so naturally he didn't pause to think about it. "Please. The paramedics can vouch for me. Elias Hunt and Waylon Ramson. Please just let me get in there and see—"

"That's not how this works. I know you're upset, but the paramedics are doing everything they can and they don't need you in the way." She looked sympathetic. "You don't want to distract them, is what I'm trying to say. What's your name?"

"Gabe O'Neil."

"Gabe, I'll keep you updated. Best I can do." Her radio squawked. "Now, I need you to step back." Office DeVivo turned back toward the parking lot.

Gabe did everything he could to try and see into the

window. The sunlight was at an angle that showed him bodies moving inside. Paramedics standing and bending down in front of the window.

They're working on someone right in front of the window. It's Rochelle.

Stop. You don't know that.

The front door opened and he braced when he saw an officer holding it open for someone behind him.

This is when they wheel out her body. It took Gabe everything he had not to break through the yellow tape and race toward the door. He needed to see her.

Sonny stepped out past the officer and the door shut. Gabe breathed a sigh of relief. It wasn't Rochelle on a stretcher. Now that Gabe could concentrate, he recognized the officer as the head of Lyons' police department, Sergeant George Williams. Sonny looked completely shaken up. He was speaking loudly to George, maybe shouting, but Gabe couldn't make out his words from the street. The wind was picking up and the most he caught was *April* and *Kevin.*

Are they injured? He felt sick at the image of the little boy around Laurie's age as a victim of a stupid, senseless crime.

Not senseless. Your fault. All your fault.

Velna's face loomed in his mind. This was her sick revenge on him and Shane for getting Plymouth and Alphie arrested—target Rochelle and April.

The paramedics in front of the broken window stood with a stretcher and started wheeling it toward the door.

Oh, dear God.

God, no.

Please don't let her be the one on the stretcher. God, please. Please. Don't let that be her. I'll make any deal with you. Any deal at all. Take all my hearing. Take my life. Just don't let it be her.

Gabe's hands shook. His mouth filled with cotton. His heart flung itself at his ribcage.

Another office held the front door open. Elias stepped outside first with Waylon, then two other paramedics exited with the rolling stretcher. Officer DeVivo directed them straight to the ambulance to keep them from crossing the place where they were scouring the parking lot for bullet casings.

"Rochelle!" Gabe yelled. Elias looked up and started shaking his head. He put his hand out, palm toward Gabe. *Stop.*

"Gabe! Over here," a woman's voice called from the doorway behind the paramedics.

Hannah Taylor stood in the doorway to the coffee shop.

But more importantly, Rochelle stood right behind her.

She was covered in blood.

NINETEEN

"She was in Japan when—"

The screech of car tires in the parking lot made Rochelle jump. Before she had a chance to turn and see what was happening, Huey looked past Rochelle as his eyes and mouth opened wide.

He lunged across the table toward Rochelle just as she watched a spray of glass appear over her head and heard a *bang*. More glass sprayed over her right shoulder just as Huey knocked over the table, grabbed her, and pulled her down, shouting. She banged her head on the floor as Huey went down beside her.

The rest of the window behind Rochelle's back cracked and shattered, covering them in broken glass. Rochelle's head swam as she tried to process what was happening. Other people were shouting now. Was everyone okay?

Why does it feel like I'm moving through water? Everything is so slow and heavy.

Even the sounds around her seemed muted, as if they were coming to her from the surface of the ocean and she was sitting at the bottom. But at the same time, everything was bright, haloed.

Her tote, Huey's book, her laptop—all of it lay scattered across the floor, covered in broken glass. That was wrong. She needed to clean them off and put them away, especially the book. It was the only copy. She couldn't lose it.

Rochelle grabbed the paper-covered book. When she dropped it into her tote, she saw blood on the paper and looked down at the floor. No—the stain had come from her own hand. Blood flowed around a piece of glass protruding from a cut on her palm. It didn't hurt, which was strange. She pulled out the glass so that she wouldn't get blood on anything else, then picked up her notebook and her laptop and put them into her tote. More blood stained them. Right—just getting the glass out wasn't enough; she needed to get a bandage on that.

She turned her head and saw more blood.

"Oh my God! Huey!" He was lying face down, his shoulder soaked in crimson.

Time sped up again.

Rochelle grabbed her coat, wadded it up, and pressed it against Huey's bleeding shoulder. He groaned and asked her if she was alright in Mandarin.

"I'm fine, Huey. We need to get you to a hospital." She looked around at everyone else. Some people were still on the floor covering their heads. Sonny was up and shouting behind the counter. There was no sign of Hannah. Rochelle hoped she was crouched down behind the counter.

"S-someone, help," Rochelle called. "We ne-need a paramedic over here. Please!"

"I'm on 911," Hannah called from somewhere.

"Stay down!" Sonny shouted again. Rochelle realized he'd been shouting it over and over.

A police officer followed by four paramedics burst through

the front door into the coffee shop. Rochelle recognized two of them.

"W-W-Waylon! Eli-li-lias, over here!"

They swung around, saw Rochelle with Huey, and started to race over but the officer stopped them. His head was on a swivel, looking for any threats before allowing the paramedics into the coffee shop.

"No shooters, George," Sonny shouted at the officer. "They shot through the window and drove away."

The officer nodded and let Elias, Waylon, and the others proceed. Elias reached them first.

"W-w-watch the glass," Rochelle told him as he dropped down.

"That's my line, Rochelle," Elias said. "How bad are you and the gentleman hurt?"

"I..." What was he asking? *Huey. Right. I'm keeping him from bleeding out.* Rochelle felt faint all of a sudden.

Elias didn't wait for her to finish. He spoke soothing words while gently removing Rochelle's hands and coat from Huey.

"N-no." She shook her head. "No."

It's Huey. He's bleeding bad. From his shoulder. He was shot. The words wouldn't come.

"Rochelle, it's okay, you did great. You kept the bleeding in check. Now I need you to step back and I need to check you out."

"We got him," Waylon said. He jerked his chin toward the counter across the shop.

Elias nodded. "Here, let me take a quick look at you. Can you stand?"

Rochelle nodded.

Elias gave her a serious-looking smile as he handed Rochelle her tote and helped her up. "How about walking? Can you walk?"

She nodded again. Words no longer existed. Only Huey lying on the floor, bleeding. Huey, who'd saved her.

Elias led Rochelle across the shop to the counter, looking her over as they walked.

"You've got blood down the front of you. Is it yours?"

She shook her head. *It's Huey's* she tried to say.

"Your knees are bleeding. I think you were kneeling on broken glass. Does it hurt anywhere else?"

Rochelle showed him her hand.

"Yeah, that's an awesome laceration you've got there," Elias said. "Let's do something about it, then we'll take care of your knees."

He opened a bag but Rochelle was barely aware of what he was doing while he quickly cleaned and bandaged the wound. Her eyes never left the man who pushed her out of the way of a bullet. He'd shouted something—

"All right, that's taken care of," Elias said. "Anywhere else besides your knees? Rochelle?" He tried to turn her but she didn't want to stop watching the paramedics working on Huey. She was irrationally afraid that if she looked away he wouldn't make it.

Elias made a full circle around her. "Did you hit your head?"

Rochelle shook her head even though she couldn't remember if she'd hit it or not. Nothing hurt.

"How about your torso?"

"N-no."

"Okay. I'm going to take care of your knees." Elias lifted her onto the counter as if she weighed nothing. "Looks like we've got some glass in there. Sorry, I'm gonna try and not make this hurt any more than it probably already does."

"It d-doesn't hurt at all."

"Rochelle?" Hannah asked. "Are you all right?" She turned

her head and Hannah was standing right behind her, on the other side of the counter. Hannah put her arm around Rochelle's shoulder.

"Looks like the last of it." Elias said. He put a bandage on Rochelle's knee. She hadn't even noticed he'd already finished with the other one. Elias stood. "Are *you* all right, Hannah?"

"Yeah, I'm fine." She looked over at a couple of patrons still kneeling on the floor. "How about you guys?"

"We're okay," a man said. The others nodded.

"Is anyone else here?" Elias asked Hannah.

"Just my dad, but he's okay, too. He's outside talking to George."

"What about your sister and nephew? Were they in the back, or...?"

Hannah looked sick for a moment. "No, they aren't here. April's picking up Kevin from school. I know Dad's gonna want to go check on them."

Elias turned his attention back to Rochelle. "You sure you're all right?"

She touched her temple. "I might have hit m-my head." Rochelle hadn't even noticed when Sonny and the officer had left. Was that from shock?

"Okay, let me take a look." Elias tested her pupils and asked her questions, which she answered distractedly. All her concentration was on the circle of paramedics working on Huey.

"I think you're all right. But, keep an eye out for confusion, headache, nausea." He looked back over his shoulder.

"Go on," Rochelle said. I'm fine. Take care of Huey, please." Her eyes prickled as she fought back tears.

Elias nodded. Then he lifted Rochelle off the counter and set her on the floor. He went back to the circle around Huey. Rochelle started shaking.

Hannah came around the counter and gave Rochelle a hug.

"Honey, here. Let me brush all the glass off." Hannah had a clean towel in her hand.

"It'll g-get everywhere. You'll cut yourself."

"No, it's fine." Hannah dropped a couple more towels on the floor and wrapped her hands in two more. "Now close your eyes. Don't want to get any in them." She gently brushed glass off Rochelle onto the towels.

The sound of the front door slamming open made both women jump.

Gabe.

Rochelle had no reason to believe it was him, but her heart didn't listen to reason. She felt him close by.

A police officer came in and walked over to where the paramedics were working. One look told him he wasn't about to get any answers out of the victim soon. He looked up at Rochelle, Hannah, and the other three patrons, then started walking over. He took out a notepad.

"Are you injured?" he asked Rochelle.

She nodded. "N-not badly. Just glass. I wasn't..." She couldn't get the word *shot* out of her mouth.

"Can you answer some questions for me?"

Rochelle nodded.

He asked her name and jotted it down.

"Did you get a look at the vehicle or shooter in the parking lot?"

"No. I had my back to the window. I j-just saw glass, and then Huey p-pulled me to the floor."

"Huey?" That's the man who they're working on?"

"Y-yes. He...he..."

The officer cut her off with a curt nod. He turned to Hannah. "Any reason why Riversong was targeted?"

Hannah's face flushed and angry red. "You just assume that, huh?"

The officer's face went stony. "Unless you can give me a reason not to."

"I get it. Wondering who we pissed off just because it's my family."

"Miss, I'm just trying to get the report here."

The paramedics transferred Huey to a wheeled stretcher and it lifted. Rochelle heard Huey cry out for his daughter. She pushed past the police officer and bolted to Huey's side.

"Huey, it's Rochelle. I'm here." She grabbed his hand.

"*Tamen zhaodaole wo*," Huey said. *Found me* Rochelle translated in her head. His eyes looked unfocused.

She spoke to him in mixed Mandarin and English. "Yes, I found you, Huey. You're going to be okay. They're taking you to a hospital."

Elias placed a hand on Rochelle's shoulder. "Let us get him through the door. I'll see if there's room for you to ride along. We could use an interpreter."

Rochelle didn't correct him—she was no interpreter but she was better than nothing. She let go of Huey's hand and they wheeled him to the door. Hannah came over as the jerk police officer ran ahead and held the door open.

"What was that about?" Rochelle asked Hannah as she stared at the officer.

Hannah huffed. "It's nothing new. My family's just always in trouble no matter what we do or don't do."

Rochelle's heart clenched. The idea that Riversong had been the target of an attack tore her up more than the idea of random violence. She grabbed Hannah's hand and squeezed it. "I'm sorry."

"Worst part of this is that he's probably right," Hannah said.

"What do you mean?"

She shook her head dismissively and they followed the paramedics to the door.

Rochelle felt his presence immediately. Her eyes went straight to the crowd behind the yellow tape.

Gabe.

He stood at the front of the yellow police tape roping off the parking lot, watching the paramedics. The look on his face was one of pure devastation.

"Rochelle!" he shouted, his voice ragged and broken.

He thinks I'm hurt. Or dead. And it's destroyed him she thought.

"Gabe," Hannah called. Gabe didn't move. He just kept staring, looking completely lost.

"Gabe! Over here," Hannah tried again.

Gabe tore his attention from the paramedics to Hannah. He looked absolutely lost, his eyes so full of despair that Rochelle's heart broke just looking into them.

His attention shifted to Rochelle and life and light came back into his eyes. His mouth opened in wonder.

Then he was ignoring the tape and dashing across the parking lot, straight to her.

TWENTY

Rochelle.

His love was alive. But covered in blood.

Gabe ran.

Officer DeVivo was a blur in his peripheral vision, her calls for him to stop barely registering. His focus was on Rochelle. She quickly signed to him "I'm all right" but it didn't slow him. He paused only long enough when he reached her to look her over and realize the blood was not hers. She threw herself into his arms and he curled around her. Gabe breathed in her scent, tainted by the coppery tang of blood. He tried not to shake with rage and fear himself. God, how close he'd come to losing the woman he loved. He held her tightly and silently stroked her hair.

"I'm all right," she told him again. "But I need to help Huey."

Gabe let her go and she brushed his cheek before moving past him toward the man on the stretcher. Gabe followed.

"Is it okay to come along?" she asked Elias.

Elias looked regretful. "Sorry, not enough room. Officer's riding along."

"We'll drive right behind the ambulance," Gabe told Rochelle.

"Um, no, you won't." Officer DeVivo placed her hand on Gabe's shoulder. "I don't appreciate you ignoring me. The crime scene's taped off for a reason."

As if they needed more chaos, Shane pulled up, got out of his SUV, and ran toward them. He looked pale, stricken.

"Where is she?" he shouted. "April—"

"Aw, shit," Hannah said. "Shane, it's okay. She's not here. She's off picking up Kevin at school."

Shane bent at the waist and braced his hands on his thighs as if he'd just run a marathon. Gabe knew exactly how he felt.

Sergeant George Williams turned his attention toward them. Gabe felt relieved. The sergeant was a good man, friendly with Watchdog.

"Carla." Williams nodded at Officer DeVivo. "It's all right. Let 'em go."

Carla rolled her eyes. "George, if you weren't like a dad to me I'd slug you right now." She turned and started walking toward the middle of the parking lot.

George grinned. "I'll send some of Cynthia's cookies your way."

"You'd better," she said over her shoulder.

Sonny was standing next to Williams. "George, I need to go, too. Gotta check on April and my grandson."

Williams held up his hand. "We're already on it, Sonny, just wanted to let you know. Got an officer there who will be escorting them home."

Shane straightened and turned. He started back toward the SUV but Williams grabbed his arm, stopping him.

"Said we have it under control, Shane."

"I'm just heading back to work."

"Son, don't bullshit me. Stay here."

Sonny glared at Shane. "My daughter doesn't need you right now."

Shane looked like he was ready to throw a punch. Gabe grabbed his other arm. It was clear to Gabe that Sonny knew Shane had something to do with the drive-by. If that was the case, the last thing they needed was for Shane to end up back in jail.

"George says they're safe, brother," Gabe told him.

"I can keep them safer," Shane said, still looking at Sonny. "Up at Watchdog." He looked at Hannah. "All of you."

Hannah started to speak but her father cut her off.

"No, thank you." Sonny walked over to his daughter and put his arm around her. "We don't need any favors from you."

Rochelle appeared confused as she looked from Hannah to Shane to Sonny.

She's not from here Gabe reminded himself. *She doesn't know the history.* Gabe wasn't sure himself about the rumors all those years ago, but this confirmed what he'd suspected back then. Shane and April had history.

"Wouldn't be a bad idea if Kyle's willing, Sonny," George said.

"I said no thank you. We'll make do."

Hannah looked from Shane to Sonny. "Dad—"

"No. Family takes care of family."

With that, Sonny turned and led Hannah into Riversong.

Shane's glare looked like it could drill a hole in the door but his body relaxed.

"You good?" Gabe asked him. He nodded. George and Gabe let go of Shane's arms.

The ambulance pulled out of the parking lot.

"G-Gabe. I'm sorry, but." She jutted her chin in the direction of the ambulance. "I've got to go."

"No, baby, wait." Gabe blew out a breath. "This is my fault. Shane, if Kyle has an available safehouse, I'd like to get Rochelle there ASAP."

Rochelle's eyes went round.

"What do you mean, your fault?" George asked.

Gabe's heart clenched.

If I say this out loud, Rochelle will bolt. But the most important thing is her safety.

"It's Velna Tobison and her crew. Gotta be. Targeting us for stopping her cousins from harassing and trying to humiliate a little girl and getting them arrested. Rochelle's here, April was supposed to be here." He looked at Shane. "That's why Sonny's pissed at you, isn't it? He knows it's about us."

George frowned. "Son, hold on. Who's this Velna Tobison?"

If George doesn't know, that means Sonny doesn't either, Gabe thought.

"I'll answer your questions just in case," Shane told George, then he looked at Gabe. "But, T-Wolf, Rochelle's safe. I don't think this is about us. Go on to the hospital. It's okay. I'll keep you posted."

Maybe it's not about us after all.

"That okay, George?" Gabe asked. "I'll answer anything you want, just let me get my woman where she needs to be right now."

The sergeant nodded. "We got a statement from Rochelle and there's an officer accompanying the victim. If I need anything from you, he can question you for me."

"Thank you," Rochelle told George. She slipped her hand into Gabe's and squeezed it. "Let's go."

In spite of his worries, Gabe's heart soared at her confidence in him.

"This way, baby." Gabe walked her to his truck, his arm around her. When they got to the passenger side he hugged her again and asked, "Are you all right?"

"I'm okay," she insisted in his arms.

Gabe only kissed the top of her head in response. He opened the passenger side door and got Rochelle situated.

"I promise I'm okay," she repeated. Gabe studied her face. Her eyes did look clearer. At least they were headed to the hospital in case she wasn't.

Elias and Waylon would have never let her go if she wasn't okay.

Gabe went around the truck, got in, and started the engine. He reached across the space between them and grabbed Rochelle's hand. As they drove to the hospital, Gabe found himself tongue-tied. What was he supposed to say after this? That he was afraid he'd almost gotten her killed? That he was relieved she wasn't a target—this time?

Gabe found a spot in the hospital parking garage. He killed the engine and Rochelle was the one who broke the silence.

"It wasn't your fault, Gabe."

Gabe grimaced and looked away. Before he did, Rochelle flinched at the pain in his eyes. Finally, he looked at her again.

"Not this time. The little girl we've been protecting, her abuser's family is not only stalking her but has threatened to retaliate against us. Against me specifically, and maybe Shane. Shane and I..." He briskly rubbed his hands over his face. "We were arrested when we stopped them from harassing Laurie at school. The assholes doing it were arrested too."

"Wait, what?" Rochelle grabbed his hand and clutched it. "You were arrested?"

Gabe felt miserable. "Yeah. And all the charges against us

were dropped. I used that to rationalize not telling you. But I should have. I'm so sorry. I should have let you know what you were getting into dating me. It was selfish of me and I could have gotten you killed."

"Is that why you stayed away all week?"

Gabe nodded. "Don't you see? If you stay with me, I'll do the same thing to you that your parents did when you were a little girl and that they're still doing to your sister. My actions, the way I live my *life*, could put you in danger."

Rochelle unbuckled herself and laid her hand on his cheek. "Listen to me. Today was not your fault."

"But what about tomorrow, or the day after?"

She laid her finger on his lips, quieting him.

"*Listen*, Gabe. The way I see it, you go after monsters who need to be stopped at all costs. That's a good thing."

"Not at the cost of your life. Rochelle, I love you."

She sat up straight at his words. He took her hands in his.

"I know it's probably way too soon to tell you that, but it's true. I was attracted to you from the moment I saw you, can't deny that, and I liked who you were just from talking to you. But I've been in love with you from the moment I realized you'd learned ASL just so we could communicate."

"Gabe—"

He shook his head. "Even my brothers haven't done that, not to the extent that you have. That tells me how kind you are, how accepting. And that you wanted to make the effort for me."

"Gabe. You still aren't listening to—"

"And all I've done in return is put you in danger—"

"*Gabe*." Rochelle pulled her hands out of his and signed, "I love you. I love you *so* much. I don't care if it's early. It's real."

He stared at her while she repeated out loud, "It's *real*. I love you too."

"Rochelle," he whispered.

"I do. And I'm not going to let fear stop me from loving you or being in your life." She stopped abruptly and laughed.

"What?"

"I'm just remembering how I ran out of the coffee shop because I was so afraid to talk to you. It's funny to me now, to think of how unsure I was. If I'd let that fear control me, I wouldn't be here now. I would have missed out on so much good. Gabe." She looked him square in the eyes. "I'm not afraid, maybe for the first time in my life. And I'm not going to let you talk yourself into thinking I'm better off without you." She narrowed her gaze. "Because I can see it. I can see that doubt in your eyes. Don't you dare doubt me."

Gabe reared back. "I don't doubt you. I'm amazed by you. Absolutely, utterly amazed."

"Then trust me that I know what I'm getting into. And I'm choosing to do that. Gabe, I'm choosing a life with you."

───

GABE AND ROCHELLE entered the ER. Rochelle approached the desk.

"A man was just brought in from Riversong in Lyons—"

"Yes," the nurse behind the desk said without looking up from her screen. "He's in surgery now. Are you—" She stopped talking when she looked up and saw the blood on Rochelle's clothing. "Oh, goodness! Where are you injured?"

"No, I'm okay. The paramedics took care of me. This isn't my blood, it-it-it's his."

The nurse's expression turned sympathetic. "If you'll have a seat, we'll let you know when he's out of surgery. I'm so sorry. It's shocking. Lyons is such a nice little town."

Gabe put his arm around Rochelle and directed her to one

of the plastic chairs in the waiting room. He looked for any sign of Elias or Waylon hoping to get more intel, but they were already gone.

"After Huey's out and we know he's okay, I'll run you by your apartment and we'll grab you some more clothes and a toothbrush and all that," Gabe told Rochelle. "But I'm taking you home with me tonight."

Rockelle covered her face. "Oh, duh. I have a change of clothes in my tote already. I should go change." She uncovered her face and gave him a smile as her eyes lit with mischief. "You were planning on taking me home after dinner tonight, right?"

God, her smile puts me at ease.

"Absolutely." He leaned in close and gave her a quick kiss on the lips. "How about this? We'll stop by your place anyway and pick up more clothes for the weekend. Maybe enough to go into next week."

"What about Greg?"

"We can bring your cat, no problem."

Her eyes widened and she laughed a little. "Really? You'd let me bring my cat to your house the first time I'm there?"

"I'd let you bring an elephant."

Now she laughed for real. "An elephant, huh? I'm sure you'd be so happy to have an elephant tromping around your yard."

"Hey, just ask Ben sometime. It was a possibility last summer."

Gabe relished the astonished look on Rochelle's face.

"Wait, Ben? The Ben I just met at Ellie and Bear's house? He has an elephant?"

Gabe couldn't keep a straight face anymore. "No, he doesn't. But, one of his friends who he works with does. Guy and his wife also have a camel."

"A...camel and an elephant? What, does Ben's friend work for the circus?" She tilted her head. "Okay, that goofy look on your face right now... Are you about to tell me *Ben* works for the circus?"

"Nope, not the circus. Or the zoo."

"That was my next guess. Vet's office?"

This is fun. And it's a good distraction. "Nope."

"Then where?"

Gabe felt his phone buzz in his coat pocket. He pulled it out and looked at the text from Shane.

"One second, baby. Gotta take this."

"Oh, no. Not fair." Rochelle crossed her arms.

Gabe kissed her again. "Go change your clothes. I'll be right back." He went out where it was quieter and hit the call button beside Shane's name.

"What have you got for me, brother?" Gabe asked. "And thanks for helping us get out of there faster."

"No problem. How's Rochelle?" Shane asked in return.

"She's better but still upset. No surprise. She's worried about the guy who was shot. He's an author she's working with, named Huey. She says he pulled her down to the floor, saved her life." Guilt filled Gabe's heart like sludge. "Brother, you *sure* it isn't the Tobisons? Velna threatened me, said I'd be sorry, that one day I'd lose someone I loved..." He trailed off. It was the first time he'd told someone that he loved Rochelle and it felt right.

"Velna's full of shit. She's not going to hurt Rochelle. None of them will. They aren't going to get near her. Plymouth and Alphie are out but they're wearing government-issued Fitbits."

Gabe smiled at Shane's term for an ankle tracker.

Shane went on. "The minute I found out about the drive-by, I thought the same thing you did. On my way over to Riversong, I called Gina and she told me her people already hacked the ankle jewelry so we know every move they make."

Gabe wasn't surprised. He didn't know Gina's full story, but from what he'd heard, she could do damn near anything.

Shane continued. "They were at home. It wasn't them, T-Wolf. Gina and Kyle are working on locating the rest of the family. But while I was talking to George, the police found the car, or at least what they think is the car. It was burning up on the side of the road on CO-7."

"No shit? Jesus."

"Doesn't match any of the Tobisons' cars. George is gonna look into any stolen cars while Gina's searching for recent car sales and rentals."

Gabe knew George would do everything he could while looping Watchdog in on whatever they found. His daughter, Sylvie, was a police officer Watchdog had helped save a few months back along with Gabe and his friends as Mountain Division, though they'd done it anonymously.

"So, you think they took off on foot after they torched the car?" Gabe asked.

"Could have, but it's more likely they had another car waiting. They were in a spot without any cameras. Police have a manhunt going in the area just in case. We're loaning them men and dogs since we were closer and faster than Boulder's K9 unit."

That must please Kyle Gabe thought. "Once Lion's off duty, he needs to join the manhunt. No one can track like him, except maybe you."

"Yeah, I'm already part of the team. At least I can help out *that* way." Gabe heard bitterness creeping into Shane's voice.

"Riversong looked pretty fucked up. They don't need this. As if anyone does. You sure it's not our fault?"

"No. It's not on us, it's..." Gabe heard Shane draw a hard

breath. "Look, I can't talk about it. Ongoing investigation and all that shit. But it's a hit on Riversong, not on Rochelle."

Gabe noticed Shane had left out April's name.

"How's April?"

"Still don't know." The bitterness grew. "Sonny went to the school and came back with her and Kevin and immediately sent them to the back office with Hannah. After that, they all circled the wagons. Wouldn't let me speak to April, just all left together. Riversong's closed until further notice and now they aren't returning anyone's calls."

"What about Badger? You talk to him?" Badger was one of their friends who grew up around Lyons and worked at Watchdog. He was engaged to April's cousin, Brianna.

"Nope. He and Brianna have been out of town. They weren't supposed to come home for another week. Radio silence there anyway. Not even Kyle can raise him."

That didn't sit well with Gabe, though he understood Badger's reasons. He was as protective of Brianna as any man could be of his woman. He'd already saved her life once—he was probably of the mind to keep her out of whatever trouble this was. Sonny's family had a sketchy background connected to illegal drugs, one that Sonny had rejected when he started Riversong, though trouble still came their way. Brianna had suffered for it, the same time Officer Sylvie did. Was this fallout from that?

"Maybe there's more to this than we know. After what happened to Brianna, maybe he went to check on April and Kevin in an overabundance of caution," Gabe said.

"Could be," Shane said, but he didn't sound so sure.

"Any word on the cops questioning Rochelle further?"

"Naw, brother. Sounds like they got what they needed from her. They'll ask that guy who got shot what he saw when he wakes up."

"Thanks. Keep me posted on the manhunt."

"Will do."

"And brother?"

"Yeah, T-Wolf?"

"Don't give up on April."

Shane paused. "Yeah." Then he disconnected.

Gabe returned to the ER waiting room. Rochelle was back, wearing her clean clothes. She stood up when she saw him, a look of relief on her beautiful face.

"Any news?" he asked.

"I ran into the officer after I changed," she said. "And then a surgeon came out. He said Huey lost a lot of blood but he's going to be fine. He's in post-op now and then they'll move him to a regular room."

"That's good news, baby." Gabe pulled her into a hug. "You wanna stay or go home?"

Rochelle looked torn. "Is it okay if we stay until he wakes up?"

"Whatever you want. You hungry?"

She shook her head. "I'm fine. He said it won't be too much longer, then they'll let me into post-op when he's more awake before they take him upstairs."

"Did the officer question you?"

"No. He's in there now." Rochelle shivered. "I hate that Huey's going to wake up to a police officer and not his family. He's afraid of authority. After what he went through in China to get to the U.S., I don't blame him."

"Ms. Carlson?" A nurse in surgical scrubs and a hair net stood in the doorway leading to the OR and post-op. "I can take you back now."

Rochelle smiled. "Thanks." She and Gabe followed the nurse down the hall, then past curtained-off beds in post-op until they got to Huey's. The officer was standing outside of the curtain. The nurse opened the curtain to let them all through.

Rochelle took one look at the man in the bed and stifled a sob. Huey's skin was pale. He moved his head side to side, blinking and squinting like he was looking for something or someone. When his eyes fell on Rochelle, he said something in Chinese and she responded, shaking her head. She went to his side and took his hand. The police officer closed in on the other side and Rochelle looked at him sharply.

"Maybe you should step back. He's very confused—"

Too late, Huey noticed the officer and his eyes went wide and he started shouting. Gabe didn't need a translator to tell him that Huey was shouting for help, scared for his life. A machine behind him started beeping wildly.

"Huey, Huey." She said something else Gabe couldn't understand, trying to soothe him even as she shot daggers at the cop who showed no signs of leaving.

"I need to question him," the asshole insisted. "Ask him if he got a good look at the person who shot him."

"I'm not asking him *anything* right now," Rochelle spat. "He's confused. He thinks he's back in China and I'm his daughter and you're going to kill us. Get out. Get *out*." She nearly shrieked the last word.

"Time to go, buddy." Gabe approached the cop, not caring if he was about to get arrested. His woman issued a command and this ass was not listening to her.

Just then the curtain opened and the nurse stuck her head in. "Everyone out, now, doctor's orders." She pushed past the men to get to Huey. "Sorry, honey, you too," she told Rochelle. "All of you can come back tomorrow when he's coherent."

Rochelle squeezed Huey's hand one last time and told him something before she turned to leave. Gabe put his arm around her and shielded her from the cop, who was glaring at both of them.

"Let's get out of here. We'll get your stuff and come back tomorrow." No fucking way was Gabe going to subject Rochelle to another minute of this bullshit.

"Gabe—"

"Baby, he'll be fine. We'll come back first thing, promise."

EVENINGS ALWAYS CAME FASTER in the valleys and eastern-facing slopes of the Rockies. The air itself seemed to turn blue as the clouds closed in, stealing some of the daylight and bringing on the night even earlier as Gabe drove home. The sun made one last pass between the bottom edge of the cloudbank and the tops of the mountains before giving up. Golden light stabbed through the blue and was gone.

Past the switchback when the road straightened out, Gabe took one hand off the wheel and grabbed Rochelle's unbandaged hand. Thank God, that was the worst of her injuries. At least as far as *physical* injuries went. He would watch Rochelle closely tonight and make sure she wasn't dwelling on—

Being shot at.

—seeing someone get shot.

He thought of how she'd talked about the day she ran out of Riversong in fear. That woman wasn't Rochelle today. She'd been steaming mad after the cop upset Huey. Gabe had never seen her so angry, but instead of being upset at her or trying to calm her down, he was proud of his woman and let her roar. Her anger was righteous and it made her strong. She was standing up for someone she cared about. That's where she found her courage.

Now I just need to teach her it's okay to stand up for herself.

When they'd left the hospital, they'd headed straight for her apartment. Her anger had ebbed on the way—more out of exhaustion than anything else, Gabe thought. Her cat hadn't greet them at the door like he usually did. She'd found him hiding under her bed and had to coax him out with treats. Greg meowed in distress—no doubt picking up Rochelle's mood. He fought her as she got him into his carrier which upset her further. The hair on the back of Gabe's neck prickled with nerves the whole time.

Gabe put Rochelle's bloodstained coat into a bag, intending to wash it for her at his house. She grabbed a handful of underwear out of her dresser drawer along with some shirts and a pair of sweats and stuffed it all into a duffel. Gabe carried the duffel and her tote with her computer, and Rochelle carried the cat carrier while Greg yowled like it was the end of the world. In the kitchen, Gabe grabbed a bag of kitty litter while she dumped kitty kibble into a bag and they were ready to go.

Greg continued to sing the song of his people all the way up the mountain.

Gabe's porch light never looked so good to him shining through the trees, welcoming them home and promising comfort. He parked in the detached garage and came around to Rochelle's side, then opened her door and helped her out. She wrapped her arms around him.

"Let's get you in out of the cold, baby," he said into her hair. She nodded, yawning.

They grabbed their things. Greg mercifully went silent as soon as he was out of the truck. Gabe walked Rochelle out of the garage to the front of the house. Her eyes were wide and her head swiveled as she took in her surroundings like a small animal checking out her new territory. He'd get her inside, make her comfortable, and they'd go from there.

"This is not the way I wanted to show you my house for the first time." Gabe turned off the house alarm, then held the front door open for her. The scent of the pinewoods, the snow, and the crisp, winter air trailed in with them. Gabe tried to see his home through her eyes—the solitude that brought him peace, the shelves lined with books, the glass-faced wood stove built into the fireplace with its logs stacked neatly and ready for a fire, the stained-glass lamps his mom loved and left with the house because that's where she said they belonged. He held his breath.

Her expression relaxed into a soft smile as she looked around.

"It's lovely, Gabe. Look at all those books." She smiled up at him. "I already feel at home."

And Gabe breathed again.

"Go ahead and let Greg out. I'll put your bags away and get your coat in the wash."

He needed to get the coppery stink off it, but first he had to make sure she was comfortable.

Maybe a fire would help settle her. Feeling the warmth and watching the flickering flames through the glass always soothed him.

Rochelle knelt and set the cat carrier on the floor then opened it. "Come on out, baby, it's okay. This isn't the vet."

Gabe watched the cat slowly make his way out of the carrier and look around. He meowed accusingly at Rochelle as if to say *The things you put me through!* and then bumped his head against her outstretched hand.

"He seems all right now," she said, stroking the cat's head. Rochelle seemed marginally better, too. "I'll get his food, water, and litter box set up."

Gabe opened the stove's door and felt residual heat from the embers left after last night's fire. While Gabe tended the coals and added logs, Rochelle got Greg's stuff squared away then studied the books on the shelves—no surprise there.

"Most of those are left from my parents. This is the house I grew up in. They retired to Florida a while back and I bought their house."

"Your mom must like romances."

"She sure does." Satisfied that he had a good blaze going, Gabe closed the door to the wood stove. "You can read any book you want. The Agnes O'Neil Library is open for business." He stood and turned to Rochelle as she smiled, pulled a book from the shelf, and studied it.

"I need to get your coat in the washer, baby. I'll be right back. Then I'll get some food cooking."

Rochelle closed the book and gazed deeply into his eyes with a look of love and trust so complete it shattered his heart. He didn't deserve her trust—didn't deserve *her* in spite of what she'd said at the hospital.

He pushed his doubts to the back of his mind. He'd sort his thoughts later. For now, his priority was Rochelle. He stroked her face and she laid her hand on top of his, telling him without words how she felt. He leaned in and kissed her softly, a gentle brush of his lips against hers.

"I'll be right back. I love you." The words left his lips without the slightest hesitation.

"I love you, too."

Gabe carried her things into the bedroom then took her coat to the laundry room and started the washing machine. He looked down at his shirt and found a couple of bloody smudges from holding Rochelle. He stripped his shirt off. He couldn't get the smell of blood out of his nose. Gabe dropped everything into the washing machine then went to the bedroom and put on a clean shirt.

The wood stove was putting out good heat when he got

back to the living room. Rochelle lay curled up at one end of the couch. She had one of his mom's romances open across her chest, but she was dead asleep. He gently brushed her hair back off her face and she didn't stir.

"Rochelle?" he whispered. She snuggled deeper into the oversized throw pillow.

Gabe picked up the paperback and found the bookmark his mom kept in the back of almost every one of her books. He tucked it into the page where Rochelle left off. Then he carefully picked her up and carried her to his bedroom.

TWENTY-ONE

Rochelle drifted in and out of sleep all night but never quite woke up. Gabe held her close and safe until she was ready to face the world again. Toward morning, she thought she heard rain falling heavy on the roof. A goose called—somewhere geese were flying. Somewhere, the world was as safe and predictable as it had always been, not a place of sudden, random violence.

Rochelle turned in Gabe's arms. She felt his breathing change.

"Sorry I woke you," she said.

"No worries, baby. I was already awake. How are you?"

"Embarrassed that I fell asleep on your couch."

He grinned. "Don't be. It was a self-defense mechanism kicking in. Your system was flooded with adrenaline, you'd had a bad shock. Your brain said nope and sent you to sleep to protect you."

Thunder boomed in the distance.

"Was that...?"

Gabe looked at her quizzically as his body tensed. "What?"

"Nothing, it's okay. I thought I heard thunder. Is it really raining? In winter?"

"Welcome to Colorado," Gabe said, a smile in his voice. "Where you can experience all four seasons in one day. Yes, it is raining. Supposed to be in the sixties today. Then it's back into the deep freeze." He propped himself up. "Now, enough about the weather. How are *you*? You've gotta be starving by now."

Sleep cleared out of Rochelle's head and she came fully awake.

God, what am I doing? she thought in a sudden panic. She sat up and started to throw off the covers.

"I'm fine, but I need to know if Huey is all right."

"Hold on, hold on," Gabe soothed. He gently settled her back into bed. "Good news. I called the hospital last night after you fell asleep. Huey is in room two-oh-eight which is a regular room, he's stable and he's going to be all right."

"But I need—"

Gabe looked into her eyes. "Rochelle. Huey will be fine."

She nodded and squeezed her eyelids shut but not fast enough to stop the tears from slipping past them.

Why am I crying now that he's safe?

Maybe because I feel safe enough to let go.

Gabe pulled her into a tight hug.

"It's all right. He's safe. *You're* safe," he said as if reading her thoughts.

It was easy to feel that way in Gabe's bed, wrapped in his arms, with the rain falling outside. But she owed Huey her life.

"I want to go see him," Rochelle said. She pulled away from his arms and wiped her eyes. "I'm not doing Huey any good here. I don't know if he has friends here or how to reach his daughter in China. She needs to know." Rochelle looked around Gabe's bedroom. "My phone, it's in my bag. I should look up Huey's agent and call him. He'll know how to contact her."

"Baby, slow down. We'll have some breakfast and then head over. You haven't eaten anything since early yesterday." Gabe took her in his arms again. "I love you and I want to make sure you're okay. Stay here, sleep some more, and I'll bring you breakfast."

———

HE LOVES ME.

The words danced in Rochelle's head as she sat on a stool at the kitchen peninsula and watched Gabe make breakfast. No way was she staying in bed like he'd insisted. She cut up strawberries while he made pancakes. Greg jumped up next to her. Startled, she dropped the knife.

"Thanks for feeding Greg while I was conked out. Are you sure it's okay for my kitty to stay here?" Rochelle picked him up and set him on the floor. He'd acted weird yesterday at the apartment and it niggled at her, but now he'd settled down and made himself right at home.

Gabe chuckled. "Of course. It's nice having him. I used to have a cat growing up." He checked on the bacon cooking in the oven.

"Oh?" Rochelle looked up. "I figured you for a dog person."

"Why? Because of Watchdog? Eh, I'm an animal person, period. Dogs, cats, doesn't matter. They're all great."

The corner of her mouth turned up. "What about skunks?"

That made Gabe laugh. Then she laughed too. She hadn't realized just how bunched up her shoulders had been until they loosened up at the sound of Gabe's laughter.

He added another pancake to the growing stack on a platter. "Okay, I'm not quite Saint Frances or Doctor Doolittle the way Bear is. No skunks allowed."

"Oh thank goodness," Rochelle said. "Though I have to admit, Spot is cute." She scooped the sliced strawberries into a bowl and added sugar and a dash of balsamic glaze. "What else can I do?"

"Nothing, babe. Go grab a book. The one you were reading last night is on the table beside the couch." He pointed at the table with his spatula.

Rochelle grinned up at him, her eyes crinkling at the corners. "Thank you."

Greg sauntered behind her to the couch. He hopped up and made himself into a furry, purring puddle beside her. She picked up the paperback as she ran her fingers through Greg's fur. Something about the way he acted the day before bothered her. Maybe it was the blood on her clothing that upset him. Then again, he hadn't come to the door when she got home. He was already hiding. A vague worry tickled the back of her brain.

Rochelle grabbed her phone off the charger on the table beside the couch. She scrolled through her contacts until she found Theo Firestone's name and hit call. It rang a few times before going to voicemail.

"Hi, Theo, it's Rochelle. I hope that by now you know what happened yesterday when I met Huey to go over the translations at Riversong. If not, he's in the hospital in Longmont, room two-oh-eight. I don't have his daughter's information so I'm hoping that you do and you can let her know that her dad is going to be okay. Give me a call, thanks."

She disconnected, hoping that her messages didn't sound too lame. She *hated* leaving messages.

While I'm at it, I'd better text April and see how she is. I need my car back, too. It had been in the parking lot, and officially part of the crime scene.

> Hey, April. I know you have to be incredibly
> stressed and busy right now, but I want to
> make sure you and your family are okay.

She traded her phone for the paperback and tried to relax in front of the fire.

Gabe plated up breakfast and carried the tray of food over to the couch. Pancakes, the bowl with the strawberries and balsamic she'd made, bacon, and toast with butter. Rochelle set the book aside and took one of the plates.

"This looks so good."

"I've never had strawberries like this, "Gabe said as he sat next to her.

"I learned how to make it in Italy on one of my parents' tours."

Gabe nodded and added a dollop to his pancake stack. Rochelle took a bite of hers. The flavor was amazing—sweet and tangy and perfect on the buttery pancakes. But she felt tense until he took a bite and closed his eyes.

"Fantastic," he said.

They ate quietly, Rochelle only then realizing just how hungry she was. When she was done, he took their plates back to the kitchen.

Rochelle stood when he came back to the couch. She melted against Gabe. He wrapped his arms around her and turned so that she was toward the fire. He stroked her hair and laid his cheek against the top of her head. They stood there softly swaying for a while, the only sounds the crackling fire and the wind outside.

"We'll leave in a little bit," Gabe said. "They'll be done with rounds by then and you can see him."

Gabe sat down on the couch and gently pulled Rochelle down onto his lap. He put his arms around her, drawing her close to his chest. She let out a small sigh of relief, leaning her head on his shoulder. Gabe caressed her hair softly, soothing her. They stayed like that for a few moments, just enjoying each other's presence. Outside, the rain had picked up, pounding against the window. The sound of the downpour filled the silence between them. The flames from the wood stove cast a rosy glow in the room, counteracting the gray weather outside.

"Are you happy here, baby?" Gabe asked.

She nodded against his chest. "I am."

Gabe kissed her. His lips grazed over hers, once then twice. He leaned back and studied her face.

"What is it about Huey's poetry that speaks to you?"

The question took Rochelle by surprise, but she had an answer right away.

"It's that I could always lose myself in his images. I could completely forget who I was for a while and be in a different world, away from all my problems. No matter where I was or what was going on, I could find myself in a better place."

Gabe smiled and looked away.

"What?" Rochelle asked.

"The same thing happens to me every time I look into your eyes."

Rochelle felt her cheeks heat up. She ran her hand through the hair at the nape of his neck. Heart pounding, she tilted her head for another kiss. The world outside Gabe's home—the mountains, the town, the whole world—faded into insignificance, leaving only the two of them in his sanctuary. The warmth between them grew steadily, the heat of their need blending into the warmth from the fire.

And that's when Gabe's phone rang.

"Argh!" Gabe groaned as he threw his head back against the couch.

"Great timing," Rochelle said, her face red hot and her breath coming in fast gasps.

Gabe snapped his head back up and planted a hard kiss on her lips. He pulled out his phone.

"Yup, Shane is indeed cockblocking me."

Rochelle laughed. He gently shifted her onto the couch. "I'd better take this." Gabe put the phone on speaker.

"Hey, brother. I've got Rochelle on speaker. Have you talked to anyone at Riversong yet?"

"Wagons are still circled there, brother," Shane said. His voice told Rochelle that question was at the entrance to a minefield. "I haven't been able to raise anyone. Rochelle, how are you?"

She gave Gabe a confident-looking smile. "Thanks for asking. I'm fine, I promise. No bad dreams last night, no shakes today." She held out her hand to prove how steady it was and her voice sounded strong even to her ears—not a hint of a stutter. "I tried texting April earlier but she hasn't answered me, either. I'm sorry she hasn't reached out to you. I'm sure she and her family are in shock."

"Doesn't matter." His tone sounded so discouraged, it hurt Rochelle's heart. She checked her phone again just to make sure that April hadn't responded, but there was no answer.

"I need to get to work," Shane said. "Let me know if you need anything, T-Wolf."

"Thanks, brother," Gabe answered, then disconnected.

"He sounds heartbroken," Rochelle said.

"They have some history." He smiled softly at her. "Are you all right? Ready to see Huey?"

"Yes and yes."

Gabe stood, held out his hand, and pulled her up into his

TIMBERWOLF ON THE MOUNTAIN   223

arms. "Then let's go see the man who saved your life. I want to shake his hand and thank him."

———

WHEN THEY GOT out of the truck in the hospital parking garage, Rochelle's phone buzzed. She looked at the screen.

"Sorry, I need to take this," she told Gabe. She hit the connect button as they walked toward the hospital. "Hello?"

"Rochelle? Hi, it's Theo Firestone."

"Theo, hi," Rochelle said. "Thanks for returning my call. I hope I didn't bother you."

"No. Not at all. I was going to call you to check on the status of the translations."

Rochelle frowned, confused.

"Did you get my message? Do you know what happened yesterday?"

"Yes, of course I do. I just wanted to make sure you were still on board with the translations. If not, I understand, but I'd need his book back right away to get someone else on it."

Her heart skipped with a jolt. "No, I'm definitely still on."

Gabe gave her a concerned look as they walked into the hospital lobby.

"Good," Theo said. "You're working on it now?"

Seriously? Theo sounded like he cared more about the project than about Huey's wellbeing. When she'd met him at the dim sum restaurant, he'd seemed protective of Huey. *This guy was all business.*

"I'm not working on it at this very moment. I was kinda shaken up yesterday."

"Oh. Sure. Of course. Sorry, that was thoughtless of me. Are you home now?"

"No, actually, I'm at the hospital right now to check on Huey."

"Good. I need to do that, too. Do you have the book with you? I could meet you there. We can all go over what you've finished so far. I'd like to take a look for myself, compare it to the original."

"Um, sure. I'll be here for the next hour at least."

"Great. I'll see you then." Theo disconnected. Rochelle dropped her phone into her tote.

"Everything all right?" Gabe asked. They got to the elevators and he hit the call button.

"Yeah." She smiled to reassure him. "That was just Huey's agent checking in. He wants to go over the translations. He'll meet us here later." The elevator opened and they got in.

"You looked upset for a minute."

"Oh, yeah. He wanted to make sure I was still on the job after what happened yesterday."

"Why would that change anything?"

She shrugged. "I guess he thought I'd be too shaken up to work."

"What's his name?"

"The agent? Theo Firestone."

The elevator doors opened and Rochelle and Gabe approached the nurses station.

"We're here to see Chen Shu-Hui. Is he up for visitors?" Rochelle asked the nurse behind the desk.

The nurse frowned and gave her a funny look. "On this floor?"

"Yes, I think so. Room two-oh-two? He goes by Huey?"

The nurse brightened. "Oh, Huey. Yes, Mr. Zhang should be in his room. Go on in."

Mr. Zhang? Rochelle thought. *That's not his name.*

A misunderstanding—they happened all the time when there was a language barrier. She was about to tell the nurse she'd made a mistake with the name, but what if it was something else? Huey had a natural distrust for authority, and who could blame him? *Maybe he told the hospital a different name, knowing that the police would get involved.*

Or, what if it was a new pen name Huey was using instead of his real name? Authors used pen names all the time to protect their privacy, and Huey had his reasons for keeping a low profile. His new book was tightly under wraps and her contract held her to keeping it a secret. Did that include Huey's identity?

"You sure you're okay, babe?" Gabe asked.

"Yes." She tried to smile but it felt all wrong. She started walking toward Huey's room.

"You don't seem okay," Gabe signed. She appreciated his discretion.

"I'm not sure if I can talk about it," she signed back.

She hated the way his face fell.

"It's not you." Her hands rushed to make the signs. Then she said, "I can't say because I'm under contract to keep quiet." She tried to give him a reassuring smile that felt totally fake. When they reached Huey's room, she stopped outside the door. "I need to ask Huey something. In private."

Gabe ran his hand down her arm. "Understood. I'll be right here."

Just like that. Gabe trusted her.

"Wait," Rochelle said. "This doesn't feel right. I...I kind of lied to the nurse just now. And so that feels like I'm lying to you."

Gabe tilted his head. The way he looked at her broke her heart. "What?"

"I can't lie to you. It kills me that you're trusting me right now. So, even if it's breaking my contract..." She covered her face.

Without a word, Gabe led her to an alcove across the hall where an ice machine hummed away.

"Rochelle, you don't need to tell me something that's private. I understand when things need to stay confidential. But, baby, you're acting like you're in trouble." He looked across the hall at Huey's door. "Or that he is."

"No, no, I'm not in any danger." Now she felt silly. If her mother was here, she'd tell Rochelle she was being dramatic. "It's just something small, probably not important."

"But?" Gabe gave her an encouraging smile.

"But... the nurse called Huey Mr. Zhang. That's not his name."

Gabe's eyebrows rose. "I didn't even catch that when you asked for him. I thought maybe that was just his first name and Huey Zhang is his Americanized name."

Her mother was firmly in her head now, telling her that Gabe was confirming that it was all a misunderstanding and now she was seeking attention.

She half-laughed. "No, you're right, I'm being dramatic. It's probably just a misunderstanding, that's all. Ignore me." Satisfied, her mother's voice in her head quieted.

Gabe shook his head. "I never said you were being dramatic. That's someone in your head telling you that."

All Rochelle could do was blink at him. *How did he know?*

Gabe stroked her cheek. "Baby, this is obviously not sitting right with you. I don't think you're being dramatic at all, okay? I think your gut is telling you something and you're not listening to it. I don't want to scare you, but when I was with the Rangers, not listening to your gut could get you hurt, even killed. If you think Huey might be in trouble, it could be connected to the shooting. Watchdog can protect him. And you."

This time, it was her father's voice.

You're wrong. Stop causing trouble. Be quiet. Be good.

Rochelle closed her eyes as her father's voice went on berating her.

Finally, she sighed and opened them. Then it all came out in a rush before her parents' voices could silence her.

"It could have been a misunderstanding or something. Huey's been through a lot, and he's not the biggest fan of authority. Huey disappeared in China right before he came to the U.S. The rumor is that he was picked up by the Chinese police for speaking out against the government. He doesn't talk about it, but I've seen for myself how jumpy he is. I believe the rumors about his arrest. When my family lived in China I could feel eyes on me, even as a kid. When we lived there, my parents told me all the time to be careful what I said or we could get arrested, so I understand how he feels. I *still* get paranoid sometimes and think I'm being watched." She laughed again. "Even if it's silly to do that here in the U.S."

Gabe smiled tenderly. "It's not silly at all, baby, it's smart to be aware. Thank you for trusting me with that."

"I hope I'm not making a big deal out of nothing."

Gabe gave her a soft smile and stroked her cheek. "One of the wonderful things I love about you is that you're ready to give everyone the benefit of the doubt. Which is why it breaks my heart right now to see you doubting yourself. Whatever this is, baby, you did the right thing."

Rochelle tried to believe him.

He looked at the door to Huey's room, contemplating. "While you're talking to Huey, I want to give Gina a call and ask her to look into him just in case, okay? She's discreet—she won't get you in trouble if nothing's there. But if there is something going on, she'll find it. Will you let me do that?"

Rochelle grinned. "I have a feeling you'd contact her anyway, just to be safe."

No one had ever looked at Rochelle more seriously than Gabe did at that moment. "I'll do anything to keep you safe. *Anything*. But I'm not going to leave you out of that decision. I respect you too much. And I don't think you've had a lot of respect in your life."

Rochelle's mouth dropped open and she quickly covered it. She felt an incredible surge of love for Gabe—one that threatened to overwhelm her.

She signed, "You aren't mad? At the lie?"

"Never," Gabe signed back. "You didn't lie to me. You told me the truth."

Her heart melted at his understanding. "I'll tell you another truth," she signed. "I love you, Gabe. So, so much."

"I love you too, Rochelle," Gabe said. He wrapped his arms around her and held her tightly. "Always. No matter what."

***

WHEN ROCHELLE KNOCKED on Huey's door she was surprised at how much her hands were shaking. What if she was right? What if something serious was going on with Huey that made him hide his identity? She appreciated that Gabe had not gone straight to the worst case scenario, the one that she didn't want to think about, either.

What if Huey was a spy?

Though, that didn't make sense. Too many people here already knew him by his real identity. If he was spying, it would be easier to do it under his real name. A false ID would raise red flags—like they did now.

Another possibility came to her. What if the Chinese government was still harassing him?

She knocked a second time, then opened the door.

"*Wéi*," Huey said. A simple hello as he picked up his glasses off the table spanning his bed to see who was coming in. Rochelle's nerves ramped up now that she was looking at him. His color was much better than the day before, but he looked like he'd aged fifty years and the expression on his face was solemn, resigned. But resigned to what?

As soon as his glasses were on and he saw who she was, his expression changed to dismay, then went neutral.

"Hi, Huey. How are you feeling?" Rochelle closed the door behind her.

Huey said nothing back for a few seconds. "You found me." His voice sounded unsure. It reminded her of what he'd said at Riversong. *Found me.*

She decided the direct approach was best. "Yeah. You probably don't remember me in post-op yesterday. It was pretty chaotic."

"I don't." Huey looked away from her.

"So chaotic, that I think they got your name wrong. The nurse just now called you Mr. Zhang."

Huey's head snapped back to her.

Rochelle went on. "I was confused, but thought maybe it was a new pen name, so I didn't correct her. Is that all right?" Her gaze never unlocked from Huey's.

"Yes, yes, good," Huey said, his voice a little lighter. He gave her a smile that didn't reach his eyes. His gaze darted behind her at the door then back again. "You must be busy today. You go on, have fun. I'm fine."

"Oh, I don't have any other plans," Rochelle pushed. "I was planning on visiting you for at least an hour."

"*Bù xíng*," Huey said, telling her it was not okay to stay. "I am okay. I will be home tomorrow. You go home. Stay home and rest."

Rochelle closed the door behind her. "Huey? Is everything all right? Do you need me to call someone?"

"*Bù xíng*," Huey said louder. "I am fine." He waved her off.

Rochelle swallowed. *Time to push harder.* "Have you heard from your daughter? Does she know—"

"*Méi mén er!*" Huey practically shouted—a firm *no way*. "I told you, I'm fine. Go home *now*, okay?"

You heard him, Rochelle. Leave. You're being a nuisance.

No.

"I'm worried about you. You saved my life, Huey. I'd do anything to help you. Anything. Just say the word." Tears stung her eyes. *Please be good. And please let me help you* she pleaded silently.

Huey's face looked like it was carved from stone. Finally he spoke.

"I thought I was doing the right thing. I wanted to send money home and they said they would help. Now, I need to *go* home. My daughter needs me. She can't get health services."

"What? Who? Who's doing this?" Rochelle balled her fists.

"She can't travel," he intoned as if he hadn't heard her. "She says they will take my grandson when he is born."

Rochelle covered her heart. "Oh, Huey, I don't know what to say." She looked over her shoulder. "But I have friends who might be able to help you."

He shook his head. "Too late. You need to leave, Rochelle. Go live your life and forget this foolish old man."

"Please. I can help."

Huey shook his head. "Third poem, first line. Read carefully. Okay?" Then he turned away, done with their conversation.

Rochelle turned and left the room.

But she wasn't done. Not by a long shot.

Gabe was on the phone, still across the hall in the alcove. If he wasn't already talking to Gina, Rochelle would make sure that was his next call.

He looked up at her and said, "We're leaving now."

TWENTY-TWO

Gabe watched Rochelle go into Huey's room. Over the past ten minutes, he'd watched his woman go from relaxed to shaken up and scared.

This isn't right.

It killed him that Rochelle had no confidence in herself and her own instincts. He'd work on that with her later. Right now, his top priority was making sure she was safe. He was beginning to wonder if they had the shooting at Riversong all wrong.

He dialed Gina.

"I'm one step ahead of you," Gina said after he told her about Rochelle's behavior.

Gabe grinned. "I'm not surprised."

"This hasn't been sitting right with me, either. I was looking into the Tobisons just to make sure it wasn't them, and like George, I'm convinced they didn't have anything to do with the attack. They're out of cash and it took a good deal of money to hire the shooters."

"You know who the shooters are?" Gabe asked.

"I've identified them, yes. A couple of hitmen out of Las

Vegas who were hired by a PI in Denver. But that's as far as I've gotten. I was about to call my friend Elissa in Los Angeles. This is exactly her jam. But it sounds like you have some intel I didn't know about."

"I'm hoping it's nothing," Gabe said, "but it's about Rochelle's client, Huey. She was having lunch with him at Riversong."

"The man who was shot, correct?" Gina asked. "You think there's a connection with him?"

"We just found out he's going under a false name, Huey Zhang. At first, Rochelle thought it was a misunderstanding. She's in there asking him about it now."

"Let's go under the assumption that it's true. What's his real name?"

"Chen Shu-Hui. He's a Chinese author who lives in the U.S. now. He actually sought political asylum when he came here. He doesn't trust authority as you can imagine. Rochelle thought maybe that's why he might be going under a false identity. I don't know if he's just being cautious or if he's in real danger, and by extension, Rochelle."

"China. Damn," Gina said. "Not my specialty. In my former job, I traveled around the Middle East and Africa. But I have friends who worked in China. I'm going to give them a call, see if they can help with this. It might take a little while. They're...reorganizing...after our last job together. Thanks, Gabe. My gut's telling me this is worth checking out. You may have saved me from a rabbit hole. And you may be saving both Rochelle and Huey."

"There's someone else, too. Theo Firestone. He's Huey's agent."

"I'll look into him as well. In the meantime, I want you to bring Rochelle into Watchdog right the hell *now*."

"I was leaning that way myself."

The door across the hall opened and Rochelle stepped out looking stricken.

Gabe's blood froze. He'd been stupid, so, *so* stupid not to take Rochelle straight to Watchdog the day before.

"We're leaving now," Gabe told Gina and hung up.

Rochelle didn't hesitate. Didn't question him, nothing, just grabbed his hand and they headed for the elevators. She didn't say a word until they were alone in the elevator.

"We need Kyle's help," she said. "Huey's in danger. They're coming for him." Rochelle told him about the conversation she'd had with Huey. It killed him that she wasn't concerned for herself at all. Her first thought was for the author.

"We're headed for Watchdog right now, baby. My first priority is *you*. I don't like the fact that Theo wanted to know where you were and that he suddenly wants to meet with you. I'm calling Gina back as soon as we get to the truck."

Her eyes widened. "I knew it."

"Knew what?"

"I've had this feeling a few times over the past couple weeks that I was being followed, but I ignored it. Once leaving Riversong, then again at a grocery store." Rochelle put her hand over her mouth. "I...I'm an idiot. Oh my God, the night I talked to my sister. There was someone outside my door at my apartment. I'd forgotten about that."

Gabe's stomach clenched. "Man or woman? Description?"

"I can't be sure. A woman, maybe? I didn't get a good look at them. Whoever it was, they were already in the elevator by the time I got to the door and I only looked out the peephole."

"Baby, you and I are going to have a serious talk about trusting your gut." He pulled her into him and kissed the top of her head. "I don't mean to shame you with this. I'm pissed right now that you were taught to ignore your own feelings as inconvenient."

The elevator doors opened. The hairs on the back of Gabe's neck stood up. He grabbed Rochelle's hand as they stepped out of the elevator.

"What does Theo look like? Do you see him anywhere?"

"No," she said, looking around as they marched through the lobby. "He's tall, thin, blond hair, maybe in his forties."

Gabe logged everyone in the lobby. Volunteers behind the desk spoke to a couple in their thirties. Three nurses laughed together as they headed for the exit. A gray-haired man with an oxygen tank sat reading a newspaper. Gabe didn't see anyone fitting Theo's description.

Good.

But his senses wouldn't stop tingling. As they exited the lobby, he pulled out his phone again and hit the contact for Elias.

"Hey, brother! I was—"

"Six. You or Ram near the hospital?"

At their signal for danger, Elias immediately went on alert. "Both of us just got off shift. We're in the ER. Where are you?"

Thank fuck for small favors.

"Approaching the visitor parking garage."

"Be right there."

Gabe paused at the entrance to the garage. Stale air and the faint whiff of exhaust fumed around them. Gabe's truck was parked away from any other vehicles. No one else was around, just a few scattered cars.

"We're gonna make a run for it. When you get in the truck, I want you on the floor."

Rochelle squeezed his hand in acknowledgement.

Their footsteps echoed against concrete walls as they ran

through the garage. As soon as they got to the truck, two men came jogging out of a stairwell.

Fuck. Feds. Gabe could smell it on them—the way they moved, the way they dressed. And yet, something was off.

Where did they come from? Had they just missed them coming from Huey's room? He clicked his key fob and the truck unlocked.

"In the truck now, baby."

Rochelle didn't bother going around the truck. She opened the driver side door facing them and slipped in. She closed the door and immediately dropped out of sight.

"Excuse me," one man shouted. "That Rochelle Carlson?"

Gabe stood between them and the truck. "Who wants to know?"

The taller man, with close-cropped hair that seemed to stand at attention, stepped forward, badge in hand.

"I'm Agent Cooper, and this is my partner, Agent Thompson," he announced, gesturing towards his companion, whose lips were a thin, unyielding line. "We need to ask Ms. Carlson a few questions about Chen Shu-Hui."

Gabe studied the men. A slight bulge in each of their jackets gave away the fact they were armed.

"And why would the FBI be interested in what Rochelle has to say?" Gabe questioned, keeping his body between the agents and the truck's cab where Rochelle now lay out of sight.

"Chen Shu-Hui is a person of interest in an ongoing investigation," Agent Thompson cut in, his voice clipped.

Gabe stretched out his hand. "Let me see your badges."

Thompson didn't move. Agent Cooper handed him the badge. Gabe studied it.

Not bad. Gabe didn't think an agent would ever hand over his badge but he couldn't find anything glaringly wrong with the ID.

Come on, Lion and Ram. Where are you?

He handed the badge back calmly. The weight of his Sig in its concealed holster comforted him as he stalled for time.

"And Chen Shu-Hui, he's a spy, you said?" He watched them closely for any tell, any twitch or hesitation that meant an immediate attack.

"Not exactly what we said," Cooper corrected smoothly, yet his gaze darted to the side for the briefest moment. "He's a person of interest. That's all we can disclose."

"Understood." Gabe's voice was even, betraying nothing as adrenaline sharpened his senses, readying him for whatever came next. Gabe tilted his head, feigning interest in Cooper's explanation. "A person of interest," he echoed, his gaze never wavering from the agent's face. The garage's fluorescent lights cast stark shadows across the concrete pillar behind him.

"Exactly." Cooper's affirmation came a heartbeat too slowly.

"Mind if I see *your* badge?" Gabe asked Thompson, keeping his voice smooth.

There was a flicker, the barest narrowing of Thompson's eyes. It was that tiny reaction—a flash of annoyance or perhaps fear—that sharpened Gabe's focus even further. He tensed, ready to grab his Sig. Thompson reached inside his jacket opposite the side with the bulge.

"Sure." Thompson's voice stumbled slightly over the word as he produced his badge, holding it out for inspection. He didn't offer it to Gabe when he tried to take it. Instead, he glanced at Cooper.

The game was almost over.

Where are they?

Gabe crossed his arms, moving his hand closer to his Sig.

"She's not answering anything right now."

Cooper's eyes flared. "Sir, Chen Shu-Hui has placed Ms.

Carlson in danger. We need to ask her some questions. We can do that here or we can do that down in Centennial. I can also have you arrested on the spot. Which do you want?"

From the corner of his eye, Gabe caught sight of Elias and Waylon moving with lethal grace into the garage.

Finally!

"Go ahead and call the police. She's not getting out of the truck."

Agent Cooper smiled and side-eyed his partner. "You heard him. Call them."

Thompson reached into his jacket again, this time on the other side.

Gabe swung. His knuckles connected with Thompson's jaw.

Cooper pulled a pistol but Gabe was quicker. His right hand shot out, seizing Cooper's wrist in an iron grip, twisting it sharply. The imposter's face contorted in pain as his weapon clattered to the concrete floor of the parking garage.

Waylon launched himself toward Cooper. He tackled Cooper from behind, driving him into the side of the truck with a formidable thud. Cooper grunted, winded, as Waylon wrenched his arms behind his back with a practiced ease.

At the same time, Elias was already moving, his training automatically kicking in, every nerve in his body wired for combat. He zeroed in on Thompson, still reeling from Gabe's punch. Elias flanked Thompson, then delivered a sharp blow to the ribs that expelled the air from the man's lungs in a whoosh. A swift uppercut sent Thompson staggering back, his nose spurting crimson as he backed into a concrete pillar.

"Secure them," Gabe commanded. He turned to make sure Rochelle was safe. She was exactly where he'd told her to be, hunkered down in the truck. His chest heaved as he allowed himself a split second to feel relieved, just as a new threat emerged. A third man appeared as a shadow on the passenger-side window, gun raised and pointed at the interior of the truck.

"Rochelle! Stay down!" Gabe shouted, his voice cutting through the tension-tight air as he took aim at the shadow.

"We just want the book," the man shouted. "Give it to us and we'll leave you alone."

Bullshit.

Gabe prayed he'd be faster than the gunman, when the truck's door flew open, sending the man sprawling.

Gabe raced around the truck. He launched himself toward the gunman with the same ferocity as a guard dog defending its home. His body was a weapon, honed through years of service alongside Bear. But as soon as he saw the guy, Gabe actually laughed. Rochelle's maneuver with the truck's door had caught the guy square in the jaw—and the balls, judging by the way he stood bent over and cradling his jewels, his face pale as a ghost.

But just for good measure, Gabe's fist connected with the man's jaw and a crack like thunder echoed in the parking garage. His head snapped back and he crumpled to the concrete, disoriented and defeated. His gun spun across the concrete, safely out of reach.

Gabe scanned the parking garage for more threats. His gaze fell on Rochelle as she stared at the man from the floor of the truck. She still had a death grip on the door handle. She looked shocked at what she'd done. Gabe's heart swelled with pride at his brave woman—though he hoped she'd never have to be that brave again.

He trained his gun on the man. Shouts and footsteps filled the garage.

"You call security?" he asked his brothers.

"Yup," Elias answered just as guards poured into the garage. The growing wail of sirens told him the police weren't far behind.

ROCHELLE SAT on Gabe's lap, tucked securely in his arms on the couch at Arden and Kyle's farmhouse—the safe heart of Watchdog. Their gold-and-black Lab, Camo, lay curled up in the crook of her legs. The dog's head rested on her knee as she scratched behind his ears. The fire in the huge stone fireplace warmed everyone—humans and dogs—gathered in the great room.

All of Gabe's brothers were there, and of course Arden and Kyle. Bear and Ellie sat on a second couch across from Gabe and Rochelle, Ellie in Bear's lap as well. Gina and Lachlan sat beside them. Two dogs lay at their feet—Sam and Fleur. Other dogs piled together on a rug directly in front of the fire, snoring blissfully. Every now and then, one or another would stand up and patrol the perimeter of the room, pausing to look out the sliding glass doors into the night before settling back down into the pile.

The last time they'd all gathered was at Bear and Ellie's house—talking, laughing, dining and dancing well into the night. This time, the mood was more serious.

Shane and Ben had gone to Rochelle's apartment after the attack to check things out. Just as they feared, the place had been tossed.

Thank God I took her home with me yesterday. And that we stopped on the way to pick up Greg. Gabe couldn't imagine Rochelle's broken heart if anything had happened to her cat. He'd become fond of the little guy too, who was sleeping safely away from all the dogs in one of Kyle's safehouses, where he and Rochelle would stay until they were positive she was safe.

But worse than Rochelle's apartment, Huey was missing from the hospital.

Huey had disappeared sometime during the confrontation

in the parking garage. Theo Firestone wasn't answering Rochelle's calls, either. The police found his home ransacked as well. Gabe, Rochelle, Elias, and Waylon had just come back from talking to the police after the attack in the garage. While they'd been helpful, the police remained close-mouthed about what they'd learned.

Good thing we have Gina Gabe thought.

Gina's phone lay on her lap on speaker. On the other end was a man she called Atlantis—one of her friends who had 'special' knowledge of China. Rochelle was going over her last conversation with Huey.

"He told me to pay attention to this line of poetry: *While the fox hunts the sheep*. I was going to ask him about it at River-song. That's where the sh-shooting happened. I thought he might mean a wolf, since foxes are too small to hunt sheep. I've had time to think about it and I think he's referring to the Chinese zodiac. Every year is named for an animal. Huey was born in a sheep year, so he could be talking about himself being hunted. But there is no year of the fox."

"Project Fox Hunt," Atlantis said over the speaker.

"What's Project Fox Hunt?" Rochelle asked.

"It's the name of the operation to hunt down people that the Chinese government sees as traitors to China and force them to return. It's run by the Chinese Ministry of Public Security. The CMP use what they call "persuasion to return" methods on former Chinese citizens. They claim the people they go after are criminals wanted in China—and maybe some of them are. But the CMP have other targets, too. People who speak out against the Chinese government, especially artists like Huey, are targeted and pressured into going back. And judging by the first line in his poem, that's exactly what he knew was happening."

Rochelle sat up straighter. "I know how they got to him.

Huey said he was trying to send money back home for his daughter and someone was helping him. Do we know who it was?"

Gina nodded. "My friend Elissa traced the money used to hire the hitmen out of Vegas. A man by the name of Wei Yang hired the PI who then hired them. Yang is a Chinese author who's been in the States for fifteen years. Guess who his literary agent is?"

"Theo Firestone," Gabe said.

Gina nodded grimly. "Yang left China for the same reasons Huey did—he'd been writing and speaking out against the government."

"So why would he betray Huey?" Rochelle asked. "Aren't they on the same side?"

Atlantis answered her. "Either he's changed his mind or he's being compromised. Elissa traced the money from Yang to a Chinese police station in Denver masquerading as an NGO service center."

Rochelle's eyes widened at Atlantis' words.

"Chinese police station in...Denver? I don't understand."

"They're in cities all over the world," Atlantis said. "They operate in secret under the guise of helping Chinese expats renew their driver's licenses or send money home. But that's not their real purpose. They make sure that anyone from China remembers their origins and stays loyal to China first."

"Oh no." Rochelle looked sick at heart.

"They'll use any means necessary, including getting family members still living in China to beg them to come home. They drop their social credit, cutting off health services and banning them from public transportation to coerce them into telling their loved ones to come home. And once they're back, they sometimes disappear."

Gabe pulled Rochelle close. She closed her eyes as she lay

her head on his chest. "Poor Huey," she said. "And his daughter. That's exactly what's happening to her."

"I've got people here watching the airports for Huey, Rochelle," Kyle said. "So does the FBI now."

"And I've got people on the ground in China who are checking in on his daughter," Atlantis said. "They'll get her to safety."

"Thank you," Rochelle said as she opened her eyes.

"Thank *you*, Rochelle," Atlantis said. "Denver wasn't on our radar. Now we can feed the FBI the intel they need to shut down the police station."

"Good."

"I'll be in touch," Atlantis said, then he disconnected the call.

Rochelle sighed. "That helps, but I'm worried about Theo, too."

"We'll find him," Kyle said. The bleak expression on his face conveyed what he didn't say—*dead or alive.*

"Maybe if I'd said something different on the phone when he called—"

A chorus of protests came from their friends. Ellie hopped up off of Bear's lap and rushed over to Rochelle.

"What we're all trying to say is, don't even start down that road, my friend. You had no idea what was happening." She sat on the edge of the couch. "I mean, we still don't know for sure if Theo was working with them or not. For all we know, they could have messed up his house on purpose to throw everyone off."

"I don't think he was. He sounded scared, now that I think back." Tears filled Rochelle's eyes. "I should have *known*."

Ellie leaned in and grabbed Rochelle in a Bear-worthy hug.

"You are so wonderful, do you know that?" Ellie said. "Your life's been threatened not once but twice in two days but you're all worried about someone you barely know." She pulled back and looked into Rochelle's eyes. "Do not second-guess or blame yourself for any of this, okay? I know what it's like to be in the middle of a mess you didn't cause. Your head can play games with you. If it starts doing that, you call me and we'll talk. Or just come up and visit me anytime."

"Careful though," Bear said. "I know from personal experience she'll have you painting and fixing things up around the place." His eyes twinkled as everyone laughed.

Gabe couldn't help but be amazed at his friend's happiness.

He's truly found his way home with Ellie. That's how I want to be with Rochelle. I just need to get her safely through all of this.

A big part of that would be making sure she had all the love and attention she needed.

Sign me up.

He thought everyone in the room felt the same way as he looked around at his friends' faces.

Upset as she'd been, even Rochelle laughed at Bear's joke.

"It's worth it," she said. Then she snuggled back down into Gabe's lap. "Can I bring this guy with me?"

Gabe's chest both warmed and tightened as he wrapped his arms around her.

Ellie smiled and nodded but Bear said, "Only so long as you keep a paintbrush outta his hands. He'll paint everything purple."

Gabe's friends laughed as Ellie, Rochelle, Kyle, Gina, and Lachlan looked intrigued.

"Bear will never let me forget the time when we were eight and I decided to help him paint his go-kart. Only, I brought leftover paint from when my mom did her craft room. I got to his house and he was off in the woods somewhere, so I started without him."

"It was like a lilac bush threw up on my go-kart by the time I got back."

"I don't know what I was thinking." Gabe laughed, and so did Rochelle.

Kyle's phone buzzed and the room went quiet. He looked tense as he held up a finger.

"Whatcha got?"

Gabe felt Rochelle's body tense.

Please, God, let the news be good.

TWENTY-THREE

Rochelle's laughter dried up as she watched Kyle's face. She was both eager for the news and full of dread.

What if they found them dead? She tried to stop the scenarios playing out in her head—scenes of Huey and Theo tied up in a van or sprawled out in a ditch, bullet wounds to the head.

Gabe held her close until she could hear his heart beating. It was slow and steady, calming her. Ellie gripped her hand. The images faded. Whatever news Kyle had, she was protected and surrounded by love.

Kyle closed his eyes.

This is it.

Her breath hitched. Gabe kissed her hair.

Kyle opened his eyes and smiled.

"Elissa tracked them on camera and Charlie found them both, alive."

Cheers filled the room, startling the dogs out of drowsing, and they sent up their own chorus of howls. Gabe hugged Rochelle as relieved tears flowed down her cheeks.

"Rocky Mountain Airport. Chartered flight. Charlie and the FBI stopped them on the tarmac."

Shane laughed and clapped. "Good old King Charlemagne."

Rochelle lifted her head. "Whoever that is, I'll have to send him a gift."

"Not him, her," Kyle said. Charlene King, one of my best bodyguards."

"Guess I'll let her have that, under the circumstances," Shane said.

"Present company included," Kyle joked.

"Was Theo...?" Rochelle couldn't say another word.

"He appears to have been a hostage." Kyle said.

Relief flooded her. Not that she'd wanted him to go through something as terrible as being held hostage—something she'd narrowly avoided—but it was a relief that he wasn't a traitor.

"What happens now?"

Gabe answered for Kyle. "Now, we keep you lying low for a while, just until we're sure you're safe. They're gonna want to question you some more, but we'll do everything we can to protect you."

Rochelle looked around at Gabe's friends. Hers now, too, she supposed. Every man in the room nodded their agreement. Elias, Waylon, Shane, Bear, and Ben. Kyle and Lachlan. Gina, Arden, and Ellie, too. Even Camo licked her arm as if to say *Don't count me out.*

She'd never felt safer.

But one last thing still worried her.

"Gina?" she said. "Your friend, Atlantis. Can he really help Huey's daughter?"

She nodded. "I'm confident he will."

"Will Huey have to...pay him?"

Gina grinned. "Not a dime."

"Are you sure?"

"Don't worry," Gina told her. "Atlantis owes me big time."

THREE WEEKS LATER, Rochelle lay in Gabe's arms in a hammock under the trees in Ellie and Bear's orchard. The branches were still bare but the temperature was in the high sixties and the sun was out, warming the day further.

"I like this kind of Colorado mood swing," she told him. "It feels like spring."

Gabe chuckled and nuzzled her hair. "Don't be fooled. It's only March. We get most of our snow in April and sometimes into May. Spring's a long way off."

"Ugh." She rolled on top of him. "It was nice of Colorado to warm up for us today though."

He studied her face. "It was. I'm sorry it's been so difficult for you these past couple of weeks."

Rochelle gave him her best reassuring smile. Yes, it had been difficult, but she'd done her best not to let on. It killed her that Gabe saw through her charade.

Her phone buzzed and she groaned.

"I thought you had that on do not disturb," Gabe said.

"I forgot to put it back on after Sandra called earlier. That might be her again."

Rochelle leaned over the hammock's frame and picked her phone up off the ground. She looked at the screen and tried her best not to pitch the stupid thing across the yard.

"Shit. Another one?" Gabe asked.

"Yup." Rochelle declined the call, blocked the number, and dropped the phone back on the ground. Not that blocking one phone number would stop the next reporter from calling her and asking for an interview.

Gabe along with Kyle—everyone at Watchdog really—had done everything they could to shield her but the press still got her name when Huey's story broke. She turned down interview after interview, only issuing a statement that Huey was a fantastic author and she hoped people would enjoy his books as much as she did. Tucked away at one of Watchdog's safehouses with Gabe, she finished the translations. It helped keep her mind off the fact that, as nice as the house was, and as friendly as everyone acted, she was still a prisoner.

Rochelle missed Riversong. She missed April, who promised to come see her but still hadn't dropped by.

"Don't take it personally," Gabe had told her the week before. "She knows Shane works here and ever since the drive-by, she's kept a low profile."

Rochelle didn't want to pry—the last couple of weeks had taught her the value of privacy. But it made her sad to think of her outgoing, boisterous friend hidden away just like she was. Once the media moved on—and they would as soon as the next scandal broke—she'd seek out April and they could go shopping.

Rochelle needed some more lingerie.

"What's *that* smile about?" Gabe asked, giving her back a sly, sexy smile of his own.

"Just thinking about my next shopping trip."

"Are you?" He ran a teasing finger down the side of her face, her throat, over her clavicle, and between her breasts, sending tingles through her entire body.

"I'm thinking I'll take April and Stephanie with me. Clothes shopping."

Gabe laughed. "*Clothes*, huh?"

"Something like that."

"Can't wait to see what you buy." He ran his finger back up the way it came and buried his hand in her hair. He found the nape of her neck and gently pushed her head down for a kiss. His hands stroked over her ass and she pressed down on his hardness. Was it bad to tease Gabe knowing that their friends were inside the cabin and could come out at any moment?

Probably. But it sure was fun.

He groaned and bit her lower lip, reminding her that two could play that game.

Damn. Well, that sure backfired. Now *she* was all hot and bothered. She'd been looking forward to leaving the house at Watchdog and getting out to see Ellie and Bear and now all she wanted to do was get back there as fast as she could and see how quickly she could strip down her perfect book boyfriend.

The creak of the cabin's front door opening made them both groan, then laugh. Rochelle rolled off of Gabe and they both sat up like a couple of guilty teenagers caught making out. Ellie and Bear appeared around the corner and by the blush on Ellie's face, Rochelle figured she was fresh from her own makeout session inside.

"It's so nice outside, I think we should have lunch out here." Ellie sounded a little too breathless just to be talking about lunch.

Makeout session confirmed.

"Sounds good. I'll help you out." Rochelle grabbed her phone off the ground just as it buzzed.

"Not again. I swear, I'm throwing away my phone."

It wasn't a reporter. It was Huey.

"Oh!" she said, surprised to hear from Huey. They hadn't spoken since the hospital. "Huey, hello. How are you?"

"Rochelle. Forgive me for not calling until now. Been so busy." He sounded happy. "My daughter is here now with her husband."

Rochelle smiled so wide, her cheeks hurt. "That's wonderful news!"

"I hope you can meet her soon. You two will be friends."

"I can't wait. I am so happy for you all."

"Thank you. She said you made this happen."

Sudden tears blurred the orchard. "It wasn't me. It was...a friend of a friend."

"It was you, Rochelle. Thank you. I will call again and we'll get together, okay?"

"Okay. Huey?"

"Yes?"

"I'm glad you're okay and your daughter is here."

"Me, too. I am sorry to have been trouble for you."

She smiled softly. "Never. We'll talk soon."

Just as she was about to tell Gabe, Ellie and Bear the good news, her phone buzzed again.

"Oh, for the love of Pete." She checked her texts and smiled.

More good news.

After putting off her visit, Sandra was finally on her way to Colorado.

GABE HELD Rochelle's hand while she waited anxiously at Denver International Airport for Sandra to come up the escalator from the trains running between concourses and the main terminal. She'd texted Sandra detailed instructions on how to navigate the busy and confusing airport, but her sister had just sent back laughing-rolling emojis.

Oh, yeah. I did nickname her Luggage for a reason. She knows her way around airports blindfolded.

There was something vague about her other responses, and yet Rochelle got the feeling Sandra was bursting to tell her something important but was keeping it a surprise. Before, she would have ignored her gut, blamed it on being excited to see her sister. But now, thanks to Gabe's encouragement, she listened to her feelings.

So, when Sandra came into view, Rochelle wasn't completely taken by surprise. But it was close.

"Is that her?" Gabe asked, pointing at Sandra.

Rochelle let go of his hand so she could sign, "Yup. And those are my parents right behind her."

"She didn't tell you?" he signed back.

"Nope."

"Whatever you need, I'll back your call." Then he grabbed her hand again.

"God, I love you," she said. She took a deep breath. "You know, I think it's going to be okay." She squeezed his hand. "I get to introduce you."

Toward the top of the escalator, Sandra caught sight of them in the crowd and waved ecstatically. Their parents found Rochelle a second later. Maman grabbed Dad's arm and pointed at Rochelle like she was some remote temple at the end of a long trek.

Stop it. Be nice. Even as she looked at her real mother, her inner-Maman voice chastised her.

Then a new voice chimed in—her own.

I will brook no BS, even if they are my parents.

Sandra broke away from their parents and wove through the slow-moving crowd at the top of the escalator. She ducked under the rope dividing passengers from the people waiting for them, not caring if there were any consequences. Rochelle lifted it an inch to avoid Sandra's backpack from snagging on it.

"Oh my God, it's been forever, Bookworm!" Sandra squealed as she opened her arms wide. Rochelle hugged her, tears at the corners of her eyes.

"I see you brought the parentals," Rochelle whispered.

"Nope. They insisted on tagging along. The surprise was my idea. So, surprise!"

"Truth—you thought I wouldn't pick you up if I knew they were along."

"Maybe." Sandra pulled away from Rochelle and looked Gabe up and down. "Wow, so *this* is the book boyfriend. Nice!"

The entire world stopped while Rochelle's cheeks turned bright red.

"Book...boyfriend?" Gabe asked, one eyebrow raised. "What's that?"

Sandra laughed. "You. Totally you."

He looked at Rochelle, his smile somewhere between amused and completely confused.

"I'll explain later," she signed quickly. Because her parents had finally made their way through the crowd and around the rope.

"Rochelle! *Mon bébé!*" Maman threw her arms around Rochelle. She kissed both her cheeks.

"I'm so surprised you're here," Rochelle said.

For all our languages, communication in our family sucks rocks.

She tried not to laugh at the daring new voice in her head. Where *did* it come from?

"*Chérie*, of course we're here!" Maman looked at Dad, who hung back a step behind her, grinning sheepishly at Rochelle. "We were so worried when we heard what happened. I remembered fleeing China ahead of the police. We don't know if they ever connected us to that gathering, but it's the only country where we don't tour. There was a part of me that thought maybe the shooting was revenge for what we had done all those years ago, and I couldn't live with myself if that were true. We love you, *chérie*. We don't ever want anything bad to happen to you."

At Maman's words, Rochelle felt her heart unclench just a little. She was still wary, still ready for Maman to say something to undercut her. But, for now, she'd take her words at face value.

Dad put his hand on Maman's shoulder. "Mind if I hug my daughter?"

"Oh! Of course not."

Dad maneuvered around Maman, who dodged his backpack while Sandra simultaneously dodged hers, and hugged Rochelle.

"You look older," he said, and Rochelle tried not to cringe.

"Well, it's been a minute." Rochelle pulled away from Dad and turned to Gabe. "Maman, Dad. I want you to meet Gabe O'Neil. He's, um."

Oh, God. Great time for my words to fail me.

But what word could she use? *Boyfriend* sounded so immature. *Man friend*—no frickin way was she calling Gabe that. There was no word that would translate who Gabe was to her and how she wanted to describe him to her parents.

She stuffed down the words *protector, champion, perfection, the one, soulmate, lover,* and *best friend,* though he was all of those.

Fiancé or *husband* would have been fine with her.

Just fine. Maybe someday.

"He's her book boyfriend," Sandra sing-songed.

Great. Who invited her here again?

Gabe grinned and offered his hand to shake. Dad took it while sizing him up.

"Pleased to meet you," Dad said. "Call me Connor. This is my wife—"

"Renée," Maman said as she extended her hand. "*Enchantée.*"

Please don't kiss her hand.

Gabe shook Maman's hand and Rochelle relaxed.

"So," Sandra said, looping her arm in Rochelle's. "I can't wait to see the apartment."

"Um." She looked at her parents. "I wasn't expecting..." Now that media coverage had died down, Rochelle and Gabe had moved out of the safehouse a few days before and Rochelle was in the process of moving her things into Gabe's house. She'd planned on letting Sandra sublet her apartment. How was she going to explain all this to her parents, especially when she was positive Sandra hadn't broken the news about staying? "I-I mean, I'm not sure I have room at my apartment for all of you."

"We've got a hotel room arranged," Maman said.

Sandra bumped her hip against Rochelle's. "I'm still staying with you, though. We've got a lot of catching up to do, Bookworm."

"Let's get your bags," Gabe said as he started to walk toward the baggage carousels.

Sandra laughed. "Checked bags are for chumps." She pointed over her shoulder to her backpack, which matched their parents' packs. "Let's get outta here, get settled in, then you can show us around."

As they walked toward the exit, Sandra threw her arm around Rochelle's shoulders and laid her head on her shoulder.

Aw!

"So, the Colorado tour had better include some more book boyfriend mountain men," she murmured in Rochelle's ear as she eyed Gabe.

Ohhh.

"Down, girl." Rochelle pushed her sister's head off her shoulder. "You have your own life to think about first."

ROCHELLE HAD to give her parents credit. They stayed for a full ten days—a record visit—before their feet got itchy and they were ready to get on with their next tour. If she was being completely honest, she had to give them extra credit for the way they got along with Gabe. Her dad especially. The two of them went off exploring a couple of times while Rochelle, Sandra and Maman went shopping.

Not for lingerie, unfortunately. That would have to wait for later.

Dad came back smiling from one of their outings and hugged Rochelle.

"He's a good man, sweetheart," he told her.

"I know. He is."

"I approve."

"Well, that's good, because I'm moving in with him whether you approve or not." She stopped her hand from flying up and covering her mouth at the last second.

Her dad eyed her, grinning. "Okay."

"Okay?" Rochelle tilted her head. "That's it?"

"Mmm-hmm." He tousled her hair like she was three then abruptly changed the subject. "Dinner's on me tonight. We're going to a steakhouse."

So after a near-perfect ten-day visit, it was time to take them back to the airport. There was only one problem Rochelle could see and it was about to go down now that she and Sandra were at their parents' hotel room.

"I'm staying here," Sandra told them.

"What?" Maman asked. "You mean for the next tour?"

"Yeah, and maybe the one after that, I don't know yet. I want to try art school, to learn more about photography. Who knows what I'll do after that."

Their parents looked at each other, dismay on their faces.

"You guys will be fine," Sandra said. "People signed up for

your tours because of you guys, not because of me. It's always been that way. You design these incredible getaways and I'm just the pretty face, see?" Sandra crossed her eyes and stuck her tongue out. Rochelle laughed, but her parents weren't finding this as funny.

"But our website, our live stories," Maman said. "You won't be in them."

"I'm not in most of them lately anyhow. It's *your* enthusiasm that draws people in, not mine. If anything, I'm not looking too thrilled on the last tour anyway."

"Are you sure, *chérie?*"

"Positive. You'll do great."

"Wow. Somehow, when we weren't looking, you became an adult with your own ambitions, making your own decisions," Dad said.

Rochelle had her own opinion on that. Watching her sister handle their parents, she thought maybe Sandra had been adulting a lot longer than anyone suspected.

TWENTY-FOUR

"That's the last of it," Gabe said as he carried Rochelle's wooden rocking chair into the house. Rochelle had moved her furniture in earnest after her parents left town, while Sandra re-furnished the apartment from crates that seemed to arrive every day from every corner of the world.

"And you're sure it's okay?" Rochelle asked for the thousandth time.

Gabe set the rocker down next to the fireplace. Greg watched him from the basket they'd eventually placed on the kitchen counter for him. He hopped down, sauntered across the room, and jumped into the rocker immediately, claiming it.

"Yes, Rochelle. It's perfectly fine," Gabe both said and signed to emphasize his point. He had insisted from the beginning that she bring more furniture with her than what she'd planned. "I want this to be *our* house. You should have your things here, not just mine. And if there's anything you don't like, we can replace it with something else that you do like." He looked at the bookshelves. "I can box some of these up—"

"Don't touch a single book." Rochelle smiled. "There are a

bunch here I haven't had a chance to read yet. I like your mom's taste in books."

It turned out when she met Gabe's mom for the first time, she liked her, too. The two women talked almost nonstop about books while Gabe and his dad looked on and shared a smile now and then.

"She's a keeper," Gabe's dad had told him as they stood out on the back deck with a couple of beers. "She's good for you. Your mom and I, well, we worried about you after we left for Florida. You had your friends and a place to live, but you didn't have someone special to make it a home again. Now you do."

"Yeah, I do. Is it crazy that it happened so fast?"

His dad thought about it for a bit before he answered.

"Life can change that quick." He snapped his fingers. "You know that from being in the Rangers. One day you were on a mission, the next you were in a hospital, and then home. That was a hard change, and fast. But I don't think you'd trade your life now for anything, would you?"

Gabe nodded. "There was a time when all I wanted was to have my hearing back. To be a Ranger again. I thought I needed that to feel whole. But now, no, I wouldn't. I wouldn't trade what I have for anything."

"Well, then maybe everything moved quickly for you and Rochelle because it was fate. Fate has no timetable, son."

Gabe sipped his beer and thought about his dad's words. "You're right. If anything, that explosion taught me that life is short and we all have to appreciate it and make the most of the time that we have. Grab the opportunities that come our way with both hands."

"Then why are you out here asking me if it's right when we could be inside there enjoying the best parts of our lives?" His dad looked back through the window where Rochelle and Gabe's mom were sitting at a table, laughing.

"You're absolutely right, our place is inside there."

"So. When are you going to ask her to marry you?"

Gabe chuckled. "I already asked Connor's permission when they were out here and he gave me his blessing. Said it would be an honor to give away his daughter on our wedding day."

Gabe's dad nodded. "Good. I wondered."

"Wondered what? If they'd bother coming to town again for the wedding?" He chuckled. "Not that I blame you for asking, given their history. Yeah, I think things are different now. Maybe after what happened to Rochelle, they understand too how short life is and what's important." Gabe laughed again. "Though, Connor did ask if we might have the wedding someplace tropical and photogenic. Said he could offer me a travel deal."

Gabe's dad laughed. "Yeah, well, people never change completely." He placed his hand on his son's shoulder and squeezed. "Let's get inside."

Then before Gabe opened the door, his dad signed, "I love you, son. Proud of you."

Gabe's eyes stung and his heart clenched. "I love you, too, Dad," he signed back. "Thanks for everything."

That night, Rochelle couldn't stop talking about Gabe's mom.

"She's so warm and funny, Gabe. Now I know where you get the light in your eyes." She stroked the hair back from his face as they lay in bed, naked in each other's arms.

"Mom's pretty crazy about you, too. Not that that's a surprise. Dad likes you, too."

Rochelle burrowed into his chest and kissed his throat. "I adore them both." Her smile turned seductive. "I adore you, too."

"Mmm." He tipped her chin up and kissed her. "I love

you." He rolled with Rochelle so that she was lying on top of him. She immediately began rubbing against his hardening cock.

"And I love when you do that." Gabe grabbed her ass and squeezed, moving her into position to take his cock. He groaned at the slick wetness waiting for him there. Rochelle sat up and gripped his cock. She teased his tip at her opening, just the way he liked it. It still surprised Gabe how much she liked to take control.

It's always the quiet ones.

"Why are you grinning at me like that?" she purred. His cock jumped.

"I can't grin at my woman looking so hot and sexy for me?"

"That wasn't an answer, that was another question." She ran her hand up his shaft, squeezing gently until a drop of pre-come glistened at the tip. It dripped onto his stomach and she rubbed his tip against it, smearing his come and driving him wild. "Why?"

"Mmm...because watching my little bookworm in the window, I could have never guessed how much she likes to be in charge in bed."

"I do not," she protested as a lovely pink blush crept up her chest, throat, and onto her cheeks.

"Yeah, you do, babe. Or else I'd be inside you right now, pounding away until you scream my name. Instead, you're driving me—"

He gasped as she ran her hand back down and up again, milking more pre-come out and onto his stomach. "You're driving me insane with your teasing."

"Am I?" she asked, all innocence and sweetness.

Her hand twisted around his shaft as she stroked him, fingers slick with his release. Her thighs tightened around his hips and he felt her warm wetness on his skin. She was driving herself wild from playing with him. Whatever it took to get her excited, Gabe was all for it, especially when she could make him feel this good.

"You know you are." Gabe bent his knees and arched his hips up, pressing against her core. "And I think you're getting off on it more than I am."

She tilted her head back and closed her eyes. "What if I am?" Her voice was heavy with need.

"Then I'm the happiest man in the world." He ran his hands up her body, over her plump breasts, nipples pebbling under his touch. He squeezed her hard, the way she liked it, then gripped her upper arms. "Now I'm about to get a whole lot happier, and I'm taking you with me."

Before she could protest, Gabe reversed their positions. Rochelle lay under him, looking up into his eyes, hunger apparent in their shine.

"You're still in charge, baby. Do you want this?" He nudged his cock against her sweet, wet warmth.

"Yes. Always."

Gabe's eyes closed as he thanked the universe for this woman—this sweet, smart, sexy-as-hell woman who made his life complete. Who brought him home. Who he was ready to make his—mind, spirit, and body—forever.

"I love you."

"I love you, too, Gabe."

He pushed his tip just inside her and felt her squeeze as she arched her back and closed her eyes. If he wasn't careful he'd come right at her entrance. This was when she was at her sexiest—right at the beginning when he first took her.

"More, she begged. "Give me more."

"Like this?" He pushed another couple inches inside her.

"Yeeess," she moaned. Another squeeze threatened to end his fun right there. God, she was so hot and tight. *Unbelievable.*

The best.

"How about more?" he gritted out.

"*Gabe,* give me all of you. Don't make me beg again."

Gabe chuckled low and deep. "Never, baby. Never gonna let you want for anything."

With one firm stroke, Gabe plunged all the way into her core. Rochelle's head tilted back as she arched into his thrust. On her face was a look of deep, wanton pleasure. She gripped his shoulders and wrapped her legs around him, pulling him as close as she could while he gave her long, slow strokes. He built their pleasure up like he'd build a fire in the wood stove, one that promised to last all night. Gabe watched Rochelle's skin bloom into a darker pink as her pleasure built. Her bookstore scent went from innocent to sensual as he smelled her need mingling with his own.

"Gabe," she moaned, and he sped up at her unspoken demand. All he needed to hear was her tone—as clear as a bell to his ears, and her body's heat made sure he understood. His thrusts turned faster and shorter as she tightened around his cock like a velvet glove.

"*Now,* Gabe. Oh, God, now. *Now.*"

With one final, ecstatic clench, she sent Gabe over with her into ecstasy.

"Rochelle, oh, damn. I fucking love you, baby."

Love you so much.

THE NEXT DAY, Gabe took the friend he trusted the most in these matters out to lunch.

Then to a jewelry store.

Gabe examined the sparkling diamond under a jewelry

microscope on the counter. He stepped aside for his friend to take a look.

"What do you think? Is it good enough for her?"

Stephanie took Gabe's place and examined the diamond while the clerk looked on, hopeful. "I can show you the grading report again," he said.

Stephanie chuckled. "A piece of paper can tell me it's a flawless diamond, sure. But my eyes will tell me if it's *perfect* for her." She leaned back and turned to Gabe. "It meets my approval."

The clerk's shoulders eased. And Gabe found his did, too. He nodded to the clerk.

"I'll take the diamond."

"Of course," the clerk said. "Now, we can put it in a plain setting for the proposal, and then you and your fiancée can come back and choose the final rings afterward."

Gabe was already shaking his head.

"Just the diamond, thanks."

"Just the...? Very well, sir." He folded a small paper envelope around the diamond and grabbed a velvet bag from under the counter. Even Stephanie looked at Gabe funny, though she didn't say anything until they were in his truck.

"What are you planning on doing? Putting it in her hand and making her carry it for the rest of her life?"

Gabe laughed.

"Yeah, Steph, that's exactly what I'm going to do. I'm going to make my wife carry a diamond around in her hand for the rest of her life as a testament to our love."

"So what *is* your plan, Romeo?"

"You'll see."

Stephanie crossed her arms and muttered, "Today, I hope."

"Today."

Gabe pulled up in front of Ben's place, an old Victorian

that reminded Gabe of Arden and Kyle's ranch. He got out and helped Stephanie down from his truck. Ben opened the door as soon as they stepped onto the broad porch. He looked Stephanie over and she returned the appraisal.

Ben looked at Gabe, a half-smile on his face. "Think you brought the wrong woman."

Stephanie's eyebrows shot up. "I beg your pardon, Hercules?"

"Ben, this is my friend, Stephanie West. She runs the rec center."

She looked at Gabe like he'd sprouted a second head. "What are you talking about? I don't own the rec center."

"I didn't say you owned it, I said you run it, and I'll die on that hill."

Stephanie puffed out her chest. "Yeah, okay. I'll let you do that."

"Come on in." Ben held the door open for Stephanie then jokingly let go as soon as Gabe started through.

Stephanie stopped just inside the room and looked around. "Nice. Family home?"

"Naw. Bought the place years ago during that real estate slump. It was in rough shape, but I worked on it whenever I was on leave." He tagged Gabe's shoulder. "This guy helped."

"We all helped, just like with Ellie's cabin. It's what brothers do."

"You did a fine job." Stephanie looked all around the front room. Ben had opened it up, removing a wall that separated the front parlor from the hall with the staircase, and taking out the ceiling so that the second floor was partially exposed. "That's beautiful metalwork on the railings. Where'd you get it?"

"That's all Moose's doing." Gabe tagged Ben back on his upper arm, which was like knocking his fist against a brick wall. Ben had guns to end all guns. "And it's the reason we're here."

"I've got coffee brewing. Any takers?" Ben led them through the front room, past the staircase, and into the kitchen.

"Oh, pick me," Stephanie said. "I can smell it already."

Ben pulled three mugs from a cabinet while Gabe studied the chaotic mess spread out across the gigantic farm table. Moose was meticulous in all aspects of his life except when it came to his passion.

"You bring it?" Ben asked. He handed a coffee mug to Stephanie, then to Gabe.

"Got it right here. Where do you want it? I'm afraid it'll get lost forever if I just set it on the table." He reached into his coat pocket where the velvet bag with its precious treasure waited.

"You ass..." Ben stopped himself as he glanced at Stephanie. "...uming that I don't know what I'm doing is rude, T-Wolf."

Stephanie rolled her eyes. "Think I never heard a naughty word before?"

"Moose is just being polite." Gabe handed the velvet pouch to Ben.

"What is this Moose and—*T-Wolf*, was it?—business?" she asked.

"It's from when we were kids," Gabe explained. "Group of us all had nicknames. Moose, Timberwolf, Bear, Lion, Elk, Ram, Badger, and Hawk, God rest his soul."

Stephanie looked the two of them over. "Animal names, that's cute. Can I join the club and you can call me Cougar?"

Ben snorted into his coffee mug.

Gabe stared her down. "Won't Doctor Boyfriend have something to say about that?"

"Doctor Boyfriend has no room to talk. He's five years younger than me." She grinned at Ben. "Made the big guy laugh. Mission accomplished."

Ben grinned. "I like you."

"I like you too, but I'm taken. I'll let you know if that changes."

"She's kidding. Now, can we get to it?"

Ben looked pleased. He pulled out a chair at the end of the table and flicked on a light beside a combination magnifying glass and soldering tool rig sitting on a black mat. Even with the magnifying glass, he took out a pair of wire-rimmed glasses that looked like he'd stolen them straight out of the eighteenth century and put them on. Ben had made them himself and Gabe was convinced his eyes were perfectly fine and that Ben wore them for show. It seemed to attract the ladies from what he'd seen.

Ben carefully removed the small paper packet wrapped around the diamond from the bag. He unfolded the paper and laid it flat, then studied the diamond.

"Good choice," he murmured, or at least that's what Gabe thought he said. Ben was off in his own world now as he blindly reached for a jeweler's loupe. The table was covered in an assortment of pliers, shears, files, tweezers, and tools Gabe couldn't begin to name. Boxes held tiny metal rings, delicate chains, and what looked like small bars of silver and gold.

"I helped him pick it out," Stephanie said.

"She rejected four other ones."

"Now I get why you took her with you instead of me. I would have done the same but I'm not as pretty to look at."

"Fresh," Stephanie said with a totally faked eyeroll.

Ben chuckled as he measured the diamond, then folded the envelope back up around it and put it back in the pouch.

Gabe looked over the table. "You got the designs?"

"Right here." Ben moved a box of chains and several pairs of pliers off of a folder. He opened it and took out sheets of paper with Gabe's sketches on them.

"Think you can do it?" Gabe asked, his voice betraying his hopes.

Ben studied the paper, nodding slowly. "Yup." He looked up at Gabe, his eyes filled with warmth. "It's going to be an honor to create these rings, brother."

"Let me see, please?" Stephanie asked.

Ben handed her the drawings. Gabe's stomach tightened. He found he was anxious for her approval.

Her eyes widened and she smiled. "Look at the designs on those bands. Gorgeous. And very thoughtful."

Gabe relaxed. "I got the idea for them after we went to an exhibition of Chinese landscape paintings at the Denver Museum while Rochelle's parents were here."

"She's going to love them, Gabe."

"Are those tears in your eyes, Steph?"

"Absolutely not!" She looked away quickly. "Coffee's hot, that's all."

TWENTY-FIVE

"All right, babe, I'm off to work." Gabe pulled Rochelle close and kissed her hard. "You remember we're going out tonight, right?"

"Yeah, how could I forget? It's all you've been talking about for the past week." Rochelle grinned up at Gabe. He'd been like a kid waiting for Christmas. Her book boyfriend couldn't keep anything from her.

He's going to ask me to marry him tonight. If he doesn't, I'll eat my laptop.

"You're still not going to tell me where you're taking me?"

Gabe grinned. "Nope. It's a surprise. So, I'll be back around six to pick you up."

Rochelle looked at the desk Gabe had bought her to use on the days the weather was too sketchy to go to town, or when she just wanted to stay in. Lately, she was... Well, *avoiding* was too strong a word, but she hadn't been back to Riversong since the shooting.

It wasn't that they were still closed—the window had been

repaired almost immediately after the yellow tape came down and they reopened a week after that. And she wasn't afraid it would happen again—the FBI had arrested everyone in connection with trying to silence Huey so she was safe—and she didn't seem to have any PTSD surrounding the event.

Rochelle hated to admit it even to herself, but she was avoiding Riversong because of April.

April had not responded to any of her texts or calls. Rochelle was beginning to believe that April blamed her for the drive-by, and that broke Rochelle's heart. The barista was her first friend in town, and the whole reason she was with Gabe now. If Gabe was proposing tonight, she wanted April for her maid of honor, and Sandra and Ellie as bridesmaids.

So why am I still hiding here?

That was the old Rochelle, the one who ran away from her problems whenever she got scared. New-and-Improved Rochelle confronted them head-on. Ever since she slammed the truck's door into the man who would have killed her over a book of poetry, Rochelle had felt a power building inside her, a quiet and sure strength that infused her spine. She walked taller, looked people in the eye. And she rarely stuttered now.

The three weeks of self-defense classes she took at the rec center helped, too.

Gabe tilted his head. "Everything all right? You look like something's on your mind."

Rochelle smiled. "Yeah, I'm fine. Tell you what. Instead of coming all the way back up here, why don't I meet you down in Lyons after work? At Riversong."

Gabe raised his eyebrows. "You hoping to see April?"

"I am. I need to know once and for all if she's mad at me. If she is, I get it, and I'll stay away. But, I just want to see if we can work things out. I don't want to lose her as a friend."

Gabe nodded and looked away for a moment. He took Rochelle's hand.

"If she doesn't come around, I don't want you to think it's all you. Her family thought they got hit for a reason."

"I know. I've been here long enough, especially over the past few weeks, to hear the rumors about them, and it makes me angry."

It seemed like everywhere she went in Lyons, someone was talking about the Taylor family and how they were nothing but trouble. Some people went so far as to say that they were selling everything from meth to grenades out of Riversong. Rochelle found herself confronting a particularly mean woman running her mouth at the grocery store. She'd gone right up to her and said, "Seriously? How many people have you seen walk out of there with a latte in one hand and a grenade in the other? How stupid can you be?" The woman had recoiled as if Rochelle had thrown a dead rat in her face. Rochelle had felt that little spark of power and confidence kindle in her chest. She marched out with her groceries, proud of herself for defending her friend.

Which only made April's silence that much harder to take.

Rochelle went on. "Those rumors are ugly and unfair, and downright dumb. But now that she knows that it wasn't an attack on her family, I just don't understand why April's still not responding. She can't think I actually believe what people are saying." She paused. "Do you know why?"

"Not exactly. I've heard the rumors too, and I know the lies behind them. But, there's always a grain of truth, too. Like I said, there was a reason why Sonny circled the wagons and put everyone on radio silence. Maybe April will want to talk about it, but just don't be surprised if she doesn't."

"I wouldn't push her on it if that's the case. I just want to let her know I'm here, and I'm her friend no matter what."

Gabe smiled softly and cupped her cheek. "That's my

sweet lady." He brushed his lips against hers then kissed her deeper.

"Mmm. Don't go to work. Stay here with me."

Gabe chuckled, then gave her a wicked-sexy smile. "You could always bring me lunch again."

Heat rose up her throat and spread over her face until even her scalp tingled.

"If you do what you did last time, I just might."

Gabe pretended to stagger backward, hands covering his heart.

"All right, I really need to go or Stephanie will have my ass for being late. Actually, picking you up from Riversong will work out better than I'd planned."

"Perfect."

Gabe signed, "I love you, beautiful."

"I love you too," she said and signed.

———

WHEN ROCHELLE STEPPED into Riversong later, she felt every gaze in the place fall on her.

It was another warm spring day so she wore a pale green summery dress that felt like it was made of gauze. She'd done her hair up and put on a pair of sparkly earrings. If Gabe was proposing to her later, she wanted to dazzle him. Judging by the way the place quieted down, she'd accomplished that mission.

Now for the next mission, one that was far more important than turning a few heads.

April stood behind the counter. As soon as she caught sight of Rochelle she turned away and grabbed a mug, then started making Rochelle's favorite latte. No loud greeting and big smile like usual.

Now I know how Shane feels.

No, that wasn't true. April only pretended to ignore Shane while her eyes held a sparkle of humor and interest. They bantered and teased each other as April tried not to laugh at Shane's jokes. April's eyes looked guarded and dull as Rochelle approached the counter.

"Hey, April," she said to her friend's back.

April didn't turn. "I'll have this ready for you in a minute."

Rochelle had expected anger in April's voice. Instead it was flat, with only the slightest quiver at the end. It wasn't an angry voice, but one that was resigned, tinged with sadness.

Do I have it all wrong? Rochelle wondered.

April turned and placed the mug on the counter without meeting Rochelle's eyes. Before she could pull her hand away, Rochelle gripped it.

"April. What's wrong? I don't even recognize you right now."

April glanced up at her and blinked rapidly before pulling her hand away for Rochelle's.

"If you blame me for the drive-by and don't want to talk to me, I get it. But just please tell me that and I'll leave you alone. If it's something else—"

While Rochelle spoke, April's eyes got bigger and shinier.

"No, God no, I don't blame you." April swallowed. "I'm not mad at you, Rochelle." She passed her hand over her face and looked around the almost empty coffee shop. This time of day it should have been full, and with a line of people zipping in and out, grabbing their to-go orders. She looked past Rochelle to the nearly empty parking lot then sighed and started around the counter.

"Grab that. It's an extra-good one." She jutted her chin at the latte as she walked past Rochelle.

She picked up her drink and followed April to the back of the store and into an office. April closed the door. As soon as she did, her shoulders heaved and she wiped her hand across her eyes.

Rochelle didn't hesitate. She set her latte on the desk and hugged her friend, whose silent sobs wracked her body.

"Don't you dare tell anyone I'm back here crying," April finally said.

"Of course not. God, I can't imagine what it must feel like to have this happen to your business. I totally misread everything when I thought you blamed me."

Rochelle felt April shake her head. "No. I've been an ass, not answering your texts and calls. I read them and listened to your messages several times, and I just didn't know what to say back. I'm crap at things like that. Someone shooting at me, that I can handle. When someone's reaching out and being all nice to me, I don't know what to do."

"I'm like that, too, sometimes. It's okay. I'm just glad we're clearing things up now." Rochelle pulled back to look at April. She was surprised to see that her cheeks were perfectly dry, though her eyes were glassy and red. She'd cried her heart out without shedding a single tear.

"I'm glad, too. Stuff like this," she gestured toward the coffee shop. "People not coming in, and knowing what they're saying..." She shook her head. "You sometimes push someone away before they can push you away first. Hurts less." She looked Rochelle up and down. "You look beautiful, by the way."

"Gabe's going to propose to me tonight," Rochelle blurted out. "I mean, I'm *pretty* sure."

"What? Are you kidding me?" April's face practically glowed as she smiled big. "That's awesome! I'm so happy for you two."

"Well, you're the one who made it happen."

April waved her off. "Oh, I did not."

"You did."

"Okay, I might have had the teensiest part in it."

Rochelle laughed. "You call what you did teensy, I'd hate to see a grand gesture."

April looked at the ceiling. "Wow, it's like she's met me."

"So. This might be early, and I'll be totally embarrassed if he doesn't ask me, but... Would you be my maid of honor?"

April covered her mouth with both hands and bent forward. "I'd love to," she said through her fingers.

"Perfect. I'll let you know the details as soon as I know them. If I know them. If he proposes."

April straightened and rolled her eyes. "If he doesn't, don't you ever buy him another coffee."

"Oh! You know what? I forgot to pay for this one." Rochelle picked up her latte and April opened the office door.

"It's on me. But don't get used to it." She winked. "Like I said, I sell them, I don't give them away."

ROCHELLE WAVED to April as she headed out the door to pick up Kevin from aftercare. She was settled into her usual spot—no way was she going to give up the warmth of sunbeams on her back—working on a new project when her phone buzzed. Only a few people could get past the 'do not disturb' she set her phone to during business hours so she picked it up expecting Gabe. She'd texted him earlier, telling him that she and April had made up and he sounded as happy as she did. Okay, she wasn't just expecting the text was from Gabe, but hoping that he was requesting a private, late lunch in his office —food not required.

Sandra's name showed up at the top of the screen.

> Hey! I decided to skip hot yoga. Can you stop by? Need to talk to you about Mom and Dad.

Sandra never skipped hot yoga, or any sort of exercise or spa treatment. Worried, Rochelle texted back.

> Sure! Everything ok with them?

> Yeah! Just need your opinion and I don't wanna text it.

Rochelle sighed. She looked at the time. Gabe would be off in half an hour.

> Can it wait until tomorrow? I have a thing tonight.

> Wow. Guess you don't love me.

"Ouch," Rochelle said aloud. Her thumbs flew.

> Actually, I think Gabe's going to propose to me. So as much as I DO love you, this is kinda important too.

She watched the three bubbles rise and fall as Sandra texted back.

> Oh WOW! Congratulations! Yeah, that's important. But this is important too. Can you just come over here? Pleeeeeaaaaaseeee????

Seriously? Why is Sandra being so selfish...oh. Oh, duh. Rochelle chuckled. Gabe thought he was being sneaky.

> Ok fine. But if you make me miss my own proposal, I'll stuff you in a suitcase and send you back to Maman and Dad.

> LOL!!!! You won't miss anything I promise! Just get over here!

> Fine! Fine! Be there soon.

Rochelle closed her laptop and put it in her tote. She smiled at Hannah behind the counter and waved goodbye. She was pretty sure she'd see April at Sandra's apartment—along with all her friends as Gabe proposed to her in front of them.

So this was Gabe's surprise destination—a party at Sandra's apartment. Her sister probably planned the whole thing. It was her style. Rochelle felt a bittersweet wave of love for the sister she'd kept at arm's length for much too long.

She didn't want to spoil her own surprise party, so she texted Gabe just for good measure.

> Hey! Heading to Sandra's real quick to talk. Maybe you could pick me up there instead of Riversong?

> Sure, babe. Hope everything's okay. I'll see you in half an hour.

> Sounds good! Love you!

> Love you too.

Rochelle grinned. Half an hour, her butt. She'd see him in about fifteen minutes, as soon as she walked in Sandra's door.

Her stomach knotted in anticipation as she approached the apartment building. Now that she no longer lived there and didn't have a parking pass, she had to find a spot in the neighborhood. She passed car after car, looking for a Watchdog SUV, but of course they were too smart to be so obvious. The neighborhood was full of vehicles and she had to park a couple blocks down.

Looks like someone's having a party. I wonder who. She laughed to herself to cover up the tremor of anxiety in her chest. She checked her hair in the sunshade mirror and got out. Butterflies careened in her stomach with every step. She could picture Gabe standing in the middle of her former apartment while all their friends popped up from behind the couch and various paper screens Sandra had placed around the apartment. She blinked back happy tears.

Don't want to go in with raccoon eyes.

Rochelle still had a copy of the apartment keys so she let herself into the building and crossed the lobby to the elevator. She felt lightheaded as a slight wave of nausea hit on the ride up. She laughed to herself again—*What if I ended up running out of the room like on our first date? Maybe I could pretend to.* Yes, running felt like the thing to do. *Why am I so nervous?*

The elevator opened and she walked on shaky legs to the apartment door.

Should I knock or just go on in?

Rochelle tried the handle and the door swung open.

"Knock-knock," she said as she walked in, her voice quavering.

Get a grip! This shouldn't feel weird.

The apartment appeared empty but she could feel people present.

Something twinged in her gut. Something about the text thread with Sandra.

"Sandra, I'm here. What'd you want to talk—"

A hand holding a foul-smelling cloth covered her mouth from behind and a woman spoke in her ear.

"I told Gabe to soften his heart. He didn't listen to me and now you're going to suffer the consequences."

Rochelle dropped her tote in shock. She felt lightheaded from whatever the hell chemical was in the cloth but several thoughts went through her mind in rapid succession:

Where's my sister?

Who is this bitch?

Hold your breath.

Gabe will be here in fifteen minutes.

I only need to survive that long.

I can do this.

Rochelle slammed her head backward. She heard a crunch as it connected with the woman's nose, followed by a howl. Thank goodness, she let go of Rochelle and dropped the cloth as she staggered backward, covering her nose.

Rochelle turned around. The woman looked to be in her late fifties. What would she have against Gabe? Rochelle's head spun from the fumes.

"Who are you and what the hell did you do with my sister?" she yelled.

Now she knew what was wrong with the text thread.

Mom.

We never call Maman Mom on penalty of death. Does Velna have her phone?

Rochelle bent to pick up her tote and grab her phone to call for help as she ran away. She overbalanced and almost toppled over. Meaty hands wrapped around her arms and pulled her back and up.

"I got her," the man said as he gripped her arms until they hurt. He started to lift her. Rochelle bent her knee, kicked her leg back, and the back of her calf slammed into his crotch.

Thanks for talking me into self-defense classes at the rec center, Gabe.

"Bitch!" he roared as he let go and covered the family jewels.

Rochelle made a break for the door.

And ran smack dab into another man blocking her way in the hall. He shoved her backward into the apartment and she lost her balance, falling beside her tote. Her phone started ringing with an incoming call. She lunged for it but the second man was faster. He kicked Rochelle in the ribs. The wind rushed out of her lungs and she saw stars. He flipped her onto her stomach, knelt until he straddled her, and wrenched her arm behind her back.

Her phone stopped ringing and something in her heart went dark. Rochelle screamed, hoping a neighbor would hear her.

He punched her in the back of the head for her effort. Rochelle fought to stay conscious. She focused on the big, round wall clock behind him.

Ten minutes. Just survive for ten lousy minutes and he'll be here.

"Want me to drug her?" he asked the woman as he picked up the foul-smelling cloth. The first man continued swearing in pain, bent in half and glaring at Rochelle.

"No, just gag her so she doesn't scream again." The woman's nose streamed red and she snuffled. She swiped her arm across her face angrily and blood spattered on the wall beside her. "This could've gone easy but I want her awake for it now."

"Where is my sister?" Rochelle demanded, hating the sluggish way her voice sounded. She struggled to get free while the man fished around for a gag.

"Oh no, are you worried about someone you love?" the woman said, her voice dripping in sarcasm. She dropped to her knees beside Rochelle. "Doesn't it suck? I lost *my* son because of Gabe fucking O'Neil and Jon fucking Behr and Shane fucking Foti and all the fucking rest of them. My sweet, sweet little boy." Red-tinged spittle flew and she spat a disgusting wad of phlegm on the carpet beside Rochelle's face.

"Oh. Now I know who you are. You're Velna Tobison." Rochelle glared at her. "Your son abused children, and having met you, I can see where he got it. He's a demon and so are you. Gabe will never soften his heart when it comes to evil, and neither will I."

She pushed up and tried to lunge at Velna. Rochelle half broke free but Velna was ready. She punched Rochelle in the face. Rochelle's head snapped back and the apartment filled with stars again. Her head swam for a moment, then all her thoughts coalesced into white-hot fury.

"Where is my sister?" she screamed.

The second man—Rochelle wondered if he was Plymouth or Alphie or Velna's brother, or even someone Gabe hadn't told her about—gripped her hair and pulled her head back. He got off her and lifted Rochelle to her feet. She ignored her pain and tried to back kick him in the groin but he was ready and dodged. A cloth went around her mouth and cut into her cheeks on either side. He marched her across the room to Sandra's coffee table—an ornately-carved wooden trunk that the first guy opened.

God, please don't let my sweet little sister be in there.

It was mercifully empty, but it wouldn't be for long. Both men tried to force her into the trunk as she fought them.

"Grab her legs, Alphie."

"I'm not going anywhere near her legs after that kick."

"Jesus Christ, just do it."

"I'll kick you again," Rochelle struggled to say. Alphie grabbed one ankle then the other and shoved them under his armpit while the other guy pushed her down into the chest.

"Somebody give me a damn zip tie."

"Me too."

Velna obliged. "Hurry up, we're running out of time."

She's passing out zip ties like candy Rochelle thought and almost laughed. She couldn't see the wall clock anymore. That bothered her to an irrational degree, as if losing track of the time meant she'd lost.

"What are you going to do with me?"

"What's that?" Velna asked. She knelt beside the chest and looked down at her. "Did you ask what we're going to do with you?" Velna grinned as more blood dripped from her nose and splattered against the rim of the chest. "We're going to take you for a long drive into the mountains to Grand Lake. Then, we're going to go for a nighttime boat ride. But you won't be coming back from that."

"No! No!" Rochelle squirmed and tried to break free as the men shackled her zip-tied hands and ankles together. Velna stood up and disappeared. When she reappeared, she held the cloth. She dropped it onto Rochelle's face.

"Now you can sleep all the way there. Maybe you'll wake up drowning."

Then the trunk lid slammed shut, trapping Rochelle in darkness.

She shook the cloth off her face and gagged at the chemical smell. Chloroform, she guessed. The blackness whirled around her. Were they picking the trunk up or was that just dizziness? Nope—the trunk tipped up on its end then angled back. She heard a ripping sound and realized they were wrapping the trunk in cellophane.

"Hurry up!" Velna shouted.

"She's not falling asleep," Alphie said.

"Good. She can be terrified all the way there. Like Jesse

was terrified." Her voice hitched. Rochelle wondered what she meant. Did something happen to Jesse?

The trunk tipped backward at an angle and moved forward. It was on a dolly. Rochelle twisted and turned, trying to tip the trunk or at least make as much noise as possible but they held it in place. They stopped moving and she heard a ding, then her stomach dropped along with the elevator. She heard the doors open and she rolled forward. Rochelle fought unconsciousness but she knew her thrashing grew weaker.

Please, Gabe. Please, find me.

TWENTY-SIX

The street in front of Rochelle's old apartment building was packed solid with cars, so Gabe circled the block. He checked the time—fifteen minutes before they were due at the restaurant. No problem since Sandstone was only five minutes away.

And besides, it wasn't like they'd lose their reservation if they were a couple minutes late—everyone was waiting for them there, where Gabe planned on proposing.

Well, everyone except Sandra. He'd texted her at the office right after receiving Rochelle's text about talking to her.

> You should be at the restaurant. Why are you talking to Rochelle first?

She'd better not be giving it away he'd thought. He liked Sandra, but she did strike him as a little immature. But, maybe that was how all twenty-one-year-olds acted and he just didn't remember.

It took her a few minutes to respond.

Because she was getting suspicious. This
way she has no idea.

Gabe smiled. Okay, maybe he needed to give Sandra more credit.

Turning down the street flanking the building, every space was full. Gabe slowed down to check the wide alley behind the apartment building. Every now and then while they were moving Rochelle to his house, he could find a spot back there.

A van was parked parallel to the building. Its nose faced the entrance to the alley with its rear beside the service entrance. Gabe glanced at the driver through the windshield. He was looking down at the phone in his hands but Gabe was ninety-nine percent sure the guy behind the wheel was Velna's brother, Michael. He immediately called Rochelle.

Gabe made a sharp turn into the alley and drove past the van as he listened to Rochelle's phone ring over and over. As he passed the van, he confirmed it—Michael was sitting in the driver's seat totally engrossed in his phone.

Gabe drove on past the van and parked it sideways, blocking the back of the alley. His call to Rochelle went to voicemail and he disconnected. Fumes curling from the van's tailpipe told him the van was idling.

Ready for a quick getaway?

Gabe called Ben.

"What's keeping you, brother?"

"We have a situation. Michael's in a van, parked and ready to roll in the alley behind Sandra's apartment. Sandra and Rochelle are inside and Rochelle's not picking up."

"What?" Ben sounded confused. "Sandra's right here."

"The fuck? Then why did she text me twenty minutes ago saying she's talking to Rochelle in her apartment?"

"Sandra?" Ben called. "You got your phone?"

Gabe waited for Ben to come back on.

"She says she thinks she forgot it in her apartment when she left for the restaurant but didn't want to run back and get it and miss the proposal."

Fuck!

"Get everyone to Sandra's apartment building *now*. Pretty sure Rochelle's inside with Velna."

"On it."

Gabe got out of his truck, jogged past the back door of the apartment building, and up to the driver's side of the van. He pulled out his Sig then yanked the car door open.

Michael looked up from the porno on his phone in time to see the butt of Gabe's Sig smash his nose. He pulled Michael out and hauled him behind the Dumpster at the back of the building beside the apartment. Gabe threw him against the brick wall. He slid down to his knees.

"Whatcha doing here, Michael?"

"This is assault." Michael glared up at Gabe.

"It's going to be murder if I find out your skank sister touched one hair on my woman's head."

"Fuck you. Your bitch is as good as dead."

Gabe grabbed Michael by the hair and slammed his head back against the wall until Michael lost consciousness. Then Gabe picked Michael up and threw him in the Dumpster. He slammed the top down and looked up in time to see the service entrance to the apartment open. The broad metal door faced him but he didn't need to see who was coming outside.

A black SUV turned into the front of the alley and blocked it. His brothers were here.

Gabe stormed back toward the door just as he saw the front of a dolly carrying the heavy, wooden trunk Sandra used as her coffee table wheel past the edge of the door. Velna appeared beside the dolly. She pressed a bloody washcloth against her face while she barked out orders Gabe couldn't make out.

He raised his Sig and pointed it straight at her face.

Velna looked up and her eyes went round in shock.

She dropped the washcloth and smiled as she spread her arms.

"Go ahead and shoot me. Jesse died in prison today. His cellmate killed him. He died afraid. Rochelle died afraid, too." She slammed her hand against the trunk.

The world stopped. The universe shrank down to the wooden trunk.

No.

"Gabe! Don't do it!"

He wasn't sure which brother shouted his name. It didn't matter. His heart was already as dead as Velna's son.

He didn't care if he went to prison. He didn't care if he lived or died. So long as Velna stopped breathing.

Gabe took aim at Velna.

The trunk shifted. By itself.

She's not dead.

He kept his gun trained on Velna while his brothers closed in on them, their own weapons drawn.

Gabe rushed forward.

"Shoot me! *Shoot me!*" Velna howled like a banshee while her cousins looked on stupidly. Plymouth tipped the dolly up and raised his hands in the air. Alphie followed suit, his head whipping back and forth between Gabe on one end of the alley and Elias, Ben, Shane, Waylon, and Bear on the other.

"Rochelle!" Gabe shouted.

The chest rocked.

Gabe reached Velna. He noticed absently that her nose looked broken.

My strong, beautiful woman did that.

"We've got her covered, T-Wolf," Elias said somewhere behind Gabe. He dropped to his knees, took out his pocketknife, and ripped at the cellophane wrapping the trunk while Elias grabbed Velna.

But that was somewhere in a different world. His universe was down to one purpose—setting Rochelle free. He ripped the cellophane loose from the box and opened it.

Rochelle fell forward into his arms. He picked her up and carried her away from the toxic smell coming from the trunk then set her down to cut her free from the zip ties.

"Rochelle, baby, it's me." He cut her loose and started rubbing her arms, trying to get her circulation going. She looked so pale, and her eyes were closed.

But not for long, She opened her eyes and looked straight into Gabe's.

In that moment, they didn't need words.

GABE FELT like he'd seen the inside of a police station over the past couple of months more often than he'd seen his own home. He gave his statement as quickly as possible so that he could get back to Rochelle at the hospital. She was going to be fine, the doctors reassured them. Gabe swore to make it his life's mission to ensure it was the truth.

As for Velna and her family, they were not going to be fine. They faced multiple felonies. In addition to breaking and entering, and attempted kidnapping, Velna had been spying on Rochelle and then on Sandra when she moved into the apartment. When she was arrested, Velna had a set of keys to the apartment in her pocket, which she'd made right after Rochelle and Gabe started dating. She'd taken a wax impression of the lock the night Sandra called Rochelle. The police swept the apartment and found two hidden cameras and mics, which Velna had installed after the night of Ellie and Bear's party.

Velna knew exactly when Sandra left for the engagement party. She confessed to the police that she had planned to sneak into the apartment and wait for Sandra to return later. Velna, Alphie, and Plymouth would take Sandra hostage and force her to lure Rochelle to the apartment.

But Velna got lucky when Sandra left the cell phone behind. She impersonated Sandra and convinced Rochelle to come over to talk. Velna's new plan had been to kidnap Rochelle and frame both Sandra and Gabe for Rochelle's murder. Now, she, Michael, Plymouth, and Alphie were the ones behind bars.

And to think, I was almost the one facing prison time if I'd shot and killed Velna.

Rochelle had saved Gabe from that fate, saved him from giving Velna exactly what she wanted—to rejoin her son in death knowing that she'd succeeded in separating Gabe from the person he loved most in the world.

It took a couple of weeks for Rochelle to heal. Gabe waited on her hand and foot, to the point that when he did go into work, Stephanie walked into his office and closed the door behind her, blocking out the blaring overhead music.

"Look, friend. I got a call from a certain lady who wishes to remain anonymous."

"Did you? I wonder who it could be." He folded his hands on his desk.

"Keep wondering and it'll come to you. Anyway, she loves you, thinks the world of you. But also, she says she's going to be just fine. You've taken excellent care of her but she's not made of glass, she promises."

Gabe eyed Stephanie. "Did she ask you to talk to me?"

"Of course not. But I'm not stupid, I can read between the

lines. Gabe, she's back to taking her self-defense classes. She's doing one of my yoga classes. She's working again. She looks radiant. She's thriving." Stephanie's lips quirked. "We went lingerie shopping and her taste is exquisite, almost as good as mine."

Gabe covered his face. "Didn't need to hear that from you."

"Too bad. So, what are you waiting for? Propose to her already."

Gabe dropped his hands but kept his eyes closed. He sighed. "It's not that simple."

"Oh, bull pucky it's not."

Gabe opened his eyes to see Stephanie staring at him.

"I don't want to trigger her. What if she gets upset when I ask, remembering what happened the last time?"

Stephanie tilted her head. "I can see now what's going on. She's fine but you aren't."

"What are you talking about? I'm fine."

"Don't kid a kidder." Her voice softened. "You've lost a lot of things in your life, Gabe O'Neil. You lost your life as a Ranger. You lost your perfect hearing. For a while, you lost your best friend. And now you almost lost the woman you love —a *second* time. You're afraid of being the one who's triggered when you ask her again."

"I...I'm not..."

Gabe stopped mid-protest. Stephanie was right. Every time Gabe picked up the phone to make a new reservation at Sandstone, his throat tightened and his pulse raced, and not for the same reasons they did the first time. He'd stumbled over his words with excitement, picturing himself down on one knee in front of all their friends, Rochelle in happy tears when she saw the engagement and wedding rings for the first time.

Now when he tried to make the call, he only saw her pale

face as she fell out of the trunk, when he thought for a terrible moment that he'd been wrong—that she was dead after all.

No. Not going there.

Gabe stood up and grabbed his jacket. "Nope. I'm not doing this. Excuse me."

"Where are you going?"

He ignored Stephanie's question as he opened the office door and walked out. The loud music overhead hit him like a punch in the face. He just needed to get out and get some fresh air, shake the memories out of his head.

Stephanie is wrong. She's wrong. I'm fine.

He watched the tiles on the floor as he stormed to the front entrance so he almost crashed into the person blocking his way.

Which would have been like slamming into a brick wall.

"Gabe," Bear said.

Gabe stopped and looked behind him toward his office.

"Wait, did she call you?"

Bear grinned. "'Bout an hour ago. She's real good with backup plans." He clapped a hand on Gabe's shoulder. "Let's go for a walk, brother."

"Fine," Gabe grumbled.

They found their way down to the St. Vrain river, where the water widened out and didn't quite crash over the rocks as noisily as it did through the heart of Lyons. The trees lining the river had budded out and the birds were building nests. A raven cawed a harsh warning at them from a low-hanging branch and Bear answered with clicking and clucking sounds. The raven clucked back almost musically before flying to its nest in the cliffs above the river.

Same old Bear, talking sense into the creatures of the world.

"So why aren't you engaged to Rochelle yet?"

Uh-huh. Same old Bear all right, not mincing words, cutting straight to the chase.

"No reason why I should rush it. She still needs to recover."

"No, you do need to rush it because Ellie's wanting to see what she needs to change about our wedding," Bear growled.

Gabe stopped walking. "*Your* wedding? What does your wedding have to do with Rochelle and me getting engaged?"

Bear grunted. "Everything, you dumbass. Ellie wants a double wedding and she wants it soon. And when my Ellie wants something—"

"You make sure she gets it, yeah, I know."

"Just like you need to be doing with your woman. Rochelle wants to marry you." Bear crossed his arms and nodded once like that was the end of the discussion.

"And I want to marry her."

"So propose."

"It's not that simple." He tapped his ear before he realized what he was doing. "One day, there's a good chance I'm going to be completely deaf."

"She's learning ASL," Bear said.

Gabe grimaced. "I know. I fucking *know*. But that's not the point. What if something else happens? If I can't protect her now, how am I gonna do it when I'm deaf? I could have kept her safe as a Ranger. But now? I almost lost her."

Bear huffed a breath through his nose. "You didn't lose her."

"It was close."

"But you didn't."

Gabe grabbed the hair on either side of his head. "It. Was. Close. Too close. Twice. Fucking *twice*, Bear. I didn't keep her safe. I should have known she wasn't safe. The first time, I had no clue, but the second time? Jesus, I should have known Velna wouldn't give up but I missed it. I don't deserve—" He looked around as if some answer to his problems would magically appear. Instead, he bent, picked up a rock, and hurled it into the water with a howl.

"I thought the same thing."

For a split second, Gabe thought Bear was talking about him, agreeing that Gabe was a fool who didn't deserve Rochelle. He whipped his head around but Bear was staring at the ground.

"I was where you are now, brother," Bear continued. "Ellie was right by my side. Right there when we were attacked. I wanted to die when I thought I'd lost her. I didn't deserve her. She needed someone who could keep her safe and that wasn't me."

Bear looked deep into Gabe's eyes. "I had my brothers to help me. But in the end, I was the only one who could save her. And she was the only one who could save me. Once I got that, I never looked back. Looking back is what kills you. Looking back is what steals your joy, brother. Ellie and me, we walked together out of the dark and into the light and now we're only looking ahead. You gotta decide for yourself—are you gonna keep looking back over your shoulder or are you gonna do the thing that scares you even more and move on with Rochelle at your side?"

Gabe blinked. "You talk a lot more now that you're with Ellie."

Bear snorted. "Ask Ellie how long I can talk. Now—which is it gonna be, Gabe? You looking forwards or backwards?"

TWENTY-SEVEN

Sunlight fell soft and warm over her shoulders when Rochelle was ready to call it a day at Riversong. She'd finished up translating a romance into English and emailed the book to an editor when April came over, steaming mug in hand.

"This is for you." She set the mug on the table.

"I thought you sold them, not gave them away," Rochelle joked. Then she looked up into her friend's face. Her smile looked tender and gave Rochelle pause.

"Who says this one's from me?" April nodded toward the door.

Gabe walked in.

The air went still. So still, Rochelle could hear her heart pounding. Gabe had never looked more like a book boyfriend than he did right then. He'd put on a dress shirt and her favorite brown leather jacket, the one that carried the scent of pine trees and fresh earth along with the leather. She could see the love in his gaze from across the room. And when he smiled at her, the warm sunlight on her back couldn't compare.

The last thing she wanted to do was run away.

The only thing she wanted was to spend the rest of her life with this man.

"Hi, Gabe," she signed.

Gabe's smile grew warmer. "Hi, Rochelle," he signed back.

Richelle was faintly aware of April and Hannah watching them behind the counter as Gabe strode across the coffee shop. When he reached her, he didn't pull out the chair across from her. He didn't sit beside her and pull her into him.

He got down on one knee.

"Rochelle. Ever since I first saw you in the window, I've wanted you. You are the love of my life and I don't know what I'd do without you. I don't know if I'm worthy of you, but I promise to spend every day making sure that I'm the man you deserve."

He reached into his jacket pocket and pulled out a box.

Rochelle covered her mouth and blinked happy tears away.

Gabe opened the box. Inside, instead of one ring, there were three—one diamond engagement ring and two wedding bands.

"I asked Ben to make these for me to show you what I want our lives to be together."

Rochelle looked closely at the beautiful rings. The wide bands were textured and as she looked closer, she realized that they were in the shape of mountain ranges. But not just any mountains.

She touched the smaller of the wedding rings. "These are the Rockies. The Front Range." She ran her finger over the man's band. "And these are mountains from Qu Ding's landscape painting we saw at the art exhibit in Denver. My favorite one."

"My mountains on your finger, and yours on mine. I would give my world to you, and I would cherish yours in return. Will you marry me?"

Rochelle's heart nearly burst with joy. "Yes. Yes, absolutely I will be your wife."

Gabe took the engagement ring out of the box. Now Rochelle could see that Ben had carved both mountain ranges on the band on either side of the diamond, which sparkled like the sun in the sky over a perfect landscape. Gabe slid the ring onto her finger and gave her only a moment to admire it before he swept her up into his arms and kissed her. April and Hannah clapped and cheered.

April and Hannah's applause suddenly sounded a lot louder. Rochelle opened her eyes to see that all their friends surrounded them, along with Gabe's parents. And to her great shock, *her* parents flanked Sandra, all three smiling at Rochelle and Gabe.

ROCHELLE AND ELLIE both crossed their fingers that Colorado wouldn't have one of its mood swings on the day of their weddings. Ellie had good-naturedly kicked Bear out of the cabin the day before so that she, Rochelle, and their bridesmaids could take it over for the night and use it to get ready the next morning.

And it was a beautiful morning—cool and clear and no sign of a storm.

"Your veil is beautiful," Ellie told her as April finished fluffing it out behind her.

"Thanks! Maman found the lace for it in Spain years ago. She—" Rochelle sniffed and tried not to cry—"she put it aside to make me a bridal veil someday."

"Oh, that's so sweet." Ellie hugged Rochelle—carefully so that they wouldn't wrinkle either dress.

"All right," April said as she clapped her hands. "Ready, ladies? We have about five minutes."

Arden, Gina, Sandra, Ellie's namesake cousin Ellen, and April lined up at the cabin door. The groomsmen waited outside on the porch to take their arms and lead them between rows of guests to a beautiful flower-covered canopy. Ellie and Rochelle watched out the window as they clutched each other's arms.

Then it was their turn. Rochelle met her dad at the door and Ellie met Kyle, who'd told her it was a privilege to walk her up the aisle. Everyone stood and turned to watch the brides make their way to the canopy. The groomsmen all looked handsome in their suits and of course their friends were the most beautiful bridesmaids ever. April's son Kevin looked adorable holding the pillow with the rings. He was on his best behavior but April still kept her hand on his shoulder as a reminder.

But the two handsomest men were Gabe and Bear. They stood gazing at Rochelle and Ellie as if they were in a dream. Rochelle wasn't so certain she was awake herself until she made it to the canopy and her father kissed her cheek over the lace and told her goodbye. That made it all real, if still dreamlike.

"Dearly beloved," the minister began, as a woman signed beside him for their friends who knew ASL. The rest of the words faded to a blur as Rochelle held Gabe's hand in hers. She could feel him trembling beside her. On her other side was her best friend and the man who loved her and Rochelle was pretty sure they were trembling, too.

Then came the kiss, and the start of the rest of their lives together.

IF THE WEDDING was a gentle dream, the reception was a joyful awakening of Rochelle's senses. The food was incredible, the cakes were gorgeous—vanilla and chocolate. Ellie insisted on an extra-large dance floor with a disco ball shaped like a cowboy hat and a DJ ready to play tunes for the next four hours —that turned into six. Rochelle kept an eye on Gabe, knowing that loud crowds sometimes got to him.

"How are you doing?" she signed after the third line dance.

"I'm good," he signed back. "Are you ready for a break?"

"I am. I need to stop in the restroom first. How about I meet you at the lake?"

"Sounds good." Gabe kissed her and headed for the water.

Rochelle followed a few minutes later. As she stepped into a grove of aspens on the path to the lake, she heard voices ahead. April and Shane.

Maybe I should wait.

But the conversation intrigued her.

And after all, it's not like April was shy about pushing Gabe and me together, she rationalized when the truth was, she was a sucker for a good story and one was unfolding right in front of her. Rochelle took a couple of steps forward until she could get a glimpse of her friends facing each other.

"Anyway," April said. "I heard about you. Well, you and your friends. What you guys did for Laurie."

Shane cleared his throat. "Yeah? How, uh, did you hear about that?"

"Whoa." April stood straighter. "Don't get all paranoid. Laurie and Kevin go to school together. Laurie couldn't stop talking about Peetie. Said a man named Shane let her keep him overnight. Said he was a watchdog. Didn't take a genius to put two and two together that it was you and Pete was from Watchdog up the hill."

Shane's usual cocky tone was gone when he said, "Yeah,

that was me. I don't do that work for attention or anything though, all right?"

Wow. Away went the easygoing Shane Rochelle was used to. The guy was serious and a little fierce.

April scoffed. "It's not like I'm gonna go blabbing it around, cowboy, and neither was Diane. I'm just saying it was nice what you all did. Us moms talk in the school pickup zone." She looked away briefly, then back at Shane. "Diane's got a little crush on you."

"Yeah?"

"Yeah."

"Why you telling me that?" Shane grinned.

April's lips turned down before her expression went carefully neutral. "Oh, just in case you might be interested. Wouldn't want you to miss out on an opportunity to go bug her instead of me."

Shane crossed his arms. "No."

"No?"

"No way."

April put her hands on her hips. "What's wrong with Diane?"

Shane's lips twitched. "Not a thing. Diane's nice. A good woman. But why would I go bug her when I can watch that pretty blush of yours every time I bug you?"

"I do *not* blush," she said, blushing to beat the band.

Rochelle decided she'd probably heard enough. She tried to back up but she stepped right on a branch which broke under the sneakers she'd changed into when the dancing started.

Shane and April both looked her direction. And it was pretty damn hard to hide in the woods when you're wearing a big white dress.

"Rochelle?" April called. "That you?"

Busted, she walked up to her maid of honor. "Yup! Just meeting Gabe at the lake. Excuse me."

"Do I blush when Shane talks to me?" April blurted out.

"No, of course not," Rochelle said. "Now, don't mind me..."

April turned to Shane. "See? I don't blush."

"Your face feeling hot right now?" The teasing tone had returned to his voice.

"No! I mean, um, no. No it's *not*. I need to go make sure Kevin's not getting into trouble." She turned on her heel and stomped back toward the reception as quickly as she could while Shane chuckled and followed along slowly behind her.

When Rochelle got to the lake, Gabe held up a bottle of champagne and two flutes.

"What kept you?"

"I ran into April and Shane talking."

"Oh? Everything all right?"

She shrugged and smiled. "I guess we'll see."

Gabe grinned. He handed the glasses to Rochelle and popped the cork. He poured the champagne and set the bottle down.

"Here's to my beautiful wife." They took a sip. "And here's to all our friends. May they find the happiness we've already discovered." He clinked his glass against hers a second time as the stars filled the evening sky one by one.

TWENTY-EIGHT

Wren Stapleton

"I'M STICKING every single needle I own into you," he said.

Oh, this is so not going to go well.

Wren Stapleton lay face down on a table, practically naked under a thin, white sheet, waiting to turn into a porcupine.

Why did I let Barbie talk me into coming here?

"Now it's not going to hurt, I promise. So just relax," Serge the acupuncturist said. "You're so tense! Your shoulders feel like they're cast in iron. We want soft shoulders, don't we?"

Wren wasn't sure if she was supposed to nod or answer vocally. She was afraid to move, despite Serge's promise that this wouldn't hurt. He was sticking *needles* into her—she didn't care how small they were. At least there was a hole in the table for her face, but lying facedown like this was wreaking havoc with her sinuses. Or maybe it was the copious incense burning on a nearby table. The smell was supposed to make her relax but instead it made her hold back a sneeze. The last thing she wanted to do was move suddenly. What if Serge stuck a needle in the wrong place and it paralyzed her legs or something?

"Yes, we want soft shoulders," she finally said, her voice already sounding stuffy.

"Good." Serge sounded distracted. At least he was paying attention to what he was doing and not to what she was saying. "We're going to start with your ears."

"My ears? Seriously? Are my ears tense or something?"

Serge just chuckled. "Funny girl. I like 'em funny."

And then she felt the slightest pinch at the top of her ear. It actually didn't hurt.

"See? Not bad, is it?" He stuck several more needles in her ear and walked around the table to the other side of her head.

"I'm withholding judgment until this is over."

"Oh, I like 'em sassy, too. I should spank you."

Wait, what? "Um."

"Just kidding with you. Relax. I'm a professional. I thought you had a sense of humor. That's what Barbie told me."

I'm going to kill Barbie and it won't be funny at all.

"Now let's tackle those shoulders. You're going to be so relaxed when this is over you won't even recognize your own body."

"Doubtful."

"Serenity is the goal, Wren. Breathe in and embrace serenity."

"Hang on. I really need to sneeze."

"Oh, good, it's working already. Just let it out. Sneezing is a sign of relaxation."

More like a sign that this incense is going to kill me before I get the chance to kill Barbie.

The smoke had gotten stronger, and there was a foul odor underneath that didn't smell natural at all. Maybe it was burning the base it was sitting on? Her nose was too stuffy to really tell.

Wren sneezed and then Serge stuck a series of needles in her back like he was making up for lost time. A couple of them made the muscle twinge underneath, but yeah, no pain. And her shoulders and back really did feel more relaxed.

This might be working.

Barbie wasn't the only one of her subjects who raved about Serge but she was the one who finally convinced Wren to book an appointment for her shoulders and back. Carting around photography equipment all day was taking its toll.

Though, Wren's shoulders were almost permanently parked up around her ears way before she ever picked up a full camera bag. She'd just ignore that little fact.

Serenity. She took another deep breath and her nose twitched at the smell.

"Just a few more to go," Serge said as he stuck another needle in.

"I need to sneeze again."

"*So* relaxed."

"No, I think it's the incense making me sneeze."

He made a disgruntled sound. "It's barely there. I don't even smell it anymore. I was thinking of lighting another cone as a matter of fact."

"Then you're totally nose-blind because it keeps getting stronger. I think it's burning the holder or something." There was definitely an acrid smell beneath the sweet sandalwood odor.

Wren sneezed, clearing her sinuses. "Wait, that's not the incense. That smells electrical."

"Huh. I think you're right." Wren heard Serge walk over to check the incense. "But it's not coming from here. Shit."

Serge walked across the room and opened the door. She assumed he was checking the hall.

A claxon sounded, and there went all her hard-won serenity. Wren *hated* sudden loud noises and a fire alarm was the granddaddy of them all.

"Serge? Is everything all right? Should I...?" Wren lifted her head and looked toward the open door.

Her acupuncturist was nowhere in sight.

"He ditched me!"

Wren sat up and looked around. Her clothes sat in a heap on the chair where she'd left them. She jumped off the table, bringing the sheet with her, and headed for the door to close it. But pounding footsteps in the hall and shouts told her she did not have time to get dressed. And was that smoke? The electrical smell was getting stronger, and now it was mixed with other chemical smells.

What about the needles in my back?

She couldn't very well slip her t-shirt on over those, could she? She reached back, trying to touch them and when her finger brushed against one, she got a horrible cringy feeling just thinking about trying to pull them out.

Just then someone stopped at the door. Thank God, Serge had not abandoned her. He could pull them out quickly.

Nope. Wasn't Serge.

"You need to get out now," some rando guy shouted into the room. "Break room's on fire."

"Shit!" After one last forlorn look at her clothes across the room, Wren grabbed her purse off the hook beside the door, slipped on her sandals, and awkwardly shuffled out of the room, trying to hold the sheet so it covered her front and her butt at least.

This is worse than a hospital gown. Thank God I didn't take off my panties. And at least she'd worn the cute ones, not her ratty old period panties. Because everyone was about to get a show.

Wren coughed as she tried not to trip down the hall toward the exit. The smell was god-awful and the smoke harsh. Her hind brain amplified her fear and she forgot she was practically naked as she started sprinting toward the open door and fresh air. Firefighters raced past her but one stopped to escort her out. He almost put his hand on her back but stopped when he saw the needles there. She wasn't sure, but she could almost swear she heard him chuckle behind his face shield thingy.

"This way, miss." He hurried her to the exit, where the entirety of the building waited in the parking lot, facing the building. All eyes landed on her as she emerged. Looks turned from concern to humor when they got a good look at her.

Great. Wonderful. Fan-fucking-tastic.

Wren tried to wrap the sheet as best she could around her backside without turning and giving everyone a money shot. The least the firefighter could do was give her a hand, but he was already gone, back in the building actually doing something more important than protecting her modesty, she assumed.

All she wanted to do was make a dash for her car, but the idea of driving home with *actual needles sticking out of her back* gave her the oogies. She kept her backside turned away from the crowd as she inched her way over to the waist-high brick wall enclosing the lot.

She scanned the crowd for Serge, the asshole coward who'd left her there like a helpless and pathetic baby porcupine. Maybe he could quickly de-quill her and she could disappear forever and forget this ever happened.

No Serge anywhere. The bastard had bolted.

Just my luck.

No, *this* was just her luck—the most gorgeous man she'd ever laid eyes on was heading straight for her, and not with a lustful look in his eye but supreme detachment. He was wearing scrubs or some sort of scrubs-adjacent uniform—she was no expert—and coming from the direction of an ambulance parked behind a firetruck.

And damn did he fill out those scrubs. The sleeves looked painfully tight around his upper arms. Fabric stretched across his chest and loosened as it fell toward his tapered waist. Same with the bottoms—he had thigh muscles that didn't quit.

Stop staring at his scrubs pants. I bet if you looked for it, you'd see he has a face.

Why, yes, yes he does.

Quite a face. Wow. Cool blue eyes whose gaze pierced her like the needles in her back, sending shivers down her spine. A broad, clear forehead, wide cheekbones and hollowed cheeks covered in golden whiskers that matched his tawny hair.

His name tag said *Hunt.* Because of course it did.

He's a mountain lion and I'm his prey.

Wren clutched the top of the sheet with one hand at her chest and the other at the small of her back, hoping that her panties weren't showing.

Just pretend you're at the Met Gala wearing an evening gown with a plunging back. Own it.

Uh-huh.

The Met Gala was for people like her gorgeous subjects, not for her. So were guys who looked like good old Hunt here.

He stopped in front of her, a full head taller, and studied her impassively.

"Did you inhale any smoke?" he asked. "Any trouble breathing?"

Oh yeah, breathing. Breathing is good she thought when she realized she'd been holding her breath. She inhaled sharply as she shook her head.

"Nope, breathing is not a problem. Been doing it all my life. You could say I'm an expert at it."

Right along with babbling when I'm anxious.

He reached for her hand, which was still clutching the sheet above her boobies, and she turned at the waist without thinking. The sheet started to slip on one side.

Ah, a tasteful side-boob for the nice gentleman. Good going.

"Sorry," he said quickly as he jerked his hand back. "I just want to get a pulse-ox on you." He held up a doodad with a tiny screen reading double zeroes.

"Right. Sure. Of course." Wren pointed her index finger at him, which he studied, frowning.

Is my finger that ugly? She looked at her bright red nail for chips in the polish but found none. *What's the problem?*

"Um, I'm going to have to remove your nail polish to get an accurate reading."

"Oh. That might be a problem. It's not polish, it's dip and requires grinding with a Dremel."

His lips pursed momentarily before those blue lagoons for eyes brightened. "No big, I can get a reading from your earlobe." He brushed a lock of her hair back. His thumb grazed her cheek which started an earthquake in her chest.

Then he frowned as he jerked his hand back for the second time.

Oh, God, now what? I know I don't have nail polish on my earlobes.

"Hmm. Before I can do that, let's get all those needles out of you. We'll start with the ones in your ears."

Her eyes widened. "The ones in my..." She started to raise

her hand to her ear and then thought better of it. "Oh yeah, he did put some there, didn't he?"

Hunt leaned in. He had nice, fresh breath—*oh God, I'm noticing his* breath, *seriously?*—and studied her right ear.

"One drew some blood."

"Really? How much?" Now she was dying to touch her ear.

"Just a teeny tiny drop. It's already dried and crusted over."

Lovely. Perfect. So attractive.

Hunt took a folded blue paper towel out of his med kit and spread it open on the top of the brick wall next to them. Then he reached up to pull out a needle and she held perfectly still.

"I don't think this will hurt, but I apologize in advance if it does."

"Nothing can hurt more than my pride right now, so pluck away."

No smile from Hunt. He was laser focused on her ear as if he were doing brain surgery. She felt disappointment tug at her chest just as she felt him tug the needle from the edge of her ear.

"Got it. One down." He set the needle in the center of the paper towel. "Wait. I need to count these first so that I don't miss one or leave one behind for someone to step on." He shook his head, looking annoyed. With himself? Her? Serge? God knew; his expression was nothing but business otherwise.

Hunt studied her ears, first the right one, then he passed in front of her face—with too-brief eye contact—and looked at her left ear. He took out a Sharpie and wrote *5 per ear* on the paper towel, then wrote *R ear L ear* and *back* across the top edge and moved the needle to the spot under *R ear*.

Very logical and efficient. I like that.

Hunt touched her bare upper arm and he might as well have had a buzzer in his hand the way her skin reacted, shooting delicious sparks straight to her tummy, heart and... other places.

Please, nips, do not poke out at him under this very thin, very white sheet.

He gently turned her. No, actually, he very gently *tried* to turn her but she stood rooted in place.

"I, um." She giggled nervously. "Didn't exactly have time to grab my clothing."

Hunt's eyes did that widening thing again that Wren was quickly growing addicted to.

"Oh, right." He glanced over his shoulder toward the parking lot. "It's okay, I'll shield you from the crowd."

Oh, yeah. Forgot about the crowd.

Somehow, her attention had zoomed like one of her telescopic lenses into sharp focus, cropping out everything that wasn't Hunt the Lionesque Paramedic.

Including an actual burning building. That I just escaped from, mostly naked.

"Are you all right? You suddenly look pale." Hunt touched two fingers to the side of her neck. Sweet Jesus, did he have live wires running through his hands because every time he touched her he sent delicious shocks through her body.

"Pulse is racing but steady. Do you feel light-headed or faint? I should get you seated." He shook his head again, the annoyed look back in his eyes.

"No, I'm fine, just reality catching up with me, that's all."

He blew out a breath. "Let me get these needles out, get your pulse-ox, BP, hydrated, tested for shock," Hunt half-mumbled to himself. Maybe he was new on the job, reminding himself of what he needed to do? He seemed very professional otherwise. He hadn't leered at all, didn't crack a single joke when the low-hanging fruit was right there for the taking.

Darn it.

Now she felt the overwhelming urge to make him laugh. To crack that professional exterior right open and get to the warm, gooey center that must exist inside this lion.

Get a grip. Stop fantasizing.

It wasn't like she didn't spend countless hours in the presence of handsome men. Men who graced the covers of magazines, whose faces were all over the internet with headings like *Hottest Bachelors of the Year* and *Top Ten Guys We'd Like to Smother in Honey and Eat Alive.*

Problem was, they were usually boring. Or total jerks. Often both. And they'd all started looking the same to her. Haircut of the season lacquered to their heads. Faces symmetrical. Perfectly balanced. Flat-out *boring.* Total Ken dolls, really —guys who visually paired well with Barbie. Sure, the camera loved them as they pouted and sneered and only sometimes smiled, but they were always looking at the camera lens, not at Wren. She was merely the human extension of a device that took their picture and increased their fame.

So, why was she going gaga over *this* guy? Handsome men did *nothing* for her anymore. Interesting faces did.

Wren braved another good look at Hunt. Yes, he was handsome, but his face wasn't symmetrical, it wasn't perfect after all. The nose was just a tiny bit crooked, like it had been broken at one point, but whoever fixed it did a good job. Not a hint of hair gel, and the messiness wasn't contrived but looked natural, like the result of Hunt running his fingers through it. Maybe his forehead was a little too broad, his cheeks tapering too extremely? Yeah, Hunt had an imperfect but interesting face that reminded her of a lion.

But those eyes were nothing except gorgeous perfection.

Now, if she could just spark some humor in them.

Wren turned a little so that Hunt could get a look at her back and felt herself instantly flush under his intense gaze as he studied and counted the needles there. Her skin prickled as if he were touching her physically.

No, don't think about...and there goes the nips. Oh, forget it.

At least he was looking at her back.

Hunt picked up his Sharpie and added the number twelve to the paper towel beside the word *back.*

"Twelve?" Wren asked. "That's a lot. Isn't it?"

He shrugged. "I don't really know acupuncture. Is that more than what you usually get? Hold still." Hunt was back at her right ear, where he plucked out another needle and set it beside the first one.

"Dunno. This was my first time. Definitely my last with Serge."

"Serge?"

"Yeah, my acupuncturist. The jerk abandoned me when the fire alarm went off."

Hunt growled. Actually growled like an angry lion.

Oh. Dear. God.

Something coiled up in her stomach and she wasn't sure if it scared her or turned her on.

"I don't like that," Hunt said.

He plucked out the rest of the needles in her ear and set them aside, then attached the pulse-ox thingy.

"Ninety-eight percent, which is perfect for altitude."

Hunt unclipped the pulse-ox and wrapped a blood pressure cuff around her arm and declared her blood pressure good, too, even though her pulse was racing.

Yeah, wonder why.

"So, how'd you end up going to this Serge guy?"

"One of my subjects suggested I get acupuncture and she gave me Serge's name. What a mistake."

"One of your subjects?" He started on her other ear.

"Yeah, I'm a photographer." Wren felt herself starting to

blush. "I do portraiture, photo shoots for magazines and book covers, things like that. I'm getting into real estate photography now, too." That wasn't all she photographed, but she wasn't sure if she wanted to get into her pet projects.

"And someone that you photographed suggested you need acupuncture? Last one." He removed the last needle and put it with the others.

"For my shoulders." She shrugged them, raising them toward her ears, and listened to the loud chorus of snaps and pops like firecrackers going off at midnight.

"Wow, that's bad," Hunt said.

"Thanks."

"I can see why someone would suggest acupuncture."

"Yeah, worked out really great for me, too. Totally relaxed."

The guy finally cracked a smile and snorted and it thrilled her probably way more than it should have.

"Maybe I should've left the rest of the needles in for your relaxation," he said.

She studied his face. Totally deadpan...except for a twinkle in his eye.

Like sunlight sparkling on water.

Game on. Let's see who loses it first.

"But I need a good de-quilling," she said. "It's that time of year when I shed them."

"So, now you're a porcupine? Maybe you did inhale some smoke."

"It wasn't *that* kind of smoke."

That got her the slightest grin.

Even better, Hunt started to strip for her.

He grabbed the hem of his scrub top and pulled it up while Wren could only stare in fascination and anticipation of seeing his inevitable six-pack—oh, hell, probably an eight-pack—emerge.

But no, not today with her luck. A white tee hid paradise from her view. Wren did get a tiny glimpse of bare skin right at the top of his pants when the tee hitched up as he pulled the scrub top over his head. Which was almost worse than nothing at all. That skin was tan and tight and she wanted more.

"Here you go," Hunt said, handing her the scrub top. Then he turned around and blocked her from the crowd so she could slip into it unseen.

Which she did as quickly as she could. Luckily, there was a row of evergreens on the other side of the wall blocking the view on the other side. The bottom hem of the scrub top fell mid-thigh and the V-neck showed off a little more cleavage than she was comfortable with under the circumstances, but this was way better than the drunk-at-a-toga-party look she'd been sporting before.

"Okay, I'm mostly decent now. Thank you."

Hunt turned around. Those lagoon-blue eyes did that fun and cool widening thing before he looked away at the building.

Oh yeah. Burning building. Forgot about that again.

Only, it didn't look like it was burning. While Hunt had been de-quilling her, the firefighters had done their job and put out the fire. There was still some smoke in the air and a godawful stench, but no towering inferno.

"Hey!" Hunt shouted to another paramedic standing next to a firefighter. "Anyone else?"

The guy shook his head. "All accounted for. How's your patient?"

Hunt turned back to Wren. "Hi, how are you?" Deadpan.

"I'm good, great, thanks. Very relaxed."

"She's very relaxed," Hunt shouted back. "Stunningly good vitals."

"Well, thank you," Wren said. "I take pride in my vitals."

Almost. He *almost* laughed. But then he started counting the needles on the towel as the firefighter walked over.

"Can I go in and get my clothes?" Wren asked the fire-fighter. She gestured at herself in Hunt's oversized scrub top. "I promise I did not show up here wearing this."

"I'm afraid not. There's still a lot of smoke, and just on the off chance that the structural integrity of the building is compromised, no one is allowed back in until further notice."

"Oh boy. There goes my favorite bra."

The firefighter gave Hunt a look and walked away without another word.

"You can keep it," Hunt said, looking at his scrub top just a little too long.

"I can't keep your clothes! You need this. It's like a uniform, right?"

"It is, but I have more."

"Well, okay. But, can I at least wash it and give it back to you sometime, Hunt?" She unpinned his nametag from the scrub top and handed it to him.

"It's Elias, actually. Elias Hunt." He stuck his hand out for Wren to shake. Then, he ran it though his hair and she was right about the naturalness of his messy hairstyle. "So... I can't really ask you out."

She blinked rapidly. *Oh. Oh wow. Ouch.*

"Okay. I wasn't asking—"

"Because it's not professional. You're kinda my patient right now."

Yeah, great, just my luck.

"But. There's this really cool place where I like to relax after work. And I know how much you're into relaxation."

Wren nodded like a bobble head. "Yeah, very much into relaxation."

"So, if I were to see you there maybe tomorrow..." He

shrugged a broad shoulder. "Or, there's this other place right in Lyons that's also really cool, and if you showed up there tomorrow *night*—"

"Wow. Two whole cool places. What are they?"

Oh God, he smiled. An actual, full-blown, gorgeous smile.

"It's up to you, depending on what you like. You know, because it's not really a date, just a couple places that you might go to, and I might be there at the same time and want to check up on you if I happen to see you."

She nodded. "Just to make sure I'm okay."

"Just to make sure you're okay, yeah, exactly."

"Because you care about my health."

"Just like any professional would care about your health after escaping a burning building, yeah."

Now *she* was trying not to smile. "So, what are these cool places where I might accidentally run into you?"

"One is a coffee shop. Low key, very public, light of day, lots of caffeine."

"Huh. Caffeine in a coffee shop. Who knew?"

He pursed his lips and nodded sagely. "They specialize in it, actually. And sometimes it gets crowded, so we might have to share a table or else I'd have to drink my coffee standing up and looking like a friendless dork."

Her chest fluttered with laughter trying desperately to escape her twitching lips. She rolled her lips in and bit down on the bottom one, not trusting herself not to burst out laughing if she tried to speak.

Finally, she gained a modicum of control. "Well, we certainly wouldn't want you looking like a friend...a friendless... dork." *Don't laugh, don't laugh, don't laugh.*

"You'd share a table with me?"

"I'd share a table with you, yes. As a sacrifice for your not-looking-dorkishness."

Now his lips twitched as he watched her. "You're a very kind person."

"I am, yes. So, what about this other really cool place? Any caffeine there?"

"Not as much. It's a bar. They have alcohol."

She lifted her eyebrows. "Alcohol in a bar? You don't say."

"It's true. *And* they do strips."

Her eyes bulged. "Excuse me, you think you're going to bump into me at a strip club?" She looked down at herself. "Sir, I think I've given you the wrong impression with my public nudity."

"*Chicken* strips." Now he was rolling his lips in and his blue lagoon eyes sparkled like the sun was shining on them again.

"So, let me get this straight. You want to meet me in a place where *live animals* strip? Isn't that illegal in this state? And to think, I let you de-quill me. Pervert."

And that did it. Elias Hunt burst out laughing.

I win, I win! Wren gave herself a mental high-five.

Elias quickly looked back at the ambulance where a couple other paramedics were watching him, arms folded. One had a definite smirk going on.

"Shit, er, shoot, I gotta go. Your vitals are fine, no signs of smoke inhalation or injuries. Do you think you need to go to the hospital for anything else?" He handed her a form on a clipboard to sign.

"Besides a chance to continue talking to you, no, I don't need a ride to the hospital."

He smiled again as he put the clipboard in his kit. "The coffee shop is Riversong and the bar is Cocktails and Chicken Strips. I like to grab my coffee around noon, or I can be persuaded to eat chicken strips and drink a beer at seven. Or both. Your choice, um..." His eyes widened. "I don't even know your name."

"It's Wren, like the bird. Wren Stapleton."

"Alright then, Wren Stapleton." Elias started walking backward, never taking his eyes off her. "Maybe I'll see you around."

"Maybe you will."

Yeah. You definitely will.

READ about Elias and Wren in Lion on the Mountain!

ACKNOWLEDGMENTS

This one is for all the Queens who got me through.

Queen Becca. I miss you, and I still carry the two-dollar bill with me everywhere.

Trinity Wilde, Queen of Everything and Chocolate Too.

Amber Hamilton the Queen of Keeping Me in Line. (Poor thing!)

Caitlyn O'Leary who remains the undisputed Queen of Kindness.

Riley Edwards who is actually a lioness and the Queen of Defending Friends.

Bella Stone the Queen of Glitterbombs and Care Packages (and who is my long-lost Irish sister.)

Kris Michaels the Queen of Writing Sprints.

Ophelia Bell the Queen of Dragons.

Susan Stoker the Queen of the North, the Bay, and the Nighttime Bonfires.

Luci Hamilton, Queen of Good Conversation who introduced me to Aperol Spritzes over dinner, hours after I finished writing my 20th novel (This one! It's this one.)

And most of all, this is for you Queens (and a few Kings) out there who read my books. You're the ones who matter most, because I couldn't write Watchdog without your constant encouragement through your messages, emails, and amazing reviews. You lift me up every day. I can only hope my stories do the same for you.

FOLLOW OLIVIA

Follow me to catch my latest releases at:

Newsletter:
https://oliviamichaelsromance.com/

Amazon:
https://www.amazon.com/author/oliviamichaelsromance

BookBub:
https://www.bookbub.com/authors/olivia-michaels

Facebook:
https://www.facebook.com/oliviamichaelsauthor

Instagram:
https://www.instagram.com/oliviamichaelsromance/

Want more? Come be one of Olivia's Lovelies on Facebook. I can always use another ARC reader or two...
https://www.facebook.com/groups/639545290309740/

Or talk to me live on Discord! Find me, Riley Edwards, Caitlyn O'Leary, Kris Michaels, Anna Blakely, and Rayne Lewis on the Protector Romance Talk Channel:
https://discord.gg/tSBBrfwR

ALSO BY OLIVIA MICHAELS

Watchdog Security Series

More Than Love

More Than Family

More Than Puppy Love: A Christmas Novella

More Than Paradise

More Than Thrills

More Than Words Can Say

More Than Beauty

More Than Rumors

More Than Secrets

Watchdog Security Series Box Set, Books 1-3

Watchdog Security Series Box Set, Books 4-6

Watchdog Security Series Box Set, Books 7-9

Watchdog Mountain Division

Bear On The Mountain

Timberwolf On The Mountain

Coming Soon!

Lion on the Mountain

Thunder on the Mountain

Blizzard on the Mountain

Avalanche on the Mountain

Watchdog Protectors

In Susan Stoker's Special Forces Operation Alpha

Protecting Harper

Protecting Brianna

Protecting Sylvie

ABOUT THE AUTHOR

Olivia Michaels is a life-long reader, dog-lover, gardener, and a certified beachaholic. When she's not throwing a Frisbee for her fur-baby, harvesting tomatoes, or writing, you can find her playing in the surf, kayaking, or kicking back on the sand and cracking open a romantic beach read.

www.ingramcontent.com/pod-product-compliance
Lightning Source LLC
Chambersburg PA
CBHW070629260626
47161CB00007B/2632